Reed assumed that Faith would fall asleep early

To his surprise when he strolled onto the porch around ten o'clock, she was standing out there.

She didn't hear him at first. It probably would have been wiser to turn around and leave her alone. But he wasn't feeling wise. All evening he'd been feeling edgy, unable to settle in. He felt irrationally as if his life was on the verge of becoming completely different, though he had no idea how.

Maybe it was just the weird feeling of having other people in the house. No one but him had slept here since Melissa died.

He was careful to make enough noise to be sure she'd hear him. Given what she'd been through lately, the last thing he wanted was to startle her.

She turned around. "Hi," she said, smiling.

"Hi," he responded casually, but his senses were suddenly reeling. She smelled of soap and some kind of perfume that made him think of pink flowers and springtime. Her hair fell to mid-arm, curving against the tender spot where he'd earlier noticed a large white bandage. The bandage had been a brutal reminder that she wasn't here for a social visit. She wasn't even here to be his housekeeper.

She was a wounded, frightened woman. A refugee seeking asylum.

He felt a sudden flash of anger. How could anyone be trying to hurt someone so beautiful?

Dear Reader,

Once, when he was little, my son told me he was tired of all this fuss about rainbows. They weren't anything special, he said. They were, in fact, kind of stupid.

I have to admit even I was shocked. He might as well have said he didn't admire Mozart, or daffodils, or God. What kind of man could grow from a boy who didn't like rainbows?

But as I watched him turn into a wonderful young man, full of kindness and imagination, I finally understood. That little boy hadn't been insensitive. He had merely been young— and very lucky. He knew nothing of struggle or fear or loss. He had no need for symbols of hope. He didn't need reassurance that, after pain, joy would rise again.

Most of us know those things all too well. And we are grateful for the rainbow's reminder that life's storms, however violent, are temporary—and that sometimes, in the most unlikely of places, beauty and love can suddenly reappear.

Faith Constable, the heroine of *The One Safe Place*, is caught in one of those storms. When she flees to Firefly Glen, she is seeking only safety. She never dreams of finding happiness and love.

But then she meets Reed Fairmont. Reed is a man who can heal anything…sick puppies, surly lizards, damaged kids and even terrified heroines. Anything, that is, except his own broken heart. For that, he'll need an unexpected rainbow. For that, he'll need Faith.

I hope you enjoy reading their story as much as I enjoyed writing it. And the next time your life gets a little too stormy, don't forget to look up. There might be a rainbow waiting for you, too!

Warmly,

Kathleen O'Brien

P.S. I love to hear from readers! Please write me at P.O. Box 947633, Maitland, FL 32794-7633 or at KOBrien@aol.com.

The One Safe Place
Kathleen O'Brien

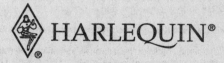

TORONTO • NEW YORK • LONDON
AMSTERDAM • PARIS • SYDNEY • HAMBURG
STOCKHOLM • ATHENS • TOKYO • MILAN • MADRID
PRAGUE • WARSAW • BUDAPEST • AUCKLAND

ISBN 0-373-71146-8

THE ONE SAFE PLACE

Copyright © 2003 by Kathleen O'Brien.

Visit us at www.eHarlequin.com

Printed in U.S.A.

The One Safe Place

CHAPTER ONE

FAITH CONSTABLE had never realized that getting shot with a .22 caliber rifle would make a person so damn *angry*.

But as she lay in the emergency room of St. Luke's having her arm stitched up by a doctor who appeared to be a teenager, a bubbling fury was by far the strongest emotion she felt.

Stronger than fear, which actually might have been more logical. Stronger even than grief, which had colored her world dead black for the past four terrible weeks.

In a way, *angry* felt better. A frightened, grieving woman walked through life with her head down, incapable of action. But an angry woman was a force to be reckoned with.

As Detective James Bentley was about to find out.

"I said no, and I meant it," Faith said. "I am not running away, and that's final. I'm going to stay here and help you catch him."

Detective Bentley had come to know Faith pretty well over the past month—intense emotion was a great social accelerator. He sat down in the guest chair, obviously recognizing that this might take a little longer than he'd expected.

"I think," he said firmly, "you'd better leave the catching part to us."

"I've *been* leaving it to you. Doug Lambert killed my sister more than four weeks ago, and he's still out there."

She had her back to the policeman, but she could imagine his face. He was fifty, lined and craggy and tough as nails. But his sad eyes were kind. The day she discovered Grace's body, he'd held Faith like a daughter while she cried.

"We're looking for him, Faith. We'll find him. But it won't help us if you get killed, too."

Faith swallowed, shutting her eyes as the pimple-faced doctor dug another stitch into her torn flesh.

Killed. The word no longer seemed preposterous, alien, abstract. That was one more thing Doug Lambert had done to her life. He had introduced the reality of death—violent, wrongful death—and now it walked beside her always.

Just five hours ago, she had decided to go out jogging, hoping that the crisp late-September New York City morning would clear her head, maybe even lift her spirits. But she had, even then, been aware of the possibility of death. Any world that held Doug Lambert was a treacherous place.

And then out of nowhere, a noise. A sharp pain. *Death.*

The bullet had skimmed across her upper arm,

leaving a burning red path. Six inches to the right, and it would have hit her heart.

She remembered her breath misting in the chilly air as she cried out. And if the other joggers hadn't stopped and gathered around, he could have pulled the trigger again, aiming a little more carefully this time.

Dead.

But wouldn't that perhaps have been some dreadful kind of justice? After all, it should have been Faith who got killed in the first place. Doug Lambert hadn't ever intended to murder Grace. In a fit of passion, coming up on her from behind, he had mistaken her for Faith.

Detective Bentley knew that as well as Faith did. But neither of them wanted to say it.

Faith tried not even to think it. If she started thinking about Grace right now, about how she had looked, lying there on her kitchen floor, her neck broken— then this hot, empowering anger might disappear in another flood of grief and guilt.

"I can't," she said. "I can't let him chase me into a hole like a frightened mouse. What if you never do catch him? Am I going to live in that hole for the rest of my life?"

"We'll catch him," he repeated doggedly. "If it really is Doug Lambert, we'll get him. And if it's someone else, we'll get him, too."

"It's Doug, damn it. It has to be. A millionaire who has been stalking me for months suddenly vanishes the day after my sister's murder, and you think it's a coincidence?''

''It might be. It's my job to consider all the possibilities. I've told you that a thousand times, Faith.''

She felt her anger rising even higher. She was breathing fast, and the air tasted horribly of hospital, a bitter concoction of alcohol and sickness. She sensed her anger was irrational, maybe even artificially induced by shock and fear, and yet she was so filled with its roiling power that she could hardly lie still for the doctor to go on working.

Bentley's attitude was frustrating to the point of madness. Doug had killed her sister. And now he was trying to kill her. She didn't want a single hour wasted looking for other suspects.

''I saw him there that morning. And he knows it. He knows I am the only one who can place him at my apartment. That's why he tried to shoot me today.''

''Maybe,'' the detective agreed calmly. ''And maybe not. Stray shootings aren't exactly unheard of in this city, you know.''

''Bull.'' She tried not to go any further with the profanity, though it was pushing at her throat, trying to explode through her fragile control. ''That's absurd. You're not an idiot, Detective. How can you possibly swallow so many huge coincidences all at once?''

''I can't. At least not without some serious chewing.'' The detective shifted in the hospital chair, which was far too small for his six-foot-plus body. "Truth is, I hate coincidences. Which is why I want you to get the hell out of this town, Faith, and let us do our jobs."

Hadn't he been listening? Faith raised up on her elbow and twisted to look at him. "I told you I—"

"Please." The young doctor had been steadfastly ignoring the debate between Faith and Detective Bentley, but at her movement he looked up, aggrieved. "I need you to be still. You two can work this out when I'm done."

"I'm sorry." But Faith couldn't lie back down. Her adrenaline was pumping too wildly, making her veins feel slightly electrified. She felt as if she could leap off this table, run right out and capture Doug Lambert single-handedly. She glared hard at the detective.

"I'm serious. I'm not going to scuttle away. I am not afraid of him anymore. Let him try to kill me if he thinks he can."

Bentley met Faith's bravado with dark, serious eyes. Those eyes had seen too much, she thought suddenly. And now they saw everything, even the things she was trying to hide.

"Okay." He paused. "And what about your nephew? If the boy is with you, he'll probably get killed, too. Is that also okay?"

Faith stared at him a minute, hating him. And then, the adrenaline leaking out of her like water from an opened drain, she lowered herself slowly back onto the table.

Spencer.

She shut her eyes, feeling herself go limp. She had been right to cling desperately to her anger. The adrenaline had been the only thing that stood between her and the razor edge of meltdown.

The doctor took advantage of her momentary quiescence, knit his final stitch and tied it off. He stood, peeling off his latex gloves, obviously eager to depart before things got emotionally out of hand. Blood he could handle. Tears obviously were a different story.

That was his youth, Faith thought vaguely. Though she was only twenty-five, she felt a thousand years older than this young man. You had to cry a lot yourself before other people's tears didn't scare you anymore.

"Tell you what," the doctor said, picking up her chart and scribbling in it. "I'll leave you two to finish this. Let my nurse know when you're ready, and she'll apply the dressing. Detective, if you need anything more, have them page me."

No one tried to stop him. And then Faith and the policeman were alone in the little alcove formed by the long white curtain. It wasn't really a shelter, but it at least offered the illusion of privacy.

Still lying on her side, Faith stared at the huge silver hooks that held the drape on its semicircular rod. But she didn't really see any of that. Instead she saw Spencer, his brown eyes wide and liquid with fear, his skinny, six-year-old body trembling, his hand creeping into hers. His pain locked somewhere so deep inside him it couldn't make its way out in words.

Spencer.

Grief and guilt seeped in again, in the void the adrenaline and anger had left behind. She felt suddenly too heavy to move.

"And even if Lambert doesn't bother killing the kid," Detective Bentley went on conversationally, as if the subject truly intrigued him. "What does Spencer do when you're gone? When he's lost his mother *and* you?"

She didn't answer. The anaesthetic was starting to wear off, and her arm had begun to throb.

The policeman didn't seem to notice her silence. He just kept talking, as if mulling over the subject with an idle curiosity.

"Well, I guess he'd just have to go into foster care. It's my understanding you're the only family he's got left—am I right? Kind of tough on the kid, though, wouldn't you say? Foster care can be pretty grim. They don't even stay in one home very long before—"

She closed her eyes. "Detective."

"Yes?" He sounded annoyingly smug, as if he had predicted to the nanosecond exactly when her resistance would vanish.

"That's enough," she said softly. "You win."

"I do?"

"Yes. I'll go. I'll go to—" She took a deep breath, though the air was sharp with disinfectant. "What did you say this mouse-hole you've found for me is called?''

''Actually, I didn't say,'' he answered politely. ''You didn't ask. But now that you have, I'm happy to tell you. This mouse-hole, as you put it, just happens to be upstate, in a rather beautiful little mountain town called Firefly Glen.''

ON THE WAY down to his veterinary clinic the next morning, Reed Fairmont looked around his quiet home, a rambling, lovingly renovated farmhouse from the 1800s, and tried to imagine strangers living here.

Frankly, he just couldn't do it. In the two years since Melissa died, he'd come to terms with solitude. More than that—he'd come to like it. He'd come to need it.

And yet, by dinnertime today, these total strangers, this Faith Constable, who had somehow tangled with a murderer, and her nephew Spencer, who apparently was emotionally disturbed, would be here.

And then what? No more quiet dinners with the newspaper, that was for sure. No more smoky jazz on the stereo when he couldn't sleep at three in the morning. No more burning off the day's tension by banging weights around in the exercise room at midnight.

And lately he'd begun to start thinking about maybe dating again, just as another way to work off tension. Well, forget that, too.

Hell. Damn Parker Tremaine anyhow. Reed should never have let Parker talk him into this. That was a lawyer for you. They started talking, and before they were finished you found yourself agreeing with them.

He slammed the door that cut the rest of the house off from the clinic, something so out of character that Justine Millner, his receptionist, looked up, a line of worry marring her clear, white forehead.

"Anything wrong, boss?"

Behind her, a baby stirred and began to whimper, probably roused by the slamming door. Justine caught her lower lip prettily between her teeth.

"Sorry, Dr. Fairmont. My mom couldn't keep Gavin this morning. My dad was home and he won't let her, you know, so I had to bring him with me. I didn't think you'd mind. I mean, you did say—"

"It's fine," he said, shaking off his bad mood long enough to bend down and let the baby wrap his fat hand around Reed's thumb. "Everything's fine."

But was it? As if he didn't have enough to worry about, he was already having second thoughts about giving Justine this job. For one thing, she was an incurable flirt. Reed had a fairly healthy ego—after all, he had won Melissa, hadn't he? And since Melissa's death plenty of women had shown themselves eager to help him recover.

But Justine was only nineteen. To her, a thirty-two-year-old widowed vet, however fit, however nice-looking, must seem ancient. Still she couldn't open her mouth without flirting.

And, though she had assured him her mom would keep the baby whenever she could, whenever her father wasn't home to forbid it, half the time Justine showed up dragging the diaper bag and baby carrier behind her.

But how could he have said no? The kid had been desperate, an exhausted former beauty queen with no husband, a hungry infant and a father who had disowned her loud enough for the whole damn Glen to hear.

The judgmental old bastard. What kind of father pinned a scarlet letter to his own daughter? Mayor Alton Millner's kind, of course. Rumor was he'd wanted Justine to give the baby up, and he couldn't forgive her for defying him.

That showed some serious backbone. And she clearly wasn't stupid, in spite of the fatherless baby, the compulsive flirtation and the tight sweaters, which were probably all parts of the same self-esteem issue.

So Reed, aware that he was one of the few employers in the Glen who didn't need to curry favor with Mayor Millner, had hired her.

The baby was sucking his finger. Reed pulled it free carefully, making a deft substitute move with the plastic pacifier. Then he straightened and headed toward the back.

"Mr. Tremaine is in room one," Justine called after him. "He's brought Frosty in for his shots."

"Is that so?" Reed changed course, heading for room one with a purposeful stride. "Mr. Smooth-talking Tremaine. Just the man I want to see."

He swung through the door with a firm push. Parker was sitting comfortably in the corner chair. Frosty, a beautiful golden retriever about a year old, stood on his hind legs beside him, paws dangling over Parker's lap, getting a lazy ear rub that had sent the dog into sleepy-eyed ecstasy.

"Uh-oh." Parker smiled, obviously recognizing Reed's foul mood and deducing the cause. "I hope we're not having second thoughts about our new housekeeper and her nephew."

Frosty bounded over to greet Reed, whom he adored. Of course, Frosty adored everyone, so Reed didn't let it go to his head.

"No," he said, petting Frosty but glaring at Parker over the dog's head. "*We're* not having second thoughts. *I* am. You're not involved in this. You're not the one whose house is being invaded."

Parker returned his glare with complete innocence. But Reed wasn't buying it. He straightened and narrowed his eyes. At six-three, he was a full inch taller than Parker, which drove his friend crazy.

"And I have to ask myself, why is that? If this Good Samaritan deed is so important, why isn't Parker Tremaine the one doing it?"

Parker stretched out his long legs and put his hands behind his head, the picture of ease and a perfectly clean conscience. "We went over this, Reed. I'm not the one with a huge house and a million extra bed-rooms—"

"Two," Reed corrected, lifting Frosty up onto the table and checking his ears, which were spotless, of course. This was one well cared-for animal. "Two extra bedrooms."

"Right. Two," Parker agreed pleasantly. "Which is the perfect number for two people. *And* I'm not the one who needed a housekeeper, which is the perfect cover for a woman in hiding. I'm not the one with fifteen open acres for a kid and his dog to play in. In fact, I've got a relatively small house, a new wife, a new baby and two dogs tearing up the place already."

Reed checked Frosty's teeth, which were fine, and began clipping the dog's toenails.

"Yeah, but you're the superhero with all those years in the Secret Service, and a stint as sheriff, to boot. You're the one who's trained to protect and defend. If a murderer shows up here, what am I going to do, neuter him and give him a rabies booster?"

Parker laughed. "With this guy, that might be the best approach. But he's not going to show up here, unless he's a mind reader. There's not a single thing to tie Faith Constable to you or Autumn House. Jim Bentley and I did Secret Service duty together five years ago, and he asked a favor. I suggested you. That's a convoluted path not even a lunatic could trace."

Reed's assistant brought in the inoculations and stayed to help Reed hold Frosty in place while he administered them. Not that Frosty was wriggling. It was actually unnatural, this dog was so well behaved. Must be the result of living with a teacher and a law-

yer. If Sarah, the teacher, couldn't make Frosty be-
have, Parker could talk him into it.

While the assistant was in the room, Parker kept
quiet, but as soon as they were alone, he started in
again.

"So what's *really* bugging you, Reed?" Frosty was
back on the ground, and Parker stroked the dog's head
absently, his intense blue gaze fixed on Reed.

Reed turned to wash his hands, buying time.

"I'm not believing that the bad guy makes you
nervous," Parker said. "I've seen you bring down a
charging bear with one well-placed tranquilizer dart.
I've seen you rope a crazed bull and wrestle it to the
ground. That's one reason I thought of you. You're
young, you're fit and you're not afraid of a damn
thing."

Reed flicked a glance over his shoulder, just in time
to see Parker grinning.

"Hell," Parker added, "I've even heard it said that
you're a whole inch taller than I am, although that
part's a dirty lie."

Reed dried his hands, then turned around slowly.

"Okay," he said. "You're right. I don't give a
damn about this Lambert character. A guy who
sneaks up on women and breaks their necks is clearly
a coward. I suspect I could handle him if I have to.
My real problem is that—"

He paused. Like most men, he and Parker didn't
discuss their emotions much. They'd known each
other so long they really didn't have to.

"What?"

Reed took a deep breath.

"I guess I'm just hoping you don't have some hidden agenda here. I hope you're not thinking that, because of Melissa, I'll be able to relate to these people in some special way. I hope you don't think I have some gem of wisdom to offer them about surviving the loss of a loved one."

Parker smiled. "Sorry. Frankly, 'wisdom' isn't the first word that comes to mind when I think of you, old buddy."

Reed knew what he meant. If anything, he had handled Melissa's death with a spectacular lack of good judgment. In fact, he'd been a mess. He'd refused to see anyone except his patients. He'd barely left the house. He had drunk himself to sleep for a full year.

But damn it, he had been married only two years. *Two years.* Melissa had been only twenty-seven. And to see all that beauty, all that life, eaten away by cancer...

Well, it didn't really surprise him that he'd drunk himself to sleep. It only surprised him that he hadn't somehow managed to drink himself to death.

"Yeah, but I know you, Parker. You probably think that, because I did survive, I learned something."

He wiped his hands on the paper towels so hard his skin burned. "But I didn't. The only thing I learned is that eventually time will put enough distance between you and the pain, and you'll be able to go on. I can't help these people, Parker. Just because I came out of it, that doesn't mean I can help them out of it, too.''

Parker leaned over to clip the leash back onto Frosty's collar. When he stood, his face was somber.

''I never for a minute thought you could,'' he said. ''If anything, it might be the other way around. Maybe I thought they could help you. Truth is, you're not as far *out of it* as you like people to think.''

Reed shook his head. ''You're wrong,'' he said.

He wanted to be angry, wanted to dispute the implication that he wasn't fully recovered. But the look on Parker's face stopped him. ''You're completely wrong,'' he repeated dully.

''Could be,'' Parker agreed, shrugging as he headed toward the door. ''It wouldn't be the first time. Just ask Sarah.''

But that was nonsense. Parker's beautiful new bride didn't think a single word Parker had ever uttered was wrong. If he said day was night, Sarah would kiss him sweetly and obediently go to sleep. And it went both ways. If she said jump, Parker would soar right over the moon.

Reed remembered what that had been like. A good marriage—two people cocooned in love. It had been soft and easy, exciting and alive, real and profound and achingly brief.

He had to fight hard against the bitter envy that welled up in him whenever he saw the blissful Tremaines. But damn it, Parker didn't know what he was talking about here. Reed didn't need a distraction. He didn't need a Good Samaritan mission. He didn't even need a housekeeper.

And he damn sure didn't need Faith Constable and her troubled nephew, with a murderer nipping at their heels.

What he needed was Melissa. Or, failing that, someone to drill into his brain and surgically remove all memories of being in love.

CHAPTER TWO

FAITH CHECKED HER WATCH in the bright mountain sunlight. She had checked her watch about ten times in the past half hour. She didn't really care what time it was. She just needed something to do, something to fidget away the anxiety that was threatening to overtake her.

At four-seventeen, just two minutes behind schedule, Detective Bentley stopped his car at a deserted mountain pass called Vanity Gap. It was time to turn them over.

His friend Parker Tremaine was waiting at the mouth of the gap, ready to receive them. It was a strange, complicated transaction, designed to make it difficult for anyone to follow them without being seen. Faith felt a little like a ransomed hostage. Or perhaps just a parcel of smuggled goods.

Parker looked very nice, and was in fact startlingly handsome. Still, as Faith watched Detective Bentley transferring their suitcases from the unmarked cop car into Parker's expensive luxury sedan, she felt a clutch of fear.

At least she knew the detective. After the past intense weeks, he seemed to have become a real ally.

A friend. Besides, he was her tie to the city, to her sister, to her real life, which for the past three hours had been rapidly receding in the rear window.

Getting into this new car with this stranger, however handsome, would be like sailing into darkness, and she was suddenly washed with uncertainty.

Somehow she had to hide it, though, for Spencer's sake. The little boy stood beside her, still as a statue. The only movement came from his Sheltie puppy, Tigger.

Tigger, whose boundless energy had earned him his name, was struggling to reconcile his excitement about the trip with his innate urge to stay close to his little master. Consequently, though he whined and writhed in place, he never got more than two inches from Spencer's left foot.

Faith patted the puppy, then took Spencer's hand and smiled down at him reassuringly.

"Okay, sweetie, here we go," she said with an attempt at brightness.

Spencer just stared at her, his brown eyes so like his mother's that Faith almost couldn't bear to look into them.

He didn't speak, of course. Spencer hadn't spoken a word since Grace's death. "Conversion reaction," the psychiatrists had called it. Or perhaps "selective mutism." But she called it something simpler—and yet far more tragic. She called it unbearable pain.

He was only six years old, and already the world

had hurt him so much he no longer had the power to express it.

No, she corrected herself. The world hadn't done that. Doug Lambert had done it.

"We're going with Mr. Tremaine now. He's taking us to Autumn House. That's where you and Tigger and I will be living for a little while, remember?"

"Please. Call me Parker." The tall, blue-eyed man came over and squatted down to get at eye level with Spencer. "Autumn House belongs to a friend of mine. It's very big and very pretty. And it has a huge yard that puppies like to run around in. I think Tigger will have a great time there."

Faith noticed that Parker didn't phrase anything as a question. So he must already know about Spencer. Detective Bentley had probably filled him in on all the pitiful details. Which was only natural, of course. Only fair. These people were doing her a huge favor, and they deserved to know exactly what they were getting into.

It was ungrateful of her to mind. And yet the idea of these strangers discussing her personal tragedies was oddly distressing. Intrusive, as if she really were just that troublesome parcel of handle-with-care cargo.

She felt a new stab of hatred toward Doug Lambert as she added this to his list. He had stolen their basic right to privacy. A small loss, compared to the loss of Grace, or the loss of Spencer's emotional peace, but another black mark on the board nonetheless.

When the bags were all transferred, Detective Brantley came over to say goodbye. His kind eyes sent courage into hers as he wished her well, and assured her that he'd keep in touch frequently through Parker, making sure she was always updated on the search for Doug Lambert.

Faith allowed herself one long hug. She had to pull herself away, finally, for fear she might dissolve into tears, which would be embarrassing. Besides, it would frighten Spencer, who needed to believe that his aunt, at least, had a firm grip on the reins of their changing, unpredictable world.

"Thanks for everything, Detective," she managed to say before her voice gave out. And then, without looking back, she took Spencer's hand and led him into the soft, leather-upholstered interior of Parker Tremaine's waiting car.

Parker and the detective must have said their goodbyes very quickly, because in less than a minute Parker joined them.

He slipped his key in the ignition, using the mirror to check Spencer and Tigger, who were huddled together in the back seat.

"Everybody buckled in?"

Spencer pretended he hadn't heard him, but Faith could see that the seat belt was already carefully pulled over both boy and dog. Spencer was so cautious now, she realized with a pang. It was unnatural to see any little boy sitting so still. Like someone frozen in the middle of a minefield.

Once Spencer would have fussed and giggled and played stalling games, pretending he couldn't find the dreaded lap restraint. But not now. Now he obviously clung to any illusion of safety he could find.

"We're all ready," she said, turning to Parker with her best attempt at a smile. He was an innocent bystander in this drama. No need to make him any more uncomfortable than was absolutely necessary.

But as they drove down the winding road that led to Firefly Glen, she gradually realized that Parker wasn't the uncomfortable type. His conversation was easy, wry and interesting. He avoided anything personal, instead amusing them with stories of how Vanity Gap got its name, and the history of the four "season" houses of Firefly Glen.

They would be staying in one of those special mansions—the Autumn House. Parker spent a lot of time describing the place, somehow making it sound both cozy and grand. Out of the corner of her eye, Faith could see that Spencer had tilted forward slightly, so that he wouldn't miss a word.

Parker was very smooth. By the time they reached the bottom of the mountain, Faith had relaxed considerably, and she could see that even Spencer's knuckles were no longer clenched white and bloodless.

"This is Main Street," Parker said as they turned into a shopping area so quaint it might have been in a picture book of charming European villages.

Faith's first impression was of clean, sparkling

color. It had rained earlier, and gleaming cobblestones wound their way through storefronts decorated with garlands of autumn leaves. Golden chrysanthemums frothed out of pots at every door and late-season daisies flowered in a hundred hanging planters.

"It's very pretty," she said inadequately. Actually, it was far more than that. It was like the schoolbook illustration for *Our Happy Hometown.*

Warm and welcoming, a little jeweled paradise where surely everyone was generous and good, and nothing ever went wrong.

But it was, of course, merely an illusion. No such Eden existed, she knew that. Even a town this beautiful had its secrets, its tears, its cruelties behind closed doors. In spite of the mountains that stood guard on every side, illness and evil and despair had undoubtedly found their way into Firefly Glen, just as they had into every other place on earth.

But none of that was visible on the surface. And a couple of months ago, before Doug Lambert had come into their lives, she might have believed it.

Parker seemed to believe it still. He clearly adored his little town. His voice was warm as he pointed out its special features.

"Main Street wraps around the Town Square. See that central area? It stretches from the church at the north end to the hotel at the south. That's the heart of the town. All the fun stuff happens here. We'll be having a Halloween party here next month."

He glanced in the rearview mirror. "It's the best

party in the world. Great rides, great games and enough cotton candy to make you puke pink.''

Faith thought she heard a noise from the back seat. It might have been a muffled giggle. But when she turned around, Spencer was studying the tag on Tigger's collar, and he didn't even seem to have heard.

"Sounds delightful," she said dryly, watching the long, open green square pass by. The streets were lined with maple trees that had already begun to hint at autumn color. It would undoubtedly be gorgeous at the height of the fall. "But we probably won't be—"

She stopped herself before she could finish the thought. *We won't be here then,* she had been about to say. Halloween was a whole month away, so surely...

But the truth was, she didn't really know what the future held. She had no idea when—or if—the police would catch Doug Lambert. She had no idea when she and Spencer could go home.

And it was extremely important that she never, ever mislead the little boy. She mustn't ever get his hopes up, only to dash them later. He had suffered so much shock, so much loss that he didn't trust anything or anyone anymore.

She was going to have to work very hard to win back even a little of that sweet trust he used to give so freely.

"It sounds terrific," she repeated, without the wry-

ness. "Maybe we'll go, if we're still here at Halloween."

And as soon as she said the words, a voice in the
back of her head added another thought…the kind of
sickening thought she'd never had before Grace's
death. The kind of ugly, shivering thought that
seemed so out of place in Firefly Glen.

Maybe they'd go. If…

If Doug Lambert didn't find them.

If they were still alive at Halloween.

REED'S LAST PATIENT of the day was a bunny that had
hopped onto a nasty piece of broken glass. Flopsy,
the beloved pet of a nine-year-old cutie named Becky,
was going to be fine. Becky was another matter. She
hadn't stopped crying for the past twenty minutes.

Otherwise, though, it had been a light day. And it
promised to be an easy night, too. They had only two
boarders—a sleepy Persian cat recovering from a routine neutering and a spoiled lizard whose doting owners were out of town and didn't trust anyone but Reed
to shove lettuce into its terrarium properly.

He appreciated the easy workload, especially today,
when Faith Constable and her nephew were set to
arrive any minute. It had given him time to make sure
the guest bedrooms were presentable—which took
longer than he'd expected.

He had opened the windows to banish any musti-
ness. He'd been too long without a housekeeper, that
was for damn sure. He hoped she was a good one.

At four-thirty, Tucker Brady, the teenager who helped him with the heavy work, poked his head in the door.

"Hey, Doc. Things are pretty quiet back here. Any chance I could dip out a little early?"

Reed ought to say no. He had promised Tucker's older sister, Mary, that he'd keep Tucker so overworked and underpaid that he couldn't acquire any more tattoos. Tucker already had a fire-breathing dragon trailing down one arm, and he was so proud of it he hadn't worn a long-sleeved shirt since he got it, not even last week, when the temperature dropped below forty.

But tonight Tucker didn't look like a boy hot for a tattoo. He had washed his face, slicked back his dark hair and waded into a vat of cologne. He looked—or more accurately smelled—like a boy with a hot date.

"Sure," Reed said, handing the bandaged rabbit back to Becky, who clutched it to her chest tightly. Actually, Flopsy was in far more danger of dying of suffocation than a cut foot. "Just toss some food out for the ducks before you leave, okay?"

Tucker agreed eagerly and disappeared before Reed could change his mind. Becky's mom dried the little girl's tears, paid her bill and departed.

So far so good. And still twenty minutes left before Faith Constable was due to arrive.

But Reed should have known that, the minute he started congratulating himself on having things under control, something would go wrong.

He was washing his hands, waiting for Justine to finish running the computer backup discs so they both could call it a day, when suddenly the room came alive with a raucous honking.

Justine covered her ears and grimaced. But Reed knew that sound. Something was bothering the ducks out by the back pond. They were making such a violent ruckus that, though the clinic was a hundred yards away, the quiet office seemed full of quacking and honking and the flapping of frantic wings.

He met Justine's bewildered gaze.

"Another fox?" she asked, worried. She picked up Gavin and held him protectively, as if she feared that the fox might decide that the plump, soft baby would make a tastier treat than an old stringy duck.

"It's a little early for that—they usually show up at dusk. But I'll see." Reed went out the back door. God, that fox was a persistent devil, wasn't he? He thought he'd scared the scavenger away for good last week.

Though he knew that ducks in the wild became dinner for foxes every day, he felt a certain responsibility toward these particular silly birds. Melissa had encouraged them to live on their pond—had named them and generally pampered them into lazy, domesticated guests.

And, as she had always said, laughing, it was very bad manners to let a predator come in and gnaw on your guests.

But, when Reed walked outside, he saw immediately that it wasn't a fox.

Instead, it was a skinny little boy and a shaggy little dog.

And it was also a beautiful, dark-haired, well-dressed woman who had kicked off her shoes and dropped her purse at the edge of the grass and now seemed to be playing a peculiar game of tag with the other two.

As best Reed could tell, the dog had started it. Just a puppy, really, he was racing up and down the length of the pond, trailing a long, limp leash. He was having the time of his life, his pink tongue flying as he ran, barking incessantly, clearly intoxicated by the power of setting the ducks into a noisy flutter.

The little boy was chasing the dog, making periodic futile attempts to snag the leash. His pinched face was as serious as a judge, and he never took his eyes off the puppy, as if his life depended on catching him.

The woman was chasing the boy, stumbling over clumsy ducks who waddled into her path. "Spencer! Tigger! Stop! Please, sweetheart. Stop."

At the same instant, Reed observed his friend Parker rounding the corner, his arms full of suitcases, which he promptly dropped when he spied the chaos before him.

"Spencer, don't," Parker called out, echoing the woman. Then he noticed Reed standing at the clinic door and gave him a sheepish grin. "This isn't exactly how the introductions were supposed to go, but that great-looking lady down there is your new house-keeper.''

"So I gathered."

Parker's grin deepened. "Well? It's your pond. Your ducks. And you're the superhero in this story. You're the gallant protector.''

"Damn it, Parker, I knew you had a hidden agenda here. I am nobody's superhero, and you damn well know it.''

"Okay, okay." Parker looked meek. "But you're in your work clothes, while I, unfortunately, am wearing Sarah's favorite overpriced suit. Maybe you should…um…do something?''

With a dark glance at Parker—a glance that reminded him whose idea all this had been in the first place—Reed moved toward the pond, which seemed to be churning with wings and webbed feet.

Suddenly, without warning, the dog took a flying leap into the pond and began to paddle furiously toward the nearest mallard.

Without a moment's hesitation, the little boy barreled in after him, making a hell of a splash.

And, of course, the woman followed frantically.

She probably thought the boy was in danger. She couldn't know, of course, that the pond was a mere two feet deep. The puppy was the only one who couldn't touch the bottom quite easily.

Reed started to lope toward them, but Faith looked over, her lovely mouth pressed tight, her wide gaze embarrassed. She shook her head.

"No, please," she said. "It's okay."

He stopped. Her voice was low and pleasant, a little husky—the kind of voice that drove men wild without even trying. But it was emphatic. She was already embarrassed, and she did not want to be "rescued."

So he honored that, standing at the edge of the pond, watching in case anyone slipped on the way out.

Now that her clothes were drenched, he couldn't help noticing that her body was spectacular. He glanced at Parker suspiciously, wondering if his friend had known that Faith Constable was a bona fide beauty when he decided she should hide out at Autumn House. It would be just like him to try a little matchmaking.

But Parker looked every bit as mesmerized as Reed felt. Parker might be happily married, but that didn't mean he was blind. And, even soaking wet—maybe *especially* soaking wet—this woman was enough to drive an army to its knees.

"Please," she called out again. "I don't want you to get wet, too, Dr. Fairmont. We're fine, really."

She was holding out her hand to stop him, and Reed realized he must have unconsciously taken another step toward her. He reined himself in with effort.

She was right, of course. They were fine. Spencer had quickly caught the dog, who wriggled in his arms, ecstatically licking mud from his chin. Faith put her arm across the boy's wet, bony shoulder and bent down, ignoring the water, to give him something that was a cross between a hug and a stern talking to.

It was quite a scene, the two drenched and muddy creatures standing knee deep in water, their clothes ruined, their hair streaming in their faces. And all around them, the ducks paddled peacefully, staring straight ahead with stately boredom, as if, sadly, nothing interesting ever happened on their little pond.

Just then, Justine appeared at Reed's elbow, chewing on some spearmint-scented gum, her sleeping baby propped on her shoulder.

"Wow," she said without much inflection, scanning the weird tableau before them. "That half-drowned thing in the pond is your 'fox'?"

"No." Reed shook his head slowly, and then, seeing that Faith's minilecture was over, he began to move a little closer. Maybe he could just lend a hand, just make sure they could climb out without any further dunking.

He glanced back at Justine briefly with a small smile. "Actually," he said, "that's my new housekeeper."

Justine stared a minute, and then she chuckled, stroking her baby's cheek softly.

"Wow," she said again as she turned to go back into the clinic. "And I thought you were nuts for hiring *me!*"

CHAPTER THREE

FAITH HAD NEVER BEEN so humiliated in her life.
What a great first impression! She couldn't imagine
what Reed Fairmont must think.

She had to fight the urge to come staggering out of
the pond, dripping mud all over everyone, and start
compulsively overexplaining, overapologizing, over-
reacting.

She hadn't realized that Tigger was essentially being theatrical and never had any intention of massa-
cring Dr. Fairmont's ducks. Tigger wasn't a bird dog.
He was just a puppy with too much energy, but for a
minute she'd forgotten that.

And she hadn't, of course, realized how shallow
the pond was. She had been too focused on the fact
that Spencer wasn't a strong swimmer. He was just
six years old, and if he'd slipped beneath the black-
gold water, she might not have been able to find him
in time.

But, though these were good reasons, they weren't
the real reasons, and she knew it. The real reason
Spencer had overreacted to the fear of losing Tigger,
and the real reason she had been so afraid of losing

Spencer, was simply that they had lost too much already.

They weren't like other people anymore. Their antennae were always subtly tuned to the disaster frequency. They had seen how swiftly tragedy could strike—even on a sunny summer morning, even in your own home, even while people were making peanut butter sandwiches—and that knowledge had changed them forever.

But that wasn't the kind of thing you walked right up to a total stranger and began explaining. "Hello, nice to meet you, sorry about the ducks, but you see my nephew and I have developed this disaster mentality."

Impossible. So instead she put her arm around Spencer's shoulder and guided him toward the bank of the pond. She stroked his hair back from his forehead, and then did the same to her own. Her stitches hurt—she shouldn't have let them get wet—but she ignored the pain.

She summoned up all her dignity and looked at Reed Fairmont with her best imitation of a normal smile.

"I'm so sorry," she said. "We seem to have made a terrible mess."

The man in front of her smiled, too. It was such a warm, sympathetic smile that for a minute Faith thought maybe Reed Fairmont did understand everything. Maybe he knew about how fear seemed to follow them everywhere, even to Firefly Glen, how they heard its whisper in the song of the birds, in the rustle of the wind and the slither of the rain, and even in the kiss of the sunset.

But that was ridiculous, of course. Reed was a doctor. That smile was probably just part of his reassuring bedside manner.

"It's no problem," he said. "I'm just sorry you must be so uncomfortable."

Her next thought was that he was a surprisingly young, attractive man. If anything, even more attractive than the elegant Parker Tremaine. She looked from one man to the other curiously.

Firefly Glen must have some kind of sex-appeal potion in its water.

Detective Bentley had never said how old Dr. Fairmont was—just that he was the widowed veterinarian of this small mountain town. Faith's imagination had summoned up a gray-haired, weather-beaten image, kind of a countrified Gregory Peck in half glasses and a lab coat, his trusty hound trotting at his heels.

She couldn't have been more wrong. No gray hair, no wrinkles, no reading glasses, no lab coat and no hound. Instead, the real Reed Fairmont was in his early thirties and good-looking enough to be an actor playing a country vet or a model posing for the cover of *Adirondack Adventure*.

Six-foot-something, with broad shoulders, trim hips and muscles in all the right places. Longish, wavy brown hair with a healthy dose of highlights. And green eyes smiling out from a forest of thick lashes.

He bent down and gave Tigger a pat. He smiled at Spencer. "Hi," he said comfortably. "You've got a pretty great dog here." Spencer just ducked his chin and stared down at Tigger.

Reed didn't seem to notice. He stood without comment and gave Faith another smile. "It's getting chilly," he said. "I bet you'd like to get out of those wet clothes."

She looked over at the house, which was gleaming now with lights in the encroaching dusk. Autumn House. It, too, had surprised her. Detective Bentley had reported that it was a large, wooden Adirondack cabin, but that simple description hadn't begun to do it justice.

Autumn House was huge, and as beautiful as the forest itself. It sprawled with a natural grace as far as the eye could see—here following the contours of a small silver creek, there wrapping around an ancient oak. The house rose three stories at its center, then sloped to two, then one, then tapered off to a long wooden boardwalk that eventually disappeared into the woods.

It had huge picture windows that looked out onto the sunsets, and porches on all three floors. She felt sure that the place had been built as a haven, a place where terrible things wouldn't dream of happening.

If only that were true.

"Tell you what," Reed said, as if he had followed her longing gaze to the warm, lighted house. "Why don't you let Parker take you up and show you where your rooms are? That way you can get a warm shower and change.''

She longed to say yes. A warm shower sounded like heaven. But she looked down at Tigger, uncertain. ''I think I'd better wash the puppy off first,'' she said. ''He'll get mud all over your lovely house.''

''I can do that.'' Reed squatted down again and tugged lightly on Tigger's muddy ear. ''I've got everything I need back in the clinic. That is, if Tigger doesn't mind going with a stranger.''

Tigger had never met a stranger. He licked Reed's hand and wriggled with anticipation. Reed chuckled. ''Guess that's my answer,'' he said pleasantly, then looked at Spencer. ''I promise I'll take good care of him.''

Suddenly Parker Tremaine stepped up, clearing his throat. ''I think you've got it backward, Reed,'' he said with a wry smile. ''It's your house—I'm not even sure which rooms you've set aside for them. So how about you take Faith and Spencer up to the house, and I'll wash the dog?''

Tigger sniffed Parker's outstretched hand and began thumping his tail in unqualified approval. But Reed gave his friend a quizzical expression that Faith couldn't quite decipher.

''What about your suit, Parker? I seem to remember that you're wearing Sarah's favorite suit.''

Parker tilted his head and grinned slowly. ''True, but, you know, Reed, there is something Sarah values even more than a good suit.''

Reed squinted narrowly at the other man, as if he suspected him of an ulterior motive. "Really. And what would that be?"

Parker hesitated—a small pause that had a distinctly teasing flavor. Faith saw that they were communicating privately—and very effectively—but she couldn't really tell about what. Maybe it was as simple as trying to get out of having to wash the muddy dog. Or having to squire the dripping guests up to the shower…

Suddenly Parker held out his hands with a smile, asking Spencer to transfer custody of Tigger. To Faith's amazement, Spencer hardly hesitated. He handed the puppy over with a single kiss to his matted head.

"Dogs," Parker said, holding Tigger up with the triumphant air of a magician pulling a rabbit out of a hat. "As you know, Reed, Sarah just loves dogs."

SPENCER AND TIGGER fell asleep early, almost as soon as they had wolfed down dinner. Reed wasn't surprised. They had both been subdued, obviously exhausted by their eventful day.

At one point, Spencer had looked up at his aunt intently, then gazed over at his bed. She must have understood, because she turned to Reed and asked whether he'd mind if Tigger slept on the bed.

Naturally, he hadn't minded at all. He'd been six years old once. And frankly he still didn't see the point in having a dog if you didn't let it sleep on the bed.

Reed assumed that Faith would fall asleep early, too, but to his surprise when he strolled out onto the second-floor porch at about ten o'clock, she was standing out there, as well.

She didn't hear him at first. Wrapped in a moon-light-blue robe and a gray cloud of deep thoughts, she was staring into the trees as if she longed to lose herself in their inky depths.

It probably would be wiser to turn around and leave her there. But he wasn't feeling wise. All evening he'd been feeling edgy, unable to settle in. He felt irrationally as if his life was on the verge of becoming completely different, though he had no idea how.

Maybe it was just the weird feeling of having other people in the house. No one but him had slept in this house since Melissa died.

And, to be honest, he was curious. He wanted to know Faith Constable's story. Parker had given him broad outlines, but, now that he'd met her, outlines weren't enough.

He was careful to make enough noise walking toward her to be sure she'd hear him. Given what she'd been through lately, the last thing he wanted to do was startle her.

She turned around. "Hi," she said, smiling.

"Hi," he responded casually, but inside his senses were suddenly reeling. She smelled of soap and some kind of perfume that made him think of pink flowers and springtime. She wore no makeup, and the blue-gray shadows under her eyes were more apparent than before, but somehow she was more beautiful than ever.

Her dark hair fell to midarm—curving against the tender spot where he had earlier noticed a large white bandage. The bandage had been a brutal reminder that she wasn't here for a social visit. She wasn't even here to be his housekeeper.

She was a wounded, frightened woman. A refugee seeking asylum.

He felt a sudden flash of anger toward this insane, vicious Douglas Lambert. How could anyone be trying to hurt someone so beautiful?

He joined her at the railing. The night was chilly, but not yet cold. The autumn sky was like a piece of heavily sequined black satin.

"So," he said, not sure how to open a normal conversation. So much about this situation was far from normal. "Is the room okay? Do you have everything you need?"

"Oh, yes, absolutely." She sounded stilted, but polite. She turned toward him with another of those strained smiles. "I haven't thanked you properly yet. It's very generous of you to let us hide out here."

"I'm glad to be able to help," he answered. God, this was like a bad comedy of manners. They were living together, for Pete's sake. They might be living together for weeks—even months. They were going to have to get past this stilted exchange of meaningless pleasantries.

"So, I was wondering… If this is a good time, with Spencer asleep, I thought maybe you'd be willing to tell me a little more about what happened."

She touched her arm. "More like what?"

He chose his words carefully. He didn't want to sound insensitive, as if he found her tragedy as morbidly fascinating and unreal as a soap opera. "About your sister, and why this guy is still after you. Why Spencer doesn't talk."

She didn't answer at first. He shouldn't have rushed her, he thought, kicking himself mentally. She wasn't ready.

"I'm sorry," he said. "I know it can't be easy to talk about. It's just that—if I'm going to help—I thought maybe I should know a little more."

She gripped the railing and stared back out at the trees. "No, that's okay," she said. "You're right. It's just that sometimes it's hard to—"

"I know," he said, wishing he could unspeak the words. What a clumsy approach this had been. He really was rusty at dealing with women, wasn't he? "It can wait."

"No. Now is better. I just—I don't really know why Spencer doesn't talk." It was as if she had to hurry up and get started, for fear she might lose her courage. "Not exactly. The psychiatrists seem to think it's the stress of losing his mother. They use some pretty impressive phrases when they talk about it. They say his 'stressor reactions of fear exceeded the normal adaptive responses.'"

She shrugged, then winced. The movement must have pulled her stitches. "Whatever that means."

"I guess it means his system maxed out."

"Right. They called it his 'breaking point threshold.'"

Yeah, Reed thought. He'd heard those terms himself, back when he was in his heavy denial and heavy drinking phase. *The breaking point threshold.* Everyone had one. You didn't necessarily see it coming, but you sure as hell knew when you crossed it.

"Anyhow," she went on, "they seem to think it's selective, that he can talk if he wants to—as opposed to a true loss of neurological function. Apparently that's a positive sign." Her eyes grew dark. "I hope they're right."

"I think they probably do know what they're talking about," he said. "Even if they like to say it in some pretty pompous ways."

She rewarded him for that supportive joke with a brief smile. "Anyhow, I guess I ought to tell you about Doug, too. He's the man…the man who—"

"They told me," he said quickly. "He's the man you believe killed your sister."

"I *know* he did," she said with a sudden vehemence. "I don't understand why no one can just believe me!"

"I believe you," he said. And he did. He had seen how her face blanched, and her lips had seemed to grow stiff when she tried to say his name. She knew Doug Lambert was a killer. She knew it in her veins, which in his book was far more reliable than knowing it in your head.

She looked at him hard, as if she wondered whether he might be merely humoring her. But she must have seen his sincerity, because she took a deep breath and went on.

"I have an interior design business. Doug was one of my clients. He had a lot of money, and he wanted his entire house done over. I worked with him for a couple of months, but eventually his interest grew... personal." She swallowed. "Personal and very disturbing."

"He wanted a relationship?"

She nodded, shivering slightly. "He was obsessed with it. It was pretty frightening, actually. He was a big man. Not as tall as you are, but bulky. Sometimes, when I wouldn't let him—" She paused, getting control of her voice. "You could almost feel the violence running through him."

Reed waited, still careful not to push. It was a little like trying to coax a hurt kitten out of the safety of its cage. He had learned through the years that you succeeded far faster if you did absolutely nothing, just provided a safe place to enter.

"I handed his work off to my partner, but he wouldn't take the hint. Eventually we had to turn the whole job over to another firm. And still he wouldn't stop. He kept calling, coming over unannounced, sending roses. Thousands of red roses.'' She glanced at Reed. "I used to like roses. You can't imagine how I hate them now.''

He didn't deny it. He couldn't know, not really. Probably no man could—especially not a healthy, physically capable man. Men generally met other men on a level playing field. But take this fragile, slender woman next to him—probably no more than five-five and just over a hundred pounds. All the self-defense classes in the world wouldn't change the fact that a six-foot man would always have the advantage.

"I had invited Grace over that day,'' she said. "Douglas was supposed to be out of town, and I was feeling great. It was lovely to know he wouldn't show up and make a scene. Grace was happy, too. Spencer's father died three years ago, but Grace had found a new boyfriend, and she was so happy—''

He touched her shoulder, careful to avoid the stitches. "It's all right,'' he said. "You don't have to tell me this part if you don't want to.''

"I do want to.'' She was standing very, very straight and her gaze was looking at something he couldn't see. "I had gone out for supplies for lunch, and when I got back, I saw Spencer sneaking out of the building. He had Tigger with him. I'm sure Grace had told him not to leave the apartment, but my apartment building was next to a park, and it probably was just too enticing.''

She smiled a little. "You likely can't believe it, but before his mother died Spencer was a very mischievous little boy. Very active. Talked a mile a minute. She used to say she couldn't keep him still long enough to tie his shoes.''

Reed smiled, too. It was a cute picture. He wanted to see the little boy like that again.

"He was sneaking out to play with Tigger at the park. He was so ashamed when he saw me coming after him. He's not naughty, just mischievous. He came with me right away. And that's when I saw Doug Lambert. Coming out of my apartment building.''

She put her hand over her eyes. "He saw me, too. I'll never forget the look on his face. It was as if he'd seen a ghost.''

"Oh, my God.'' Reed hadn't heard this part. He hadn't realized that Doug Lambert had killed the wrong sister. Suddenly he could feel the pit of guilt that must yawn before Faith Constable, and he marveled at her ability to keep her balance, to keep from falling into it and never coming out at all.

"That's right. He thought he had just killed me. I honestly believe it wasn't until he saw me on the street with Spencer that he had any idea he had killed Grace instead.''

It was too horrible. "You and your sister—were you twins?''

"No, but she was only a year older than I was, and we looked so much alike. She wore her hair the same way. We even shared clothes. I think he was just so angry, when he came in and heard her talking to

Kenny on the telephone, when he heard what she was saying. Kenny told the police that they had been so playful, kissing each other through the phone, and talking about—''

He heard the moment her voice broke. She made a choking sound, struggling to hold back. And then, defeated, she ducked her head, trying to hide the tears. ''I hate him,'' she said. ''I hate him so much.''

He didn't think. He just reached out and pulled her up against him.

''It's all right,'' he said. ''Go ahead. It's all right to cry.''

She didn't try to free herself. But she didn't surrender to the emotion either.

''No, it isn't,'' she said tightly. Her voice was muffled against his shirt, but he could still hear that it was thick with tears that needed desperately to fall. ''I can't let Spencer see me crying.''

''Spencer is asleep,'' he said. Her hair was as soft as the black satin sky, and he ran his hand down it over and over, as if he could stroke the tears out of her with the rhythmic touch. After a few minutes, he imagined that her muscles were relaxing, just a little

''Go ahead,'' he said. ''Let it go. It isn't good to keep it all inside.''

He knew that all too well. He hadn't cried, either, after Melissa died. He had taken refuge in liquor the way Faith was taking refuge in her anger. Either way, the unshed tears would poison you, until you hardly knew who you were.

She shook her head, but his shirt was warm and wet where she had been, and he knew she was losing the fight.

"Crying is weak," she whispered. "I haven't cried since the day she died. I can't afford to be weak, can't you see that? I have to be strong until they catch him."

It was too cruel. He tightened his arms around her. And as he felt her slender body press against him, he was suddenly reminded of a small, broken bird he had once treated. It had been brought to him much too late. The bird had died in his hands.

Determination shot through him like a burning streak of light. She had come here for protection, and by God he would make sure she got it.

"No, you don't," he said softly. "You're not alone anymore. Just this once, let someone else be strong for you."

She tensed again, holding her breath. And then, weeks and weeks too late, this brave, grieving woman finally allowed herself the luxury of tears.

DOUG LAMBERT laughed to himself as he passed a policeman on the street. For a minute, he considered asking the cop for a dollar, just to enjoy the thrill of looking into his eyes and knowing the dumb bastard had no idea who he was.

But ultimately it wasn't worth it. Cops were too stupid to live—fooling them wasn't even very much fun.

While they scrambled around, putting out their as-
inine all-points bulletins about millionaire murder
suspect Douglas Lambert and scouring all the obvious
places in vain, Doug was hiding in plain sight.

Living at a squalid, smelly homeless shelter.

See, that was the key. The cops had no imagination.
They never even thought of looking there. They believed he was rich, spoiled, incapable of enduring
hardship, unwilling to sleep on anything but his expensive Turkish sheets or to eat anything but five-star
cuisine.

Morons. They didn't know a damn thing about
Doug Lambert. He came from a filthy, wretched noth-
ingness, and he was perfectly comfortable returning
there for as long as it took.

Actually, it had been almost embarrassingly easy.
Get a box of Clairol do-it-yourself color and go a few
weeks without a shave or a hundred-dollar haircut.

Take out your expensive front bridgework and let
your lips cave in over a toothless mouth. He felt smug
to think how everyone had urged him to get implants—he could certainly afford them. But he didn't
like doctors, he didn't like pain, and so he had settled
for the best damn dentures on the market. See, now,
what a good decision that turned out to be?

Then splurge five bucks on cast-off jeans and a
T-shirt and a pair of stained sneakers. After that you
could walk right up and spit in that flatfoot's ugly
face, and the damn fool would never know the difference.

Still, Doug knew he had to find out where Faith had gone. He could feel the urge building inside him, until it was so big now it was almost a physical pain. Sometimes he thought he couldn't breathe around it.

He had to find her.

He wasn't stupid enough to hire a private detective. The police would be looking for that. But there were other ways. A man like him knew plenty of useful people whose names weren't in the Yellow Pages.

By the time he arrived back at the shelter, he had come to a decision. He wouldn't wait any longer, with this anger, and the desire that was its twin, building inside him like a tumor. He was patient, but he wasn't a waffler. He liked action.

He sat down, put his hand into the pocket of the drunk slumped next to him and pulled out a couple of quarters, staring in the man's eyes the whole time, daring him to object.

And then he dropped them into the pay telephone in the hall and dialed a number he knew well but almost never used.

He needed relief, and there was only one way to get it.

Faith Constable had to die.

CHAPTER FOUR

"LET GO OF THAT, you diabolical son of a—"

Faith squatted down by the vacuum cleaner, tugging with all her strength at the drapery pull that was half-in, half-out of the Hoover-monster's long silver snout. But she'd forgotten to turn the motor off, so the monster was still roaring, sucking in, as if green tassels were the most delectable treats on earth.

"I...said...let...go!"

It was too late. By the time she reached the power switch, the tassel had disappeared. The monster's roar dwindled to a sick choking sound, and the air smelled ominously of burned rubber.

She bit back a curse, remembering just in time that Spencer was in the room. She glanced at him.

"Sorry," she said. "This machine is giving me a hard time."

Tigger had been watching her the whole time, whining and growling and thumping his tail. But Spencer just kept staring out the large picture window, which offered a spectacular view of the hickory, birch, sycamore and maple that dotted the Autumn House property, thickening until gradually they blended with the untamed woods beyond.

It was gorgeous. But she was pretty sure Spencer wasn't communing with nature. His shoulders were stiff, his arms tightly wrapped over his bony chest, his eyes unblinking, probably fixed on his own tragic thoughts.

He was so unhappy, she thought with a twist of pain. And she had no idea how to help him.

Suddenly overcome by her own incompetence—if she couldn't control a simple vacuum cleaner, how was she going to cope with parenting a traumatized little boy?—she sank to her knees. She glared at the vacuum and wondered what on earth to do now.

Frankly, she had no idea. As anyone could tell you, Faith was the world's worst housekeeper.

It wasn't something she'd ever been ashamed of before. She worked hard all day, and her interior design company was successful. So she hired a "domestic technician" to perform lemony magic at her apartment once a week.

Sometimes on Fridays Faith opened her door with her eyes shut, just to savor the sparkling fresh smell that said Delilah had been there. She valued a clean house, all right. She just didn't have a clue how to make it happen except by writing a check.

Still, how hard could it be? She wiggled her middle finger down the tube of the vacuum, but encountered nothing but smooth plastic. She squinted into it, but saw only blackness. She tapped it against the floor as hard as she dared, but nothing emerged except a puff of dirt that billowed up into her eyes and mouth.

Coughing, she scanned the room. She could *not* face Reed Fairmont and tell him that she had lost a wrestling match with a vacuum cleaner. Especially after she'd so stupidly wept all over his shirt last night.

He undoubtedly already thought she was a weakling. She couldn't add hopeless incompetent to the mix.

She was smart. She was creative. She could think of something...

Of course! A metal hanger.

Five minutes later she'd broken two fingernails, the stitches in her shoulder ached and the hanger was wedged down the long snout, as lost as the tassel. She rubbed her stinging, sooty eyes and made a mental note to give Delilah a raise. A big one.

"Well, well," a dry voice observed. "You must be the new housekeeper."

Faith looked up. A tidy little woman, probably seventy-something, stood in the doorway, a casserole dish in her hands and wry amusement in her sharp brown eyes. The woman was all skin and bones, but somehow so authoritative in her plain—but very expensive—black pantsuit that Faith found herself scrambling to her feet.

"Hi," she said, trying to brush the dirt from her white polo shirt. How stupid to have chosen white! "I'm sorry. I didn't hear you knock."

"I don't knock," the other woman said. "I'm Theo Burke."

Faith hesitated, unsure whether that was a non sequitur.

"Good heavens." Theo Burke chuckled. "That was pretty cocky, even for me. I just meant I have a key. Reed and I go way back. I've been bringing him dinner three days a week since Melissa died. Not that he needs it anymore, the lazy scamp. It's just a habit now, but we both like it."

"I can understand why. It smells fantastic." Faith held out her hand, hoping it wasn't too grimy. "It's nice to meet you, Theo. I'm Faith Constable, Dr. Fairmont's new housekeeper."

"I knew it. They're talking about you in town. They said you didn't look like a housekeeper." Theo let her gaze skim the mess on the floor. "I'm inclined to agree."

Faith took a breath. "Well, I—"

"Not that it matters. You're pretty enough, and young enough—no one will ever care. It's only when you get to be an old prune like me that people expect you to be good at things."

Faith stared at the older woman, wishing she could explain why she was here, why she was posing as a housekeeper, when even a blind person could tell she was nothing of the sort. She knew it didn't really matter what Theo Burke, whoever she was, thought of her. But darn it—she was good at things. Lots of things. Just not domestic things.

"We'd better get this straightened up." Theo set the casserole, which was wrapped in a thermal covering, on one of the elegant wooden end tables. "Don't want Reed to come in and find the house a wreck on your first day. Melissa spoiled him rotten, of course. She was the perfect wife. She could scrub tubs, baste a pheasant and win the Miss America contest all at the same time. If she hadn't been such a sweetie, every female in Firefly Glen would have hated her gorgeous guts."

Faith blinked. This level of candor was rather amazing. The small-town style, no doubt. In the city, you were lucky to get a hello grunt.

"Anyhow," Theo continued, "let's see what can be done. How bloody was the battle? Did you actually kill the poor vacuum, or just maim it?"

"I—" Faith shook her head and numbly picked up the long gray nozzle. The looped end of a metal hanger stuck out like a rude tongue. "To be honest, I don't know. It all started when I pointed that thing at one of the curtain tie-backs. It just got worse from there."

Theo laughed, a surprisingly warm, pleasant sound, considering how acerbic her conversation had been so far. "Oh, this is just a flesh wound. Let Dr. Theo do a little surgery."

As Faith stepped back, she noticed that Spencer had brought Tigger over to get a better look at Theo. Boy and dog were peeking around the edge of a large rose-colored armchair.

Theo saw him at that moment, too. "That your son?"

"My nephew." Faith tried to motion Spencer out of hiding. "Spencer, this is Ms. Burke."

But Spencer wasn't moving. He was just a pair of round, dark eyes under a mess of spiky brown hair. He held Tigger tightly in his arms.

"None of this Ms. Burke stuff. Everybody calls me Theo. Everybody I like, that is, and I already know I like you, Spencer. Know how I know?"

Spencer's brow wrinkled subtly. Faith could tell he was curious, but of course he didn't say a word.

Luckily, Theo didn't seem to require an answer. "I'll tell you how I know," she said, unscrewing the body of the vacuum with a tiny silver tool she had whisked out of her pocket. "I know because your dog likes you. Dogs know who the good people are."

She held out the loose screw. "Hold these for me, would you, Spencer? And don't drop them."

To Faith's amazement, Spencer inched out from behind the chair. He took three steps closer to the vacuum cleaner and opened his small palm. Theo dropped the screws into his hand and went on working, as if nothing peculiar had happened.

Faith, too, tried to pretend nonchalance. It was such a little thing, compared to the old Spencer, who had always been sociable and talkative. But the new Spencer rarely even made eye contact with strangers.

After a few minutes, Theo tugged out the green tassel. It was crumpled and dingy, but intact. Then she wiggled the hanger free, too.

She held it up with a smile. "You were lucky.

Could have done some real damage with this, but you just melted the belt.''

She tilted her head and scrutinized Faith, who was sucking on her index finger, trying to soothe it where the nail had broken below the quick. Faith stopped with a guilty start and tucked her hand behind her back as if she had something to hide.

''Okay, I've got to know.'' Theo grinned, suddenly looking twenty years younger. ''It's none of my business, but I'm going to ask you anyhow. I always do. Anybody can tell you that.''

''Ask me what?''

''What made a woman like you decide to take a job as a housekeeper? I'd be willing to bet the cost of that glamorous manicure that you've never actually touched a vacuum cleaner before.''

''Well, of course I ha—''

Theo's prim silver eyebrows arched, and Faith's fib died on her lips.

''You're right,'' she said. ''I am very new to this. I've never used one of these canister vacuums, and I haven't a clue how to baste a pheasant, either. Sadly, I'm no Melissa Fairmont.''

Theo let out a gruff bark of laughter. ''You can say that again. Melissa could have built you a whole new vacuum cleaner with just this hanger, two stamps and a thumbtack.''

Faith smiled ruefully. So Reed Fairmont was used to living with a domestic goddess. Poor man. He volunteered to do a good deed, and look what happened.

A domestic dummy invaded his lovely house, drenched his shirt and melted his belt. He was probably already kicking himself hard for being such a patsy.

She took a deep breath. "It's all right, Theo. I think I know what you're trying to tell me, and I really do appreciate the warning."

Theo rose with a grunt and handed the screwdriver to Spencer. "Put that back together for me, would you, please? You saw how I took it apart, right?"

When the little boy accepted the screwdriver, Theo nodded briefly, then turned to Faith. "What exactly do you think I'm trying to tell you?"

"Well…" Faith felt herself coloring. "Just that Melissa Fairmont was a very unusual, very accomplished woman. And that Dr. Fairmont may be disappointed to discover how little his new housekeeper has in common with her."

"Well, that's part of it." Theo smiled. "You may disappoint him in some ways. But you may also make him laugh." She looked at the broken vacuum.

"In fact, I'm absolutely positive you will. And a little laughter may be what this house needs most of all."

REED HAD TOYED with the idea of skipping dinner— he had plenty of work to do in the clinic—but he'd finally decided that would be too cowardly.

He had to sit down and share a meal with his new houseguests sooner or later. And, as he'd learned the

first day at med school, when it came to facing a
problem, sooner was always better.

It wasn't, in the end, quite as awkward as he'd
feared. Theo's chicken-mushroom casserole was delicious, of course, and Faith had obviously worked to
set a homey tone. She'd filled a small cut-glass bowl
with yellow apples for a centerpiece, and she had
found Melissa's favorite green-flowered napkins,
which looked great against the maple table.

She was good at keeping the conversation going,
too. She showed an intelligent—though undeniably
artificial—interest in every detail of his veterinary
practice. To help her along, Reed trotted out his silliest stories—the duck that bit the sheriff, the lizard
that liked to have his tummy rubbed, the bunny that
hatched an egg and the cat that delivered her kittens
in a birdcage.

He even mentioned that he was heading out after
dinner to see those newborn kittens, and suggested
that Spencer and Faith could join him if they liked.

But, though both he and Faith kept sending en-
couraging glances down to Spencer's end of the table,
the kid never cracked a smile.

When it was over, Spencer had dashed upstairs to
his room, Tigger close on his heels. Now Faith and
Reed were in the kitchen washing dishes in a silence
that was strangely comfortable.

Suddenly the telephone rang. Faith whirled toward
it so eagerly Reed thought for a moment she planned

to answer it herself. She seemed to remember just in time that this wasn't her house.

"Sorry," she said. She backed away with a sheepish smile and returned to the sudsy water. But her posture was tight and wary. He could tell she was listening intently as he picked up the receiver.

It was just the Petermans, the overprotective owners of the spoiled lizard. Reed managed to assure them that Spike was quite contented, eating well, but not too much, missing them, but not too much, getting plenty of attention, but not too much.

Finally he hung up the phone with a chuckle and turned to Faith. "Spike's owner. Apparently Spike suffers from separation anxiety. If he looks lonely, I'm supposed to give him extra food. Unfortunately, I'm having trouble reading the nuances of his facial expression. It always looks like a cross between superbored and mildly ticked off."

She smiled half-heartedly. "Well, maybe lizard nuances are more in their body language."

Reed shrugged. "Maybe. Or maybe the Petermans are nuts."

Truth was, though, Reed did believe in body language, in animals and in people. And right now Faith Constable's body language screamed tension. She had wanted that telephone call to be someone else. But who?

He took Theo's rinsed casserole dish from her hands and began rubbing it with his thickest kitchen towel. "I wondered—the way you went for the telephone. Are you expecting a call from someone?"

"Not expecting, really." She tried to smile again, but it clearly was becoming more of a strain every minute. "Just hoping, I guess."

He looked at her sad mouth and wondered if there was a boyfriend back in New York City, a guy who was ordinarily in charge of making her smile. "But I thought—I mean, who even knows you're here?"

"Detective Bentley. He promised he'd keep me posted. About the investigation. About whether they're closing in on...on—"

"On Doug Lambert."

"Yes."

"But it's only been one day. Surely it's too soon?"

"Yes. I know." She took a deep breath. "I know it is."

They worked in silence another moment, and then she spoke again.

"It's just that...they did expect to hear from the florist today. The one who might have sold him the roses."

"The roses?" Reed was careful to keep any overly curious quality from his voice. He didn't want to pry, but he wanted to know everything he could. And it would do her good to talk about it. After her tears last night, she had seemed much more relaxed. She had let him guide her to the bedroom door as limply as an exhausted child.

"They found three rose petals in my kitchen that

day, next to my sister's body.'' She scrubbed at an already clean glass so hard her knuckles turned as white as the suds. ''The problem was that these roses hadn't come from Doug's regular florist. He sent me roses all the time, but not this kind.''

Reed wanted to take the glass out of her hand. She was holding it much too tightly. But he didn't dare break the flow of words.

''These roses were a much rarer variety. At first the police thought that meant it hadn't been Doug after all. But Detective Bentley sent the petals to a botanist, who said it was a variety called 'Faith.'''

Reed made a noise in spite of himself.

A shiver seemed to pass through her, and the glass slipped, plopping into the water. She fished it out again with trembling fingers.

''I think that was when Detective Bentley began to believe me. He finally found the little shop that sold them. It was two blocks from my apartment. We're waiting for the owner to get back from vacation, to see if he can identify Doug as the man who bought the roses that day.''

''Of course it was.''

''Yes.'' Her voice was even huskier than usual. ''But they need evidence. For a jury. For a conviction.''

Reed moved closer to the sink. ''I'm sorry,'' he said. ''I'm sorry that call wasn't Detective Bentley.''

''It's all right.'' But her voice cracked, and he knew it wasn't true.

She turned to hand him the glass. As he reached out, it fell from her shaking fingers and smashed on the wooden floor, splinters of crystal scattering in all directions.

He bent quickly, and so did she. As they knelt, their faces were only inches apart, and he could feel waves of stress pulsing from her. Her brown eyes were almost black, and a sharp sliver of glass glinted on her shirt, right over her heart.

"I'm so sorry," she said, and he could feel her struggle to hold herself together, to keep her emotions from flying into a hundred different pieces, just like the glass. She gathered shards quickly, filling her palm. "Please. I'll clean it up."

He caught her by the wrist. "It's all right," he said.

"No, it isn't." She bit her lower lip hard and inhaled deeply. The pulse in her wrist was like a jackhammer under his thumb.

"I hate this," she said. "This isn't me. I'm not like this."

"Like what?"

She held out her palm full of sparkling bits of glass. "Like this. Clumsy. Incompetent. You probably won't believe it, but I have my own business. I'm good at what I do. I don't break everything I touch."

"Of course you don't."

"And I'm not weak. I never cry. Never. I don't know what happened to me last night. I'd hate for you to think that I—"

A sudden noise in the kitchen doorway stopped her.

She looked up and saw Spencer standing there, staring at them curiously. She glanced at Reed, who let go of her hand. She stood up, all the ferocity instantly draining from her expression.

"Hi," she said to her nephew. "Don't come in, honey. I broke a glass, and it's all over the place."

The little boy didn't protest. He waited in the doorway, holding on to Tigger's collar to keep the puppy safe, too. They finished cleaning up the shards quickly, and then, at a nod from Faith, Spencer walked in, holding out a large piece of paper.

She took it with a smile. "What's this? Oh—how cute! I'll bet you drew this for Dr. Fairmont, didn't you?"

Spencer didn't answer, of course, but he didn't snatch the paper back, either, and even Reed could see that the little boy was comfortable with Faith's deduction. His somber brown gaze transferred to Reed, as if he were waiting for his reaction.

"Look," Faith said, handing it over. "It's the kittens you were talking about at dinner."

The kid was pretty good. Reed could clearly see three tiger-striped kittens sleeping inside a large, domed birdcage. Spencer had even added a colorful parrot on top of the cage, staring down, bewildered by what had become of his home.

Reed chuckled and looked over at Spencer. "Nice job," he said. "It's very good, and it's funny, too."

Spencer didn't smile, exactly. But he worried at his lip, as if he had to work to keep himself from smiling, and that was good enough for Reed. It felt good to see even the tiniest bit of pleasure on that pinched, freckled face. Kids weren't meant to be so sad.

"Spencer, what's that?" Faith bent down and tugged on a bit of leather that stuck out of the little boy's back pocket. "You brought Tigger's leash? Why?"

Spencer darted a quick look over at Reed, and Faith made a low sound of sudden comprehension. "Oh, I know. Maybe you've decided that you would like to go out with Dr. Fairmont to see the kittens?"

The little boy answered by leaning down and affixing the leash to Tigger's collar. The puppy immediately began turning around in frenzied circles of joy.

Faith looked up at Reed, delighted surprise written all over her lovely face. Apparently it was something of a miracle that Spencer would actually be willing to go out into the night with a stranger, even to see newborn kittens.

"Sure," Reed said easily. "I'd love to take him along."

Oops—he must have phrased that wrong. Spencer's brow wrinkled deeply under his shaggy brown bangs. He tugged on Faith's sweater. When he got her attention, he walked to the far counter and grabbed her purse. He came back and handed it to her.

The implication was unmistakable. Spencer wasn't going anywhere without his aunt.

"Reed?" She lifted her eyebrows. "Do you have room for all of us?"

"Of course," he said. "It'll be fun."

And he realized that, much to his surprise, he actually meant it. He had thought he'd have trouble relinquishing his accustomed solitude—and yet here he was, downright pleased that he wouldn't have to make the long drive out to the Lofton estate alone.

Someone knocked on the kitchen door. Spencer froze, then sidestepped behind Faith's legs, dragging Tigger with him. Soon all you could see were his little white-knuckled fingers around her hips.

"It's probably just Theo," Reed said reassuringly. "She'll be wanting her casserole dish."

Faith put her hand behind her back to stroke Spencer's head. "Can't be Theo," she said with a smile. "Theo doesn't knock."

Reed grinned back—he could easily imagine Theo saying something as haughty as that. So who was it? Mentally crossing his fingers that it wasn't any kind of emergency, he opened the door.

It was an emergency, all right. Somehow he managed not to groan out loud. It was a bona fide, four-alarm, social faux pas emergency.

It was Pauline Ferguson, the young owner of Waterworks, the newest retail store on Main Street. Pauline, the red-haired beauty from South Carolina who had been chasing Reed for months, trying to coax him into casting off his mourning and rejoining the social scene at her side.

He was supposed to be at her house right now, picking her up for their first real date.

She was angry, but far too clever to show it. Only the bright flash of her green eyes gave it away. Reed had once seen that same flash in the eyes of a furious, wounded fox.

"Oh, hell, Pauline. I'm so sorry. I completely forgot."

That didn't help, naturally. But it was the truth. And if she wanted to date him, she was going to have to accept the truth. He'd forgotten their date because it honestly didn't mean very much to him. He wasn't ready for a "relationship" and he'd told her so, a hundred times. He'd only said yes because she wouldn't accept a no.

She had assured him that she wasn't interested in anything serious, either, her divorce was too recent, couldn't they just keep each other company? But in those two flashing seconds he saw that she'd been lying.

If only he could just call it off. He'd much rather see whether the kittens, who were as small as hamsters, as blind as bats and as cute as hell, could make Spencer smile.

But he was stuck, of course. He wasn't selfish enough to insult Pauline like that. He introduced Pauline to Faith—and to Spencer, though Pauline had to take his word for it that a little boy was actually attached to those clutching fingers.

"I hope you're feeling flexible about tonight's date," he said with a smile. "I need to go to the Lofton farm before I can do anything else. And I promised Spencer and Faith they could come along. Dina Lofton has some newborn kittens that are pretty darn cute.''

Pauline was no fool. She smiled, the picture of flexibility. The wounded fox was completely hidden behind the easygoing Southern charm.

"Of course I don't mind. You know I adore kittens."

But Spencer began tugging frantically at Faith's sweater, pulling at her purse, trying to make her take it off her shoulder. His meaning was clear. He was no longer interested in going anywhere.

"It's okay, Spencer," Reed said. He felt irrationally annoyed with Pauline, who didn't realize the damage she'd done just by showing up. "We can still go. We'll all pile into the truck together. It'll be fun."

Spencer froze—and then he came out from behind Faith's legs slowly. He gave Reed one long, blank look. He reached over and plucked his kitten sketch very carefully from the kitchen table. And then, with Tigger prancing in happy ignorance behind him, the little boy left the room.

FOUR HOURS LATER, Reed let himself into the house quietly, hoping he wouldn't wake his houseguests. He was tired, and he needed to be alone.

The date had been a disaster.

Pauline hadn't done anything wrong, exactly. She was as clever as a chameleon, and she'd adapted herself to his mood, going from gaily high-spirited to sensitively low-key in a blink. Her message came through neon-clear: *See? I'm the perfect woman. I can be whatever you want.*

But there was one thing she could never be, no matter how clever she was. She could never be Melissa.

Oh, heck, that was a stupid thought, and he knew it. He could almost imagine Melissa rolling her eyes at his maudlin nonsense. She had told him toward the end that if he never married again she would consider it a personal insult. Hadn't she shown him how wonderful a good marriage could be?

For the first time in a long time, he wished he still drank. He'd like to forget everything about this blasted night, from the mute betrayal in Spencer's face when he realized he wasn't going to get to see the kittens, right up to the disappointment in Pauline's face when she realized Reed wasn't going to kiss her good-night.

Damn it. Damn it. *Damn it.*

Why did everyone want something from him that he didn't have?

He yanked the lid from the garbage can, deciding that action would have to replace the easy oblivion of liquor. Luckily, Autumn House never ran out of chores to exhaust his body into sleep. He might as well start by taking out the trash.

Right on top, though, were a dozen torn pieces of sketch paper with strangely familiar colors all over them. Two of the pieces fluttered to the floor. Picking them up, he tilted his head, trying to imagine the picture intact again.

The orange and brown of tiger-striped kittens. The blue, red and yellow of a parrot.

Damn it.

"I was going to take that bag out," Faith said suddenly from the kitchen doorway. "But I wasn't sure exactly where to put it."

He looked over at her, the pieces of paper still in his hand. She was already dressed for bed. She looked washed out, exhausted.

"It's okay," he said. "You're not really the housekeeper, here, you know. You don't have to vacuum, or dust, or take out the trash."

"I know," she said, twisting the sash of her moon-blue robe a little tighter. "But I have to do something. And you've been so generous, letting us stay here—"

She stopped as she noticed the torn papers in his hand. "Oh," she said, slightly embarrassed. She obviously hadn't meant for him to see the evidence of Spencer's anger.

"It was a rough night," she said. "He was a little...emotional."

"I can see that."

"I'm very sorry about what happened earlier," she said. "Spencer didn't mean to be rude. It's just that he—"

"Faith, stop apologizing." Reed hated those shadows under her eyes. When had she last had a good night's sleep? "You can't take the blame for everything that happens. It's not your fault Doug Lambert fell in love with you. It's not your fault he killed your sister. It's not your fault you had to leave New York so that he wouldn't kill you, too."

"I know," she said. But she bit her lip, and he felt a pang of remorse. She was probably struggling to avoid apologizing for apologizing too much.

His words were still vibrating in the empty kitchen, where low lights and midnight silence were creating an odd intimacy. They were like a married couple arguing softly so that they wouldn't wake the children. Except that they weren't married. She was his guest.

He rubbed his hand over his face, as if that might clear his head. He looked down at the torn picture again, and then looked at Faith, who had turned to leave the kitchen.

"I couldn't stay," he said abruptly. "I couldn't send Pauline away. It would have been too rude."

He heard a sort of apology in his voice, which was, of course, absolutely ridiculous. Why should he feel guilty for leaving? He hadn't had any choice. Besides, he didn't owe either of these people anything but common courtesy and a safe place to sleep.

"Of course you couldn't," she said. "It's fine. Spencer is fine. Please don't worry."

"Faith, I mean it. I would help him if I could, but I can't."

"It's all right. You don't have any oblig—"

"I don't even know what he needs. I'm a vet, not

a psychiatrist. I simply don't have the first clue what to do.''

She paused, turned and smiled just a little, the tired shadows shifting across her face in a way that was both hauntingly sad and beautiful.

''That's okay,'' she said. ''The psychiatrists don't know what to do, either.''

He stood there a long time after she left.

Damn, damn, *damn*.

Maybe it was because she had cried in his arms. Maybe it was because of the way the kid held on to that dog, like a life raft. Whatever the reason, for the first time in a long time, Reed wanted something.

He wanted to hear Spencer talk. He wanted to see Faith smile, really smile, all the way to her eyes, all the way to her heart. He wanted them to be free to go home again, to live a normal life without fear.

And he most definitely wanted that bastard Doug Lambert to pay for what he'd done to this little family.

He threw the papers into the trash and closed the lid quietly.

Damn it.

If he hadn't been ready for Pauline, he sure as hell wasn't ready for this.

CHAPTER FIVE

"TIME OUT!" Faith collapsed, breathless, and let the football roll to her side on the grass. "You win. I give up. Time out!"

Spencer barreled over and threw himself across her legs, tackling her just for the fun of it, even though she was already down. Tigger scampered into the heap of body parts and tugged excitedly at the cuff of her jeans.

She wriggled her legs, huffing and pretending to be trapped, but Spencer held on tightly. When she subsided, he lifted his head and grinned at her.

For a moment she held her breath. Suddenly, as if her sister had appeared before her, she was looking at Grace's smile. An irresistible smile, everyone said so. Slightly higher at the left corner, dimpling deep in the cheek.

Grace. An agony of love washed through her like rain.

Oh, Grace...he's going to be so handsome.

It had been weeks since Spencer had really smiled—Faith hadn't realized that new front tooth was already halfway in. Somehow she stopped herself from reaching over and wrapping him in her arms. At this moment, he was all boy, all mindless energy and wriggling mischief, and she wanted it to stay that way.

"Maybe you'd better take Tigger in and let him have some water," she said. The puppy was lying across her legs, panting happily. He didn't need to know the rules of the game to enjoy it. He just needed Spencer. His bright black eyes were fixed on the little boy adoringly.

Spencer looked at his watch, and his mouth made a small *o*. Faith glanced at hers, too. "Hey, it's time for *Mac's Treehouse,* isn't it?" That was Spencer's favorite TV show, the only one that would drag him indoors these days. "Better hurry."

Spencer climbed to his feet, but he hesitated, looking down at her. His hair was a mess. Blades of grass tattooed one cheek, a smudge of mud the other. He was the cutest thing she'd ever seen, and she had to fight another urge to smother him in kisses.

"It's okay," she said. She got up and brushed leaves from her knees and backside. "You and Tigger go on in. I want to pick something pretty for the table, and I'll be there soon."

He went. He made sure Tigger was at his heels, and he paused at the door before opening it, but he didn't look back even once. Faith put that on her list of small victories. Someday, when the list was long enough, Spencer would be well again.

Had she, through sheer dumb luck, stumbled onto the right therapy? For the past three days, she and

Spencer and Tigger had spent several hours outdoors. Each day Spencer had seemed a little more relaxed.

At the beginning, she hadn't thought of it as therapy at all. She'd thought of it as keeping the three of them out of Reed Fairmont's hair.

It helped that the autumn weather was bright and breezy. The air tasted as crisp and sweet as a freshly picked apple. Lying on your back in a pile of cinnamon-gold leaves, you could watch fat, low-hanging clouds race flocks of noisy geese across the sky.

On TV, the weatherman noted that the Glen was unseasonably warm, which might delay the full turning of the leaves, apparently a problem for the tourists who had booked the hotel rooms and crowded the cafes.

But for Faith and Spencer, lifelong city dwellers, it was perfect. Every inch of this wooded estate was packed with treasures—bright red cardinals busy at the bird feeders, mysterious knotholes winking from tree trunks, blue patches of chicory blooming furiously at the edge of the road and, once, a woodchuck staring out at them, his mouth full of grass.

And Autumn House had so many acres of open land. You could play leapfrog for hours and never reach the low log fence that ran along the outer boundary.

Reed must have noticed their makeshift games, because this morning, when Faith got up, she found that he'd left a football on the kitchen table.

She'd have to think of a way to thank him. Running

and tackling and tossing that little ball had kept Spencer busy all day, too busy to dwell on his losses.

She collected a basket and a large pair of cutting shears from the potting shed and began looking for flowers. It wasn't easy. This late in the season, even a garden as lush as this was fairly well spent.

She had almost decided to settle for a nice pine branch with a couple of interesting cones when she remembered the chicory out by the front road. It would look beautiful with the yellow napkins and the ivory stoneware plates.

Her basket wasn't quite full when the commotion started. Someone slammed the clinic door, and suddenly she heard a female voice raised in clear distress.

"Mom, please. Try. There has to be a way!"

It was Justine. Faith realized that, kneeling at the edge of the meadow, she might be obscured from sight. She didn't know whether to stand up or—

"I am trying," an older woman, presumably Justine's mother, said in an exhausted voice. "But you know your father. You know how he is if anyone defies him."

Justine made a pitiful noise, sounding for just a moment like her own infant crying. "This isn't about Daddy, Mom. This is about Gavin. He's my son, what was I supposed to do, throw him away? Would Daddy have thrown one of us away if we'd been inconvenient or embarrassing?"

Her mother's small hesitation was enough. Even Faith, who had no idea what was really going on, realized that Justine's mother couldn't swear to her husband's unconditional love for his children.

Justine's voice turned bitter.

"Oh, right, I forgot, that's exactly what he *has* done, isn't it? I embarrassed him, so he threw me away."

"Maybe if you'd just tell him who the father is—"

Faith had to let them know they had an audience. She arranged her face in a convincing expression of surprise and stood.

"Oh!" She smiled, as if she had just now realized anyone was there. "Hello."

Even if she hadn't heard the women quarrelling, she would have recognized trouble. Justine had a sleeping Gavin draped over her shoulder, and her beautiful face was red and blotchy. These weren't crocodile tears—she was in true distress. Even when she saw Faith she couldn't stop crying.

Justine's mother was petite and elegant, and she probably had once been as stunning as her daughter. But, though Faith guessed her to be only in her early forties, her beauty was so faded she was like a walking ghost. Her watery blue eyes were deep-set and shadowed. A worry line neatly bisected her pale brow like a knife cut.

"Hello," the woman said, trying to smile. "How are you?" Her voice was toneless and automatic, like a tape teaching English phrases. "I'm Mrs. Alton Millner. It's nice to—"

A raucous honking interrupted her robot speech.

All three of them looked over to the road, where a long, sleek convertible full of people had just crested the hill and rolled into sight.

Faith quelled her instinctive anxiety. It wasn't anything to be afraid of. It wasn't Doug. Doug Lambert owned a hearselike black Mercedes, not a bright blue vintage Cadillac convertible. And even if he had found her—which he hadn't, which he couldn't, how could he?—he would come for her quietly, in the dead of night. He wouldn't arrive with horns blowing and laughing people spilling out all over.

"Oh, terrific," Justine muttered. The noise had awakened the baby, and she bounced him gently to reassure him all was well. "What do those old geezers want, anyway?"

"Justine," her mother said. "Stand up straight. Wipe your face."

Justine pointedly refused to do either. But Faith watched, amazed, as the older woman shrugged inside her designer suit, squared her shoulders and surreptitiously fluffed her silky blond pageboy. Mrs. Alton Millner clearly did not want to meet these people, whoever they were, without her game face on.

As the Cadillac purred to a halt in front of Autumn House, Faith finally was able to see the occupants of the car. Two very large, very handsome white-haired men dominated the front seat, and in the back two beautifully dressed ladies in their sixties perched on the trunk of the car, their feet on the seat, as if they were princesses in a homecoming parade.

Oddest of all, between the lovely ladies sat another handsome old man, his face ruddy beneath longish hair the color of a slightly tarnished silver teapot. He was sound asleep, and probably would have keeled over if the ladies' legs hadn't held him up.

The man at the wheel, who, Faith noticed, really was shockingly handsome for a man who must be nearly eighty, spoke first.

"Why, if it isn't the mayor's gorgeous wife! Dee Dee Millner, climb on board, my lady! We're auditioning beautiful women who would like to ride with us in the Halloween—"

"Now, Granville," the smaller of the two women in the back interrupted irritably, adjusting her bright, flowery skirt. "You can see there's no more room. Boxer's already drooling all over our legs."

She sniffed and tried to tilt the sleeping old man upright with one finger. "I think he's just pretending to be asleep."

"Madeline Alexander, you're such a prissy little number." The other woman, who had flaming dyed-red hair, green eyes and the statuesque body of an Amazon queen, gave the little white-haired woman a scornful look. "Boxer is passed out cold. If he's bothering you, just kick him." She patted her hair. "But she's right about the room. There isn't any."

"Nonsense, Bridget." Granville grinned and winked at the other white-haired man. "There's always room for one more beautiful woman, isn't there, Ward?"

His friend nodded. "Or three. I see three more gorgeous ladies here. You're all welcome to audition, if you'd like."

Justine made an incredulous sound that stopped just short of being truly rude. But it didn't seem to faze either of the old men, who merely exchanged another devilish grin.

The driver, the one called Granville, eyed Faith curiously. "Hello! I'm not sure we've met," he began, but then his face broke out in a fresh smile. "Oh, of course! You're the gorgeous new housekeeper everyone's buzzing about. Ward, this must be Faith Constable, remember Theo was telling us?"

"Of course!" With a sudden spring, Ward levered himself out of the car without opening the door, a youthful trick he undoubtedly knew would impress the women. He plopped on the ground in front of Faith, who couldn't help smiling.

"Ward Winters," he said, holding out his hand. "The guy behind the wheel is my friend Granville Frome, but he's just a pale imitation. I'm the real thing."

"Don't listen to that jealous old fool, Faith." Granville Frome shook his head, the autumn sunlight sparking off silver threads. "I taught him everything he knows, which God knows isn't saying much."

"It's nice to meet you both," Faith said with a small laugh. She shook Ward's hand, her own disappearing into his. He was huge, well over six feet, with hair as richly white as his Irish wool sweater. His weathered face was full of life.

Heavens. Were there any men of any age living in Firefly Glen who weren't sinfully handsome and charismatic?

"Well, this is fun, but I've got work to do." Justine's voice was flat, and Faith wondered whether her unhappiness left her unable to enjoy anything, even these roguish charmers. Faith herself was enchanted.

"Ouch," Ward murmured as Justine strode away, Gavin watching them round-eyed as he bounced against her shoulder. "Seriously sour. Guess that's what happens when you pluck the fruit from the tree too early."

"That's enough, Ward," Mrs. Millner put in coldly. "I don't think it would particularly please Alton to hear you talking about his daughter like that."

Ward laughed. "Hell, Dee Dee. You know better than I do that nothing has *particularly pleased* Alton in thirty years."

Mrs. Millner seemed to puff up, her chest thrusting out indignantly, her blue eyes popping and flashing. Faith was shocked to see that much energy in the woman. Apparently all the emotion she had left resided in her ego.

"Don't you dare talk about Alton, either, or I'll—"

The impressive redhead made a disgusted sound between her teeth. "For God's sake, Dee Dee, don't bust a vein. Believe me, nobody has the slightest interest in talking about your idiot husband."

"You'd better watch your tongue, Bridget O'Malley."

Mrs. Millner marched over to the Cadillac, and Faith decided that this might be a good time to retreat. A catfight could erupt any minute. Judging by size alone, Amazon Queen Bridget O'Malley might seem to have the advantage, but Faith suspected that Ice Queen Dee Dee Millner might know a few tricks herself.

She looked over at Ward, who was watching the women with eager anticipation. Apparently he expected a similar outcome.

"I'd better get back to work myself," Faith said with a smile. "It was lovely to meet everyone, though."

He grinned, showing strong white teeth. "You'll miss the good part."

"Still." She tilted her head toward the house. "I think I'd better get inside."

"Ah, well, maybe so. You're new here—no need to let you see all our warts in your very first week."

He gave her an adorably sly wink and held out his hand again.

"I have a feeling our friend Reed wouldn't like it if we ran you off."

ON AN IMPULSE, Faith stopped at the clinic on her way back to the house. She could hear a baby's furious bawling even through the closed door. She didn't take time to think. She just went on in.

Justine was pacing the waiting room, bouncing Gavin on her shoulder, begging him to stop crying. But she was still crying herself, shiny tracks of tears crisscrossing her cheeks. The baby obviously had picked up on the tension and was screaming himself red.

"May I try?" Faith held out her hands. She didn't know much about babies, really, but she'd always been good with Spencer, and besides, what this child needed most was a pair of calm hands to hold him, a breast to rest on that wasn't heaving with misery.

She thought Justine might refuse, just out of stubborn pride. But desperation drove her, and, almost angrily, she held out the squalling baby. Her eyes were so swollen Faith wondered how she could see.

"Hi, sweetie," Faith said softly to Gavin, who had paused in his wailing long enough to eye her curiously. "It's okay, little guy. It's okay."

He gave her a wet stare that seemed to say she must be kidding.

But she kept at it, talking low and soothingly, and gradually the baby settled down. He was exhausted, anyhow, and had practically run out of steam. Within minutes, he had completely stopped crying, and his eyes were drooping. He was ready to sleep.

Faith waited an extra two minutes for good measure, then arranged him gently in his portable crib, which had been set up just beside the desk. He mewed once, rooted around in the blanket sleepily and then subsided with a sigh.

Justine hunched in her seat, her elbows on the blotter, watching the whole thing from behind a soggy Kleenex.

"I think he was just tired," Faith said softly. "He'll probably be out for a while now."

Justine nodded, but she didn't say a word. Faith couldn't quite decide whether the teenager was too embarrassed to speak, too upset to think or just too spoiled to realize a "thank you" was called for.

Not that it mattered. Either way, this girl was clearly overwhelmed and miserable, and Faith's heart ached for her. She remembered how exhausted Grace had been when Spencer was an infant—and Grace's situation had been ideal, a loving, helpful husband, a weekly housekeeper, plenty of money and friends and health care. And, of course, a doting Aunt Faith who couldn't get enough of her new little nephew.

"Justine." Faith didn't want to admit she had overheard Justine and her mother talking, but anyone could see Justine was in distress. "Is there anything I can do? Any way I might be able to help?"

Justine raised bloodshot, swollen eyes and tried to laugh. The result was a brittle sound, like treading on eggshells.

"No," she said. "Not unless you can pay my goddamn rent."

Faith didn't let the rudeness bother her. That was just the misery talking. Interesting, though, how her perspective had changed. Compared to the loss of

Grace and the threat of Doug Lambert, this snippy little teenager was nothing.

"I'm sorry," she said. She moved toward the door. Spencer's show was probably just about over. She didn't want him to worry where she was. "I guess I'll see you later."

"Faith, wait," Justine called suddenly, just as the door was about to close.

Faith turned.

"I meant to say thank you," Justine said awkwardly. "Really, I...I don't know what I would have done if you hadn't made him go to sleep. I was at the end of my rope."

Faith smiled. "You would have been fine," she said. "Funny thing about that rope. It's always a little bit longer than you think."

FINALLY, two days later, just after lunch, Detective Bentley called.

As usual, he got right to the point.

"Lambert definitely bought the roses," he said. "Florist got back yesterday. He decided to tack a few extra days on his vacation. Must be nice. Guess the guy is independently wealthy, huh? Not that I'm bitter." Detective Bentley laughed. "But anyhow it was worth the wait. He ID'd Lambert's picture this morning."

Faith closed her eyes and let the kitchen wall prop her up. "He's sure?"

"He's sure. Good witness, too. Neatnik, alphabetizes his canned goods, irons his boxers, you know the type. No juror could imagine this guy getting anything mixed up.''

''Okay.'' She took a deep breath. ''Now what?''

''Now we find the bastard.''

She opened her eyes and looked out the kitchen window. Spencer and Tigger were lying beneath the branches of an old maple, tousled and sweaty, worn out from an energetic game of fetch. The canopy of leaves above them fractured the sunlight, covering both sleepy little figures in a patchwork of amber, green and gold.

She couldn't take her eyes off them. Impossible, really, to believe that such sweetness could exist in the same world with murderers.

''Are you getting any closer? Do you have any leads?'' She forced herself to filter any frustration out of her voice. If she badgered him every time he called, he might stop calling.

''We've always got leads. Doug Lambert sightings are a dime a dozen. He's been spotted everywhere from the Grand Canyon to the Brooklyn Bridge. The real problem is—''

She'd heard this before. ''You don't know which sighting is the right one.''

''No, the real problem is we don't know if *any* of them is the right one.'' He sighed. ''Faith, look. I promise you we're on this. We're actually putting a helluva lot of muscle into finding this guy.''

''I know,'' she said, tracing a pointless pattern with

her fingertips on the woodwork. "I know you are. Thank you."

"So." He self-consciously made his voice a little more hearty, signaling a change in subject. "What about Spencer? How's he like country living?"

"He likes it. We both do. It's a beautiful house, and there's so much room. He runs around all day."

"Well, that's gotta be good for him." He paused. "Guess he's still not talking?"

"No. Not yet."

"Pretty soon, maybe. When he forgets a little."

"Maybe," she said politely. But she wondered if Detective Bentley had any idea what it did to a little boy to see his mother's dead body on the kitchen floor. Forget? How?

As they said their goodbyes, she looked out the window again, just checking. These days she was always checking.

Still the picture of autumn innocence. Spencer, wearing his favorite beat-up jeans and a heavy brown sweatshirt, was stretched out, his chin propped on one hand. He was petting Tigger. The puppy sat at attention, his tail wagging, his ears pricked up high, as if he were listening, as if Spencer were....

She leaned forward, trying to see more clearly. The splintered sunlight threw odd shadows, which were misleading, so she couldn't be sure...

But it looked very much as if Spencer were talking to Tigger.

Spencer shifted just then, and rested his back

against the tree trunk. His face was thrown into a square of golden sunshine, which acted like a spotlight.

Her stomach tightened. Yes, it was true. He was talking. In the chilly air, his breath puffed out in misty white circles as he lectured Tigger about something. Once he pointed toward the pond, toward the ducks. Maybe he was trying to teach Tigger to leave the poor ducks alone.

Faith dropped the phone onto its base with a clatter. She grabbed her sweater from the hook by the door, no room in her racing mind for anything but the one glorious fact. She wanted to scoop him into her arms, to hear the blissful sound of his high little voice.

She didn't know what stopped her. Perhaps it was the same instinct that made her hold her breath when they saw the woodchuck the other day. An inner sense that sometimes, if you were too clumsy or loud, too rough or too impulsive, you could startle a miracle right back into hiding.

Reed came through the side door, his cell phone tucked between his chin and his shoulder, drying his hands on a paper towel.

He spoke a few last sentences, then clicked off the phone. He tossed the towel into the trashcan, grabbed an apple from the bowl on the counter and smiled over at her.

"Hi. Just had to get out of the clinic for a minute. Gavin got spooked by a sick snake. He's been screaming bloody murder for the past twenty—"

Suddenly he seemed to notice something odd about her posture, her sweater dangling half-forgotten from her hand, dragging the floor. He followed her gaze out the window. "Everything okay?"

"Yes." She nodded. "Oh, yes. Look. Spencer is talking to Tigger."

"He is?" Reed stood behind her, and together they watched silently for several seconds. Spencer, unaware of his audience, was still chattering, his puppy still listening, tapping agreement with his expressive tail.

"Oh, my God." Reed put his hand on her shoulder, a single light touch that said so much. It said he understood, he knew, maybe not everything, but enough. It said he shared her joy.

Faith drank in both the touch and the sight like strong medicine, and she felt the first hint of healing move slowly through her.

"I wasn't sure," she said. "I tried to believe, and of course I always hoped. But somewhere, deep inside, I wasn't sure."

His hand tightened just a little, a bracing pressure. "This probably is only the first step, you know. He may not be ready to talk to people yet. He may not talk to us."

Us. For one prismed fraction of a second she allowed herself to imagine what it might be like if there really were an "us." If she were not alone in this terrible battle to save Spencer. To save herself.

She blinked the thought away, discarding it like the

useless fantasy it was. She was alone, except for the impersonal machinery of the law. And maybe it was better that way.

Besides, she had just been handed a miracle. She wasn't going to start complaining that she didn't have more.

"I know," she said. "I had thought of that, but—"

Before she could finish her sentence, she saw Spencer jerk to his feet. His whole body tightened, and he stared across the yard with wide eyes. Suddenly he grabbed Tigger's leash and began to run toward the house.

Both Faith and Reed moved to the door quickly, their alarm too hot and basic to have time for words. She reached it first and threw it open just as Spencer came barreling up the stairs.

"Honey, what's wrong?" Spencer flung himself into the kitchen and scrambled to hide behind her. Faith tried not to become tangled in Tigger's leash, but the puppy, thinking this was just another romp, was racing everywhere, tying their ankles together in an uncomfortable web.

"Spencer." She kept her voice calm, though her heart was drumming furiously all the way up to her ears. "Honey, what is it?"

Reed had positioned himself to block the doorway, and she noticed that he had his cell phone in his hand. He'd already punched in 911, and his thumb hovered over the send button.

But then she heard another voice, a slow, pleasing

baritone, and the sound of shuffling footsteps on the back stairs. Reed's body relaxed subtly, and then he stepped back, opening the door wide.

"Jeremy Wilson," he said pleasantly, just loudly enough for Faith to hear. "What a surprise."

"Hope it's not a bad time."

"Not at all. How are things? That's a gorgeous basket of apples you've got there. Any chance some of them are for us?"

The newcomer walked into the kitchen, holding a large basket of shining red apples in front of him. He was middle-aged, with a weathered face, dressed in a plaid flannel shirt and blue jeans so worn they had a faded white stripe from hip to toe. He was clearly a farmer, a man who worked the land.

Hardly a cocky millionaire from the Upper East Side. But Faith knew what Spencer had thought. From a distance, the two men were just similar enough— same height, same bulky, muscular frame, same dark brown hair.

Just similar enough to send a small, terrified boy streaking for safety. Though he obviously knew now that the stranger wasn't dangerous, Spencer still clutched her hips so tightly a sharp pain dug into her bones. Tigger had wound himself into a knot and finally had to plop down on her tennis shoe.

"Well, Dr. Fairmont, you know I still owe you for Maggie." The man set the basket on the counter. He touched his hand to his forehead, acknowledging Faith the old-fashioned way, before turning back to

Reed. "It'll be a while till I can pay you, so I thought meanwhile you might like a few of these."

"Jeremy, I told you not to worry about all that. You've paid me plenty through the years. I looked after Maggie from the time she was a newborn."

"Yes, sir, you did. And you kept her going a good month when everybody everywhere was telling me it was too late." The big man's eyes were shining in the kitchen light. "That month meant a lot, and I'm gonna pay you for it, that's for sure. But it'll be a while, so meantime I brought you some apples. They're sweet this year. Make a damn good pie."

He looked back at Faith. "Sorry, ma'am," he said, putting his finger to his forehead again. "I didn't see your boy there."

She smiled to show she didn't mind. It wasn't easy looking friendly and dignified, standing there lashed to Spencer. Tigger, bored, had decided to chew the laces of her sneakers.

"Say, Jeremy, do you have a minute?" Reed bent down and briskly unclasped Tigger's leash. The puppy didn't notice, completely absorbed in lace-chewing, but Reed was able to begin unwinding the leash from Faith's legs.

"Sure. I suppose so. What's up?"

"I'm building a stable for the bigger boarders, and I'm not sure I've got it right." Reed kept unwinding as he talked. "I could use another opinion."

Finally he stood and handed the neatly folded leash to Faith. She smiled her gratitude, flexed her ankles to restore the blood flow and reached behind her back to stroke Spencer's shoulder. His fingers had finally relaxed, thank goodness, and now his embrace was more a normal hug than a death grip.

"Help yourself to some apples, Faith," Reed said, putting his arm around the other man's shoulders and guiding him toward the door, away from Spencer. "Jeremy's orchard is the best in the Glen."

As soon as they were gone, Spencer came out from behind Faith and stood on tiptoe to investigate the apples, which really did look delicious. He was probably starving. He usually was—he was that age.

He loved apple pie. Grace always used to say she had to hide any she bought, or Spencer would eat the whole thing in one sitting. But right now his expression was full of disbelieving wonder, as if he had never in his life realized where those sweet boxed pies actually came from.

She had a sudden inspiration. He had been happy only ten minutes ago. He could be again. She just needed a distraction, something to keep the momentary terror from camping out in his psyche.

"Spencer," she said. "Think you're old enough to handle a little knife?"

He looked at her, his brown eyes wide and bright.

"Well, I think you are. So wash your hands, kiddo, and get ready to peel some apples. We're going to make an apple pie."

He paused, frowning. The doubt in his gaze was almost comical. He knew darn well that his Aunt

Faith was a terrible cook. Grace used to joke that Faith needed only ten minutes in the kitchen to turn a rump roast into roadkill.

"And you can wipe that look off your face, buster," Faith said, rummaging through the small flowered box of recipes that stood beside the toaster. *Apple butter, apple cobbler, apple jam, apple jelly.* These Firefly Glen people could create a week's worth of gourmet dinners from nothing but apples.

But what on earth was *pectin?*

She turned around. Spencer was still gnawing his lower lip.

"Come on," she said. "If you're old enough to learn how to use a knife, I'm old enough to learn to cook."

She saw the look Spencer gave Tigger, but she chose to ignore it. She opened the cabinet doors and scanned the shelves.

She could do this. She could.

Except…how on earth did a person *bleach* flour?

CHAPTER SIX

JEREMY HAD a million good suggestions for the stables, different angles, roof pitch, beam placement, but Reed could hardly concentrate on a word of it.

His mind kept drifting back to the kitchen. Had Spencer spoken to Faith? Had he at least spoken to Tigger where Faith could really hear him? Reed could imagine how Faith must ache for the sound of that lost voice.

Finally, thank goodness, Jeremy ran out of ideas. Reed saw him out to his truck, thanked him again for the apples and headed straight to the kitchen.

At least he thought it was the kitchen.

Though he'd lived in Autumn House all his life, he'd never seen the kitchen look quite like this. A big, wood-paneled room, it could absorb a lot of activity and still appear serene and efficient.

Not tonight, though. Reed looked around, incredulous. Apparently a bomb had gone off in here, a white bomb that weirdly coated the tabletop, as if it had snowed indoors.

A rickety Dr. Seuss tower of bowls and pans rose precariously from the sink, and a dozen containers of spices cluttered the counters, their lids half-off.

Spencer sat at the table, struggling to slice apples into tiny cubes with a dull knife. Half the pieces rained onto the floor around his chair, exciting Tigger, who obviously felt compelled to sniff every one.

Faith sat beside Spencer, studying one of Melissa's hand-written recipe cards with the same mystified intensity the first Egyptian explorers must have turned on a cave full of hieroglyphs.

"Reed?" She looked up with a sheepish smile. A fleck of dough dotted the edge of her lips like a birthmark. "Oh, darn. I wanted to get this cleaned up before you came back."

Spencer looked up, too, the butter knife frozen as he waited to see if Reed would be mad.

Faith tapped the recipe card. "I thought we'd make you an apple pie, but, sadly, the only thing I know how to make is a mess."

An unfair, momentary discomfort flashed through his blood. He didn't care about the mess, not really—

But the cards belonged to Melissa. The whole kitchen, in fact, had been Melissa's special kingdom. Sometimes when he tried to picture her, it was difficult to think back, back before the last ravaging year of her illness. But he could always summon up one clear vision—Melissa standing right there, bending over the stove, graceful and competent and completely in control.

The picture was so vivid it felt almost real. Her hair the same honey-blond as the paneling. Her feet bare, her arms bare, her legs bare under her favorite shorts. Humming sweetly while she stirred something that smelled like heaven.

He needed that picture. He didn't want to lose it. He didn't want to reach for it some cold, endless night, and find that it had blurred, tangled like a confusing double-exposure with this other picture of Faith and Spencer and Tigger, so strangely poignant, helpless amid the chaos.

But, hell, he should have thought of that before he invited them to live in his house. They were here now.

He moved into the room. "Creativity is always messy," he lied. "That's why it's fun. Can I play, too? I'm actually pretty good at pie crusts."

Faith leaned back with a sigh. "That would be wonderful. I think I goofed with the crust. It's a wreck."

He glanced over at the pie pan, which was lined with something that looked like clumps of beige glue. *Oh, boy.*

"I don't know what happened. Maybe I shouldn't have skipped step five—" she pointed at the card "—where you chill it in the refrigerator for an hour."

"Maybe not," he said with a smile. "Maybe before we put the top on you should cool down the dough for a few minutes, at least."

"Yes. That might help." She picked up the remainder of the dough and moved toward the refrigerator. "I should have thought of that. Yes, maybe this will help."

When her back was turned, Reed looked over at

Spencer with a small grin and shook his head slowly. The little boy grinned back, and then he subtly shook his head, too. It wasn't talking, exactly, but it was a clear, classic male communication. The two of them knew that this particular pie was beyond help.

Still, for the next hour they worked on it as a team, and Reed did what he could. He and Spencer formed a silent alliance. They traded the dull knife for a real paring knife, which Reed taught him how to use. They popped cubes of apple into their mouths when Faith wasn't looking. They grimaced behind her back when she added a tablespoon of salt instead of a teaspoon and then tried to scrape the excess off with a knife.

She caught them that time and broke out laughing when she saw their faces. "I know, I know," she said, plopping down on one of the chairs beside them. "I'm hopeless. It's going to taste like poison."

Reed controlled his own laughter. "No, it'll be fine. Really, it'll be great, won't it, Spencer?"

Spencer wrinkled his nose. He reached out and with one forefinger drew a squiggly line in the light coating of flour that covered the table. Then he put two dots above it. Reed tilted his head. It was a face. A cartoon rendering of a slightly queasy grimace.

He glanced over at Faith to see whether she'd caught on.

She had. She seemed to be holding her breath. Without speaking, she reached out and drew a face of her own. A bright, curving smile—the classic happy face. Then, next to it, she wrote *XO*. Hugs and kisses.

Spencer put out a finger. The room was utterly silent.

XO, he wrote.

Faith's eyes were glistening. Reed was afraid she'd cry, which would definitely spoil the mood and might even frighten the boy.

He could feel her eagerness for more—more communication, more assurances. But he could also feel Spencer's uncertainty, his fear that he might have ventured too far outside his safe cocoon of silence. He had already moved from his chair and gone over to the corner, where Tigger was sleeping.

"Okay, time to put the top on," Reed said quickly. He stood up. "Come on, Julia Child, do your magic."

As if in a daze, Faith obeyed. She rose, walked across the kitchen, pulled the ball of dough from the refrigerator and began to work on it.

The rolling pin wouldn't cooperate. Her hands were shaking as she tried to flatten out the ball. Dough kept sticking to the surface of the pin.

"I can't, I—" She turned to Reed, her brown eyes wide and deep. "Oh, Reed. Did you see?"

"Yes," he said. "I saw."

She glanced toward the corner, where Spencer was trying to interest Tigger in a piece of apple. "He's never done that before. Hasn't communicated so directly."

"I know. It's another step. A big step."

A tear clung to one corner of her eye, shining silver, like a sequin. Funny, he thought, how happy tears were brighter than tears of pain. Cleaner, somehow, and strangely beautiful, like an exotic nectar.

She started to dash it away, but her hand was sticky from the dough, and she paused.

"Hold still," he said. He reached out and smoothed his thumb under her eye. She blinked, and he felt the soft glide of her lashes across his skin.

Something moved inside him. He tried to ignore it.

But she was so lovely, her pale face dusted almost white with flour, and her dark eyes wet with tears. And she was so vulnerable, her need for comfort and hope and joy so strong they were like magnets drawing him in.

This was a mistake.

But he couldn't resist. He bent his head, said her name once. And then he kissed her.

She smelled of vanilla and tasted of apples and sugar and cream. At first she was utterly still, as if she didn't understand. And then, as his lips moved, finding cinnamon and a sweet lick of nutmeg, she came quietly alive.

She made a sound that fell over him as softly as flour sifting through the air. Her lips grew warmer, fuller. They pressed and parted, asking for more.

More? Oh, yes, he had more. So much more…

He went deeper, catching her apple-scented breath and the tiny, hard tip of her tongue between his teeth. She put the palms of her hands on his shirt, and they were warm, sticky with melting dough. He didn't care. He wanted her hands on him.

But suddenly, without warning, she pulled away. Her dark eyes were textured with flecks of hazel, green and gold, like autumn leaves in a pool of stormwater. Her lips were as red as the apple peel that littered the kitchen floor. She breathed fast and shallow.

"Faith?"

"Spencer," she whispered.

He looked, and he saw Spencer climbing to his feet, tired of trying to rouse his sleepy puppy. The little boy had his back to them, and Reed felt sure he hadn't seen anything.

Faith clearly wasn't as certain. She licked her lips, then glanced at Reed. He knew what she had found there—the taste of him mingled with the cinnamon.

She shifted toward the little boy. "Can you bring us the bowl of apple pieces, sweetie?"

Spencer obediently went to the table.

Reed took a breath and put out his hand. "Faith—"

"No." She backed up. "It will confuse Spencer."

She looked away quickly, but he had seen the hot flush on her cheek, beneath the sprinkling of flour, and he knew who was really confused.

They all were.

EVER SINCE Spencer was a baby, whenever Faith was around at bedtime she sang him a lullaby. Her voice was nothing special, but the song was sweet and full of love, and even as he got older Spencer insisted on hearing it. Up here, in the cozy Autumn House gable room that had become Spencer's bedroom, the simple notes resonated beneath vaulted pine beams and sounded even more beautiful than ever.

Since Grace had died, Faith sometimes needed to sing it five or six times before Spencer could relax enough to drift off. But tonight, exhausted from hours of romping in the brisk mountain air, he conked out in the middle of the first verse. Faith sang the final words to Tigger, who kept his ears politely perked to show that someone, at least, was listening.

"Thanks, buddy," she whispered, ruffling the puppy's ever-thickening mane. Shelties looked a little like lions, and this one was going to have a particularly majestic coat. Tigger stretched out close to Spencer, rested his muzzle on his paws and finally shut his eyes, too.

Faith sighed, tucking the soft blue quilt under Spencer's pointed chin. Now she had no more excuses. She was going to have to go downstairs and talk to Reed.

Awkward as it was, she owed him an explanation. She had overreacted to a fairly innocent kiss.

And she also needed to explain why, as innocent as it had been—and as pleasant as it had been—it must never be repeated.

Reed didn't seem to be in the main house, but his truck was parked out back, so she decided to check the clinic. A brick path lined with small landscaping globes lit the few short yards to the neat structure. Sure enough, the clinic was still completely bright, though it should have closed hours ago.

She opened the door, and instantly she heard Reed's voice coming from behind the front wall. He must be in one of the examination rooms, probably with a patient, though she hadn't seen any other cars out front. Maybe a neighbor had walked over with a sick pet?

In the small, quiet clinic she could hear him clearly, though he was talking in a voice so gentle and sweet it made Faith smile. She paused, enjoying the sound. It was nice to remember there were such men in this world. Men who stood for all that Doug Lambert was not.

"Come on, sweetheart," Reed said, his voice a blend of teasing and coaxing. It was, Faith realized suddenly, a very sexy voice. "Why don't you just relax, and I'll take that sweater off for you?"

A pause. A whispering rustle. "That's right. You don't need this, do you? There. Doesn't that feel better?"

Faith's eyes widened. Who on earth was he talking to? Now that she thought about it, no neighbors lived within walking distance of Autumn House. Who else would be here? Justine? Suddenly she remembered that Justine hadn't brought her beaten-up old car to work today. It had broken down yet again.

Was he back there with Justine? She frowned, rejecting the idea. Justine was only a teenager, for heaven's sake. Reed was a fully grown man, far too much man for that unhappy little girl to handle....

"Hey—it's okay, little girl," he said. Faith held her breath, hearing the unwitting echo of her own phrase. "I'm just going to slip this bow out of your hair. You don't need that, either. You're pretty enough just as you are."

In Faith's horrified mind, she could see Justine's blue satin bow sliding across her shining blond hair. Faith began to back up. She had to get out of here.

She reached out behind her, feeling for the door-knob. She mustn't make a sound. Her fingers touched something, her feet stumbled, and she collided, back first, with someone who had just come in the door.

Justine yelped. "Faith! What are you doing here? Man, you scared the hell out of me!"

Faith turned, bewildered. If Justine had just walked into the clinic, then who was in there with—

Reed came around the corner, a small poodle in his hands. "Hey," he said, frowning slightly. "Everything okay?"

Justine smoothed her hair, adjusting her blue satin bow irritably. She settled herself with a couple of calming smacks on her gum before answering. "Well, yeah, I guess so. Except that Faith just about gave me a heart attack."

"I'm sorry," Faith said. "I was just leaving, and we bumped into each other."

"You were leaving?" Reed frowned. "I didn't even realize you'd come in. Did you want to see me?"

"No, you're busy, that's okay." She glanced at the poodle, which, now that she focused, was the silliest dog she'd ever seen, with white cotton-ball tufts of fur around its chest and legs. It looked like a piece of topiary.

And it had one ridiculous pink bow tied on one ear. The other ear was bare.

Reed, who was holding a loose pink ribbon in his free hand, smiled. "You must have needed something."

"Well, yes, but then I heard you talking to someone—" She tried to keep from looking at the ribbon. "To the dog, I mean. Honestly, it was nothing important, I can just come back another time. I need to get back to Spencer anyhow."

"I'll walk you to the house. We can talk on the way." Reed held the poodle out toward Justine. "Do me a favor? Get Fifi settled for the night. And take that fool bow out, okay? Let the poor thing be comfortable."

The excited poodle wriggled its absurd legs, as if it could swim through the air toward Justine, who was eyeing it with significantly less enthusiasm.

"But Mike will be here soon," Justine said. "He's giving me a ride home."

"He'll wait five minutes." Reed smiled and plopped the poodle into her arms. "I always got the impression Mike Frome had been waiting for you a lot longer than that already.''

Justine shrugged, but she dimpled coyly and planted a pleased kiss on the poodle's head. The tiny, tense dog shivered with excitement. ''Oh, Mike's a fool,'' Justine said. ''But I can't stop him, can I? I guess there's no law against wishful thinking.''

Reed gave the poodle's head a friendly fluff and turned to Faith. ''Ready?''

She nodded. ''Sure.''

''Hey, boss,'' Justine called as they went through the clinic door. ''One thing. If I put Fifi to bed, that means I'm working, right? It means I'm still on the clock.''

Reed smiled pleasantly over his shoulder. ''I guess there's no law against wishful thinking.''

The October moon was full and yellow, a circle so perfect it looked as if it had been hole-punched out of a black construction paper sky. A light breeze carried the sweet hint of someone's wood fire and sent little curved birch leaves skittering ahead of them on the path.

The temperature was dropping quickly, and Faith realized the night was already colder than when she'd first walked out to the clinic. She should have brought her coat. She wondered how Reed managed to look so comfortable in only his jeans and soft plaid flannel shirt.

They covered the few yards to the house quickly— it wasn't long enough to do more than make a couple

of comments on the beautiful moon, and then they
were there.

As they climbed the steps to the back porch, she
looked at him, unsure how to broach the subject.
Maybe she should just let well enough alone. He
didn't seem uncomfortable—and he certainly didn't
seem flirtatious, as if he believed the kiss had been
the beginning of anything. Probably he felt the same
way she did—that the kiss had been surprisingly nice,
but completely inappropriate.

She put her hand on the doorknob, but at the same
moment Reed put his hand on the chain of the porch
swing.

"Want to sit out here for a minute?" His eyes
gleamed in the cold moonlight. "We really should
talk."

She hesitated. The night was so full of subtle sensuality—restless little leaf whispers, haunting calls
from throaty owls, the cold kisses of a blind night
wind, goose bumps rising and falling on your skin.

On a night like this, it was more intimate to be out
here, in the open, than to be inside by the fire. And
considering the fact that avoiding real intimacy was
what she had wanted to discuss…

He touched her shoulder. "Sit," he said. "It's
comfortable, and it's private. We can be sure no one
will hear us."

"All right."

She arranged herself on the large wooden swing,
which, though it had no cushions or pillows, really

was astonishingly comfortable. When he joined her, she was relieved to see that it was big enough to let them both sit without actually touching.

"So." He set the swing into a small, rocking rhythm that he controlled easily with the heel of his foot. "I know this is a little awkward. Considering it's my fault, maybe I should go first."

She looked over at him. His dark, wavy hair was rimmed in silver. Moonlight sculpted his rugged face with dramatic angles and shadows.

"Your fault?"

He nodded. "Absolutely. I stepped over the line in the kitchen earlier. I owe you an apology, and I want you to know that it won't ever happen again. Frankly, I can't imagine what made me act like such a fool."

He chuckled suddenly. "Wait, that didn't come out right, did it? I know perfectly well why I kissed you, of course. What I don't know is why I ignored the obvious fact that I had no right to do it."

"It's not a matter of 'right,'" she said, braiding her fingers in her lap. "It's just… It's Spencer. He's been through so much. He lost his dad three years ago, and now he's lost his mother, too. He needs stability. I want him to know he's the most important thing in the world to me right now. I don't want him to wonder if I'm…"

Her voice dwindled off. She couldn't think how to put it. It had been just one casual kiss. She didn't want him to think she had read too much into it.

But thankfully Reed was nodding. "You don't

want him to wonder if you're distracted. If you're more interested in being with me than you are in being with him.''

"Yes. Exactly.'' She looked down at her hands again. She ought to be completely honest, though this part was harder. ''And it isn't just Spencer, completely. It's also that I'm not really ready for anything...anything sexual. I shouldn't even be— I don't know how I could even have thought of—''

She swallowed. ''After Doug... After my sister—''

To her horror, she found herself near tears again. God, would this weakness never go away? But the word was so powerful. My *sister*. No one could ever know the thousands of memories that word held in its few short letters—Barbies and boyfriends and beach weeks, fights and fevers and finals, laughter and dreams and so many hundreds of inconsequential little plans. Grace had talked her into signing up for a belly-dancing class. It would have started this week. It would never happen now.

She shut her eyes. What had she been thinking? Just being alive when Grace was dead seemed unfair. But being so alive that she could enjoy a man's touch, his scent, his gentle, determined lips...

That felt like a sin.

''Faith, look at me,'' Reed said suddenly. She looked up and realized that he'd been watching her. She wondered how much her face had given away. ''It's okay, you know. It's normal.''

''What is?''

"To want to live."

It was an arrow straight to the heart of things. She didn't trust herself to speak. She just stared at him, her eyes burning, though the rest of her was shivering.

"It's a perfectly normal instinct. When you've been cold inside too long, it's human to reach out for a little warmth."

She wrapped her arms around herself. "Is it?"

He rocked the swing slightly before answering, staring out into the rustling, autumn night. "Yes," he said finally. "I think it is. I don't think they would want us to be cold forever."

They. Oh, God, grief made you selfish, didn't it? She put out her arm and touched his hand, ashamed that she had forgotten that he, too, had lost someone he loved. If she felt she had betrayed Grace with that kiss, how must he have felt?

"Reed, I'm sorry—"

"No more apologies." He smiled at her, and she could see him working to shake off the pensive mood. "Our new official limit is one a day, and I've already made it."

"But—"

He placed his free hand over hers and chafed it lightly. "Hey, your fingers are like ice. We'd better get you inside before you freeze."

They both stood and moved toward the door. The swing creaked gently on its chains, swaying from the sudden freedom. A night bird somewhere in the hemlock trees whistled something in a solitary contralto.

When he opened the door and stood back to let her go through first, Faith paused. She wanted to say something, but she wasn't sure where to begin.

Maybe she just wanted to say thank you. But for what? For sharing his warm, beautiful home, for letting it be her haven? For sharing his wisdom, for easing her guilt at being alive?

Maybe for the kiss itself, which had strangely taken root inside her, like one small green shoot in the cold winter of her heart.

She opened her mouth, but to her surprise he put his warm forefinger across her lips. It made shivers spiral down her spine, and whatever words she'd been about to say disappeared.

"Go inside, Faith," he said. "If you keep looking at me like that, I'm going to do something I shouldn't. And we don't have any apologies left for today."

She nodded. He was right. Hadn't she just said they needed to be sure nothing foolish happened again?

She crossed the threshold, but to her surprise, he didn't follow.

"'Night," he said with a smile. "Sleep tight."

He closed the door quietly. She heard his footsteps across the wooden porch, and then the soft creak of the swing as he lowered himself onto it.

The bird sang one more time. And then there was nothing but silence.

DOUG GRIPPED the phone so tight he could feel his blood in his fingertips. He could hear it whooshing in his ears, too.

Shit. His blood pressure must have gone through the roof. He hadn't been able to fill his prescription in more than a month. Having to deal with morons like this didn't help calm him down any, either. For a minute there he had actually seen a red wash spread across his vision.

"What do you mean you can't find her?"

"I mean I can't find her." The voice on the other end took on a whiny tone. "I mean she's nowhere."

Doug forced himself to talk quietly, though he had a sudden urge to take this phone cord and wrap it around someone's neck. That disgusting drunk in the corner, for instance. He'd be no loss to the human race.

"Nonsense," he said slowly, forcing himself to focus. "Everyone is somewhere."

"Yeah, well, this broad isn't. I'm telling you, I've looked everywhere. I guess I can keep looking, but you're throwing your money away. She's smart, and she's gone."

"She's not smart." Doug laughed at the idea. If Faith Constable was so damn smart, why hadn't she jumped at the chance to have a millionaire lover, a big shot boyfriend who was ready to shower roses and gifts at her middle-class feet?

She was stupid. And this jackass he'd hired was stupid, too. "You're fired," he said, and he hung up the phone with such force that even the drunk in the corner looked up.

He moved down the corridor slowly, feeling the frustration building inside his veins. It wasn't the same kind of frustration he used to feel when he thought about Faith. Then he had just wanted to screw her. He'd wanted it pretty bad. Sometimes his whole groin had pulsed raw with it, and then whichever bitch was under him really got herself knocked around big time. It had taken a ridiculous amount of cash to shut them up about it.

This was different. He didn't particularly want to have sex with Faith anymore. He wanted to kill her.

He bumped into the drunk. He knocked over the man's small bag of belongings, which had been loosely tied up in a moth-eaten T-shirt. Cigarette stubs and pennies and old socks tumbled out in all directions.

"Hey," the drunk said. "Pick that up."

Doug paused and stared at the man. His hands made fists at his side, fists so tight they throbbed with every beat of his heart. Maybe, just as it had helped a little to use other women when he really wanted Faith, maybe it would help to kill some dumb bastard like this until he could get his hands around the right lily-white neck.

But he couldn't afford to attract any attention to himself. He needed the anonymity. Apparently finding Faith wasn't going to be as easy as he thought.

The drunk's red eyes narrowed. "I said pick it up."

"Sorry, pal," he said, kicking a smelly gray sock

out of his way like a dead rat. "That's not the way it works. Here's a tip, cost you nothing. If you want a thing done, and you want it done right, you've got to do it yourself."

CHAPTER SEVEN

THE NEXT FEW DAYS, as temperatures in Firefly Glen kept dropping and the leaves began to hint at tones of russet and bronze, Faith felt herself finally settling in.

While Spencer still didn't talk, he seemed much more relaxed. He smiled and nodded and did everything short of making an actual sound. He had even allowed Faith to put a picture of his mother by his bed. Faith began to believe it was just a matter of time before he was nearly back to normal.

She and Reed were growing more comfortable together, too. The kiss seemed to have broken the ice. It was as if, once they had openly acknowledged the attraction and agreed it wouldn't be appropriate to act on it, they could concentrate on building a friendship.

The sexual awareness didn't ever completely disappear, of course. When they tackled one another at football, it flared a little. When they washed dishes side by side in the kitchen, it hummed softly between them. When they said good-night on the stairs, it hung like candle glow in the shadowy air. It was ever-present, but unobtrusive, like half heard background music.

Yes, most things were settling in just fine. Unfortunately, though, she wasn't getting one bit better at housekeeping.

Just before lunch that Saturday morning, she found herself in Reed's bathroom, as usual making the most ridiculous mess. She had climbed into his large shower to scrub the back tiles. She'd forgotten her rag, so she used one of his plump green hand towels to apply the cleanser. To her horror, it suddenly developed a large white spot in the center.

She looked down. Her denim shorts were covered in tiny white spots. She looked out. The green mat outside the shower was speckled, too.

She picked up the new bottle of cleanser she'd just opened. What on earth was in this stuff? The old bottle hadn't done anything like this.

But then, for the first time, she realized that this new bottle was just slightly different from the last one she'd used. The same brand, the same color on the label. But where the old one had said "basin and tile cleanser," this one said "mildew remover."

Mildew remover. She frowned, uncertain. Was that bad? She sniffed the nozzle and recoiled sharply. Oh, good grief. It was pure bleach.

Spencer and Tigger trotted into the bathroom, obviously looking for her. Spencer stopped at the threshold, wrinkling his nose dramatically as the stinging odor of bleach reached him. Tigger stopped, too, and began barking his disapproval.

And suddenly she saw that Reed was right behind them.

"Oh, Reed, I'm sorry, I've made such a stupid mista—"

Flustered, she tried to whip around quickly and climb out of the shower. But she had sprayed so darn much of this evil stuff, and its oily wetness was diabolically slippery. Her bare feet slid around comically, and she knew she was going to fall.

Oh, why, why was she doomed to look like one of the Three Stooges every time he caught her trying to clean house? As she did her humiliating dance of desperation on the slick tiles, her arms flailed, clutching out for balance. She caught hold of one edge of the shower curtain, but it was too late. The curtain tore from its hooks with a loud ripping sound, and she went down, right on her rump in a pool of oily bleach. The shower curtain cascaded on top of her, draping itself across her head.

For a split second the entire room was silent. Even Tigger was too shocked to bark. But suddenly she heard the sound of laughter. A beautiful sound. Light, high, uninhibited.

It was Spencer.

For a moment she forgot her own embarrassment, her guilt at ruining Reed's bathroom, even the rapidly spreading dampness across her sore rear end. Right here, right now, where everyone could hear him, Spencer was laughing.

Reed was laughing, too. He was trying not to, of

course. But he and Spencer kept looking at each other, then back at her, and exploding in new waves of uncontrollable mirth.

She shook the shower curtain off her head, ran her fingers pointlessly through her hair, and smiled over at them.

"Well, thanks, guys. It's nice to be reassured that I didn't make a *complete* fool of myself."

"Are you okay?" Reed moved into the bathroom, his hand outstretched. Halfway to the shower, he paused and sniffed the air. "God. Is that bleach?"

"Yes." She gripped the spigot and carefully dragged herself to her feet. "That's what I was trying to tell you. I used the wrong stuff by mistake and—"

She stopped, realizing that they were both looking at her rear end with expressions that pretty much promised more gales of laughter.

"What?" She craned her neck, trying to see the back. *"What?"*

"Your shorts," Reed said. "They're all white where you…" He choked from trying to swallow an oversize chuckle. "It's just that you've got these two amazingly cute white circles on your bottom."

She twisted and saw what he was talking about. The bleach was everywhere. On her hands, on the shower curtain, on her clothes.

Reed and Spencer looked at each other. Reed arched one brow mischievously. "So, Spence," he said. "Are you thinking what I'm thinking?"

Spencer grinned. He looked at Faith, and then he nodded.

Reed turned back to her. "Okay, here's the deal. Spencer and I took a vote earlier, and we decided to go into town for lunch."

"Out? But I was going to make some—"

"Nope." Reed's eyes gleamed with amusement. "We're going out. But first we have to get you cleaned up."

She tilted her head, suddenly catching on. "Oh, no, you don't," she said. She put out her hand. "Reed, no—"

But once again she was too late. Reed had reached in and twisted the spigot. She looked up. The high-tech nozzle overhead sizzled and opened, and suddenly hundreds of jets of warm spray came pulsing down like summer rain across her face.

Within seconds, the water had soaked her hair, her T-shirt, her shorts, washing away the sharp scent of bleach in soft, wet rivulets that ran down her bare shins, across her toes and into the shiny silver drain.

She peeled her wet hair from her face and turned toward the two grinning males. Baring her teeth, she gave them an indignant growl. Tigger growled back and trotted to the edge of the shower, snapping, trying to catch droplets of water that ricocheted onto his nose.

Reed handed her the soap.

"Hurry up," he ordered gruffly, but his eyes were warm and gentle. She knew they were both listening to the magical sound of Spencer's laughter in the background. "While you're in here playing around, the guys in this house are starving."

REED EYED Granville Frome coming toward him across Theo Burke's Candlelight Café. *Don't say it,* Reed instructed him mentally. *Give me a break, okay? Just don't say it.*

But of course the old guy said it.

"Good to see you in here, son. Time you started to get out and about. Heard you're dating that red-headed Ferguson gal. That's great. Melissa was a damn fine woman, but can't stay at home licking your wounds forever."

"Yes, I suppose you're right." Reed tried not to show his irritation—but he and Faith and Spencer had only been in the café for ten minutes, and Granville was the fifth person to come up and congratulate Reed for "finally" getting sociable again.

Maybe this hadn't been his best idea ever. It had seemed healthy to get Spencer out of the house, even though they'd had to leave Tigger at home, which hadn't been easy. Even that tiny parting frightened the little boy. Spencer had hugged the dog at the front door for five minutes straight, until Tigger had begun to squirm impatiently.

Still, Reed had thought it was worth it. But he had forgotten about the constant Firefly Glen gossip. To-day, they were the equivalent of the daily trifecta. People could indulge their curiosity about Reed's pretty new housekeeper, monitor the healing progress of his broken heart and get the dirt on his date with Pauline Ferguson all at once.

He hadn't really expected the part about Pauline. She must have stretched their skimpy date into an amazing feast of gossip. He'd be willing to bet that by now their one pitiful outing, with its anticlimactic cheek-peck at the door, had morphed into something downright torrid.

He unwrapped his silverware so roughly the fork clattered onto the floor. Oops. He shot Theo an apologetic look. She hated for people to make a mess of her pristine café.

But damn it. When it finally sank into Pauline's one-track brain that there wasn't going to *be* a second date, she might regret having broadcast this first one quite so far and wide.

Luckily, Granville had an eye for pretty women, so he let the subject drop quickly and began flirting with Faith. He seemed to be trying to talk her into riding in his car for the Halloween parade, and she was quite deftly turning him down.

Reed caught himself staring. He liked the way she smiled—it was a two-stage deal, as if she weren't sure she should give into the urge. First, her mouth seemed to close more tightly, the corners tucking into a couple of cute-as-hell dimples. Sometimes, most of the time, it ended there.

But every now and then her lips parted, and the second stage took over, her smile broadening, stretching, sparkling. Showing pretty white teeth and spreading sunny warmth all the way up to her eyes.

It was a fantastic smile. And he felt absurdly personal about it. It was as if the smile had been lost in some dark place far, far away. And he had found it, saved it, returned it to her face, where it belonged.

How ridiculous. Reed Fairmont, conquering hero? Not in this lifetime.

Finally Granville gave up and excused himself. He had spied Madeline Alexander in the corner with Ward Winters, and he was obviously eager to get over there and cause some trouble. *Jealous old rascal.*

Reed chuckled as he picked up his thick, juicy veggie-burger, one of Theo's specialties. He turned to Spencer. "So, was I right? Is it the best burger you ever had in the world?"

Spencer, whose mouth was chock-full of burger, shot Reed the "thumbs-up" sign, then reached for his thick chocolate milkshake.

Faith was watching Spencer, too. And then, when the little boy took another giant bite of his burger, she gave Reed one of those wonderful smiles.

Maybe coming into town hadn't been such a bad idea after all.

"Reed Fairmont. Damn it, man, I've been looking for you."

Oh, hell, it was Alton Millner, Justine's father. Reed's opinion of coming to town took another nosedive. It wasn't ever a good idea to risk running into Alton, who was Firefly Glen's mayor and a world-class pain in the ass.

"I'm at my clinic five days a week." Reed wiped his mouth with Theo's soft cloth napkin. "If you have anything to discuss with me, maybe we'd better do it there, because I'm with friends right now, and we wouldn't want to bore them."

"To hell with your lunch. Tell me why you—"

Reed tightened his jaw. "Alton. Call my receptionist. Make an appointment."

"Your receptionist?" Alton looked as if he might have a heart attack right on the spot, which would infuriate Theo. Spencer's eyes were wide as he sucked down the last of his milkshake. "She's not your receptionist, damn it. She's my daughter."

Reed shrugged. "I didn't know the two were mutually exclusive."

"They damn well ought to be!" Alton jabbed him in the shoulder with his forefinger. "What right do you have to interfere in my family?"

Reed turned to Faith. "Could you do me a favor? Could you and Spencer please go ask Theo if we could get some hot-fudge sundaes? She knows how I like mine."

Faith understood perfectly. She glided up from her chair and took Spencer by the hand. Reed knew she would manage to keep the little boy out of harm's way until this annoying man and his hostility were gone.

"All right, Alton," he said as soon as they were alone. "What exactly is on your mind?"

"I want to know what the hell you were doing hiring my daughter to answer your goddamn telephone. You know I didn't want anyone to give Justine a job around here. If it weren't for you, Justine wouldn't be in that rattrap apartment. She'd be at home where she belongs."

Reed gazed at the man calmly. "And where would Gavin be?"

Alton's face swelled up, suddenly so red and bloated that Reed had a momentary image of his salt-and-pepper mustache popping right off and shooting across the café. He looked like a cartoon character, but the truth was the man was probably in terrible health. All that rage, all that sick need for control. Reed tried to feel sorry for him, but all he could see was Justine's frightened face when she came in asking for a job.

"I refuse to talk to you about that—that child. He's no concern of yours, Fairmont."

Reed smiled. "I'll have to remember that next time I change his diapers."

"Change his—" Alton's eyes suddenly narrowed. He leaned forward. "Damn it. It isn't you, is it, Fairmont?"

Reed made his voice even steadier. "What the hell are you talking about?"

"The father. God, you're not the father are you?"

Alton tilted his bullet-shaped head, trying to figure

things out, which wasn't easy, considering he had a brain the size of a pea trying to support an ego the size of a small planet.

"It would have been last winter. You were pretty out of it last winter, I remember that. Drank a lot. Damn. I hadn't thought of this. Lonely guy up there all alone, no woman in the house. Surely you didn't—Justine didn't—"

Reed pushed his chair back slowly. He wasn't sure exactly how he planned to do it, but this bastard was going to shut up.

"Gentlemen." Theo appeared like magic. People didn't brawl in her café. People didn't even burp in her café. "Or should I say *morons.* Sit down, Reed. I'm not going to let you deck this idiot in my café, no matter how much he deserves it."

She turned to the mayor. "And Alton. If you think Reed Fairmont got your daughter pregnant, you're even dumber than you look, and what are the odds of that?"

"I'm not saying I think he did," Alton said slowly. "I don't know what I think."

"Precisely." Theo handed him his hat and jacket. "Now you run on home and sort it out in your own house. People are trying to eat here, and the smell of burning brain cells puts them off their food."

Even the mayor of Firefly Glen wouldn't dream of arguing with Theo. When she bounced you, you stayed bounced. Alton shot them both a dirty look as he exited, which made Theo laugh.

"Idiot," she said. "Wouldn't he just love it if he could pin this on you? He's spent the past two months trying to prove it was poor, besotted Mike Frome."

Reed had considered that possibility himself. "You don't think he could be right?"

"Hell, no. Anybody can tell that boy's never gotten to first base with Justine. He still thinks she's some vestal virgin goddess. She can breast-feed that baby right in front of him, and then have sex with the milkman, and he'll still think she's a saint."

Reed had to agree. "Poor kid," he said. Love was hell.

"Yeah, well, Daddy Millner has gone ever so slightly psycho, so don't be surprised if you really are his next target. If Justine can't be forced to give the kid up for adoption, he desperately wants Mr. Paternity to be any rich Glenner with a good pedigree."

Theo chuckled. "Truth is, he's scared to death it's going to turn out to have been some doped-up ski bum who blew into town last winter for a little cold-weather fun and games."

Suddenly Faith returned, her hands full of hot-fudge sundaes. Spencer was lagging behind, poking curiously into a basket of Indian corn and colorful gourds Theo had set up by the cash register.

"Everything okay?" Faith asked quietly as she set the sundaes on the table. She looked worried, and he wondered how much she'd heard. He realized suddenly that he would absolutely hate for Faith to even consider the possibility that he had fathered an illegitimate child by his teenaged receptionist.

"Oh, everything's fine," Theo said, patting him on the shoulder merrily. She smiled at Faith. "Don't mind grumpy young Doc Fairmont here. He just doesn't much like the feel of a shotgun at his back."

"I WON'T TAKE FOREVER in here, Spencer, I promise."

Spencer looked up at Faith with a look of resigned skepticism that was so typically male she had to laugh. "Really. I *promise,*" she said again. "Cross my heart."

He nodded. That had been their solemn vow since he was a baby, and he obviously still believed it.

Which meant she had to make good on it. She couldn't linger in the Firefly Glen Home and Hearth store, no matter how tempting it was. She hadn't been shopping in a long time, and she did love creating special looks with beautiful colors and textures.

She hadn't expected a small town like this to have such a lovely selection. Obviously Firefly Glen was a town of well-heeled, tasteful millionaires. Home and Hearth could rival any similar store on Fifth Avenue.

As she moved through the aisles piled high with fluffy pillows and elegant knickknacks, she could almost read Spencer's mind. She would bet a dollar that he wished he had gone with Reed to the hardware store down the street. He stood by her side like a patient little soldier, but he sighed heavily every thirty seconds or so to remind her of her promise.

She picked a shower curtain as quickly as she could, a nice manly forest green one that would go beautifully with the few towels she hadn't yet ruined. She bought a new bathmat to match, and some replacement towels.

Ten minutes. It had to be a personal record. "Tada!" she said, holding up the receipt for Spencer to see. With an I-told-you-so smile, she gestured formally toward the door.

They were supposed to meet Reed at the pet shop, which was midway between Home and Hearth and the hardware store. Obviously Reed hadn't expected them to finish up so quickly. They got there first.

Which was fine with Spencer. The sign out front announced that every Saturday the store and the Humane Society jointly hosted a pet giveaway. Tables, boxes and cages full of puppies and kittens and hamsters and gerbils lined the sidewalk.

With a low gasp of delight, Spencer knelt immediately in front of a litter of basset hound pups. He loved dogs, and dogs loved him. These were no exception. They squealed and tumbled and yipped and licked with joy.

Spencer giggled as one rambunctious puppy nearly knocked him back on his heels. Faith held her breath, listening for every glorious note of the little boy's laughter.

"Faith! Spencer!" Justine's voice called from a nearby table. "Want to adopt a kitten?"

Faith looked over. With Gavin sleeping in a carrier at her side, Justine presided over the most motley litter of tiny kittens Faith had ever seen—some tiger-striped, some cream-colored, one even a Viking red. But, tumbling together in their box, all mixed up and fuzzy, not much bigger than the hamsters at the next table, they were so cute it took your breath away.

Faith couldn't resist picking one up. It was warm and wiggly and as soft as a cloud. It immediately began to wrestle with a curling strand of her hair. "Oh, Justine," she said. "How darling."

"Yep. He likes you. You should definitely take him. Only four more to adopt out, and then I'm safe."

"Safe?" Faith could feel the kitten's heart beating under her fingers. "You mean then you can go home?"

"No, I mean I'm *safe*. You know, from their evil little kitten charms."

Faith smiled. "They are dangerous, that's for sure."

Justine picked up the Viking-red kitten and rubbed its head against her cheek. "Don't you go falling in love with me now, Leif," she said with a transparently mock severity. "As if I could afford an animal. Every cent I make goes to buying Gavin diapers."

"I can imagine." Faith remembered the constant emergency trips to the corner drugstore for more diapers when Spencer was a baby. Grace had bought boxes of them by the busload, but it was never enough.

How did a single mom, living on a receptionist's wages, manage? Faith had told herself she wouldn't speculate on the bits of conversation she'd overheard between Theo and Reed. It wasn't any of her business, really.

But it was hard to remain objective when she looked at Justine now, the teen's face sweetened by the innocent pleasure of cuddling the kitten. Over the past few weeks, Faith had wondered whether Justine might be growing up—sobering up, just a little.

The responsibilities of motherhood could do that, no doubt—especially if you had no support. No husband to make some of the diaper runs, handle some of the middle-of-the-night colic bouts, wash a few sheets and tiny little shirts and socks.

She gathered that Justine wasn't revealing the name of her baby's father, which apparently infuriated Mayor Millner. Faith had even clearly heard Theo say that the Mayor was desperate enough to consider Reed as a candidate.

The man must be insane. Faith hadn't known Reed three weeks, and she already knew such a thing was categorically impossible. Reed was a nurturer, that was all. He took in strays, and he didn't count the cost.

Faith should know. As different as they might seem, she and Justine had two things in common. They were both desperately unprepared single moth-

ers, and they were both dependent on Reed Fairmont's protection.

"You lying punk-ass creep!"

Lost in thought, Faith had only half registered the
commotion that had started on the sidewalk behind
them, but at that moment it grew too loud to ignore.
Just ten feet away, a couple of teenagers were having
a completely uninhibited squabble.

Spencer left the puppies and came to stand close
to Faith. He didn't like arguments. She put her kitten
down so that she could hold his hand.

"Man! I can't believe I'm such a fool!" The teenage girl slammed the heel of her hand against her
forehead so hard her shiny black ponytail danced.
Wearing a black turtleneck sweater and black cordu-
roy slacks, she was all big dark eyes and lanky arms
and legs.

"Damn, Suzie, chill. Keep it down, for God's
sake." The boy with her looked pained. He was very
young, no more than eighteen, but his still-developing
face and rangy athletic body promised that, in a few
years, he would definitely join the Firefly Glen glam-
our brigade. Faith might have smiled at the thought—
where did all these gorgeous genes come from?—if
the two kids hadn't looked so upset.

"Yessir, I'm a fool—but you're a double-barreled
bastard." Suzie apparently had no intention of keeping it down. She was on fire with fury. "Like you'd
ever just do me a favor. Like you'd ever just spend

your precious Saturday taking me to the pet store. I should have known *she'd* be here.''

The boy glanced nervously at Justine. ''How could I have known she'd be here?''

But his cheeks colored. He wasn't much of a liar. Faith glanced over at Justine, too. She was pretending to be oblivious to the fracas. She was murmuring something to the kitten and stroking its ears without even looking up.

Suzie knew the boy was lying, obviously. She blinked a couple of times, as if she might be holding back tears. Then she drew her skinny body into a rigid line, lifting her chin in a way that gave her a sudden, shocking elegance.

''No, you know what, Mike Frome? I take that back. I'm not a fool. You are. If you don't see how that bitch is stringing you on...'' She blinked again. ''Well, you're the only one in town who doesn't. Maybe you ought to start thinking with your brain for a change. If you've got one.''

It was a good line, and she knew it. She turned on her heels and stalked away. Mike Frome stared at her, then looked over at Justine, who had finally stopped petting the kitten and was smiling at him sympathetically.

''Don't sweat it,'' Justine said. ''Suzie Strickland's a freak.''

The boy frowned. ''No, she's not,'' he said. ''And maybe, just maybe, she's right.''

Justine tilted her head, her soft blond hair cascading over one shoulder. "Is that really what you think, Mike?"

It was like watching a fisherman reel in a marlin. The boy kept casting anxious looks toward Suzie's departing figure, which was by now only a black speck in the Saturday afternoon crowd. But his feet were moving slowly, edging him closer to Justine, who had begun to file her nails.

Poor Mike Frome. Faith suddenly remembered where she'd heard that name. This was the boy Mayor Millner wanted to nominate as the baby's father.

Oh, dear. This wasn't just a teenage tiff. It had the potential to be a very serious entanglement. Maybe they needed some privacy.

Faith put her hand on Spencer's shoulder.

"Let's walk down to the hardware store," she said. "To see if we can find Reed."

He nodded vigorously, apparently as eager as she was to get away from the scene. They moved off. Faith called a polite goodbye, but Justine didn't seem to notice. She was handing a kitten to Mike Frome, who took it like a robot, as if he had been programmed to do whatever Justine Millner ordered.

Poor kids. All three of them were too young to be in such a mess. Mike Frome ought to be heading off to college soon, just beginning his life. Faith remembered that Theo hadn't believed Mike was the father—and Theo seemed extremely perceptive. She was probably right. Faith held on to that thought.

She and Spencer made slow progress down Main

Street, because all the store windows were charmingly decorated for Halloween. Spencer wanted to stop and look at every pumpkin, every maple-leaf wreath, every corncob-pipe-smoking scarecrow wearing overalls and a straw hat.

But finally they reached the hardware store, just as Reed was coming out.

He walked beside another man, a hefty blond farmer-type in faded jeans who was talking very fast, bending his head toward Reed and worrying the rim of a soft cap between his hands.

The other man fell silent as Faith and Spencer came up.

"Hi," Reed said. He glanced at her packages. "I guess you were able to find what you needed?"

"Yes." She smiled a hello over at the other man, who tried to smile back and didn't quite succeed because he was busy gnawing on his lower lip. "Is everything okay?"

"It will be." Reed gave the big blond man a reassuring smile. "It will be, Mark, you know that."

The man nodded, but he didn't let go of his lip.

Reed turned back to Faith. "I hate to do this, but I need to go over to Red Tree Farm with Mark. His prize mare is about to foal, and she's acting a little edgy. Mark's afraid she might hurt herself, so I'm going to take over a tranquilizer." He winked at the other guy. "For Mark."

The blond giant actually blushed. "I hate to be a bother, Reed, but she means a lot to me—"

"It's not a bother." Reed raised one brow questioningly. "As long as Faith doesn't mind driving the car home for me. Are you okay with that, Faith? Mark will take me to Red Tree in his truck."

"Of course I don't mind," she said, smiling. "If you trust me with your car."

Reed chuckled. "I might not trust you to clean it, but I trust you to drive it. And there's only one road back to Autumn House, so there's no way you'll get lost. You sure you're okay?"

"Of course."

Reed knelt in front of Spencer. "Have you ever seen a baby horse be born?"

Spencer shook his head slowly.

"Would you like to?"

Spencer hesitated. Faith could feel that he was rigid with excitement and anxiety. If he hadn't found the courage to go to the hardware store alone with Reed, could he possibly go all the way to Red Tree Farm, wherever that was?

And yet, what six-year-old boy could resist such an offer?

"Think carefully," Reed said in a man-to-man tone. "If you come, I'll need your help. You'll have to see if you can get the mare to relax. She's frightened right now, and she needs someone to help calm her down."

Spencer gripped Faith's hand so tightly her fingertips were numb. Her heart ached. He wasn't going to be able to do it.

"So what do you say?" Reed stood. "Want to come along?"

Spencer took a deep breath. He looked up at Faith, his face so pale his freckles stood out like pennies on his nose.

He looked back at Reed.

And then, very slowly, he let go of Faith's hand.

CHAPTER EIGHT

FAITH DROVE SLOWLY, not because the narrow roads frightened her, but because the view was so divine. She could hardly take her eyes off the sloping green mountainsides, the tumbling orange rows of pumpkins, the placid silver ribbon of a winding creek.

Eventually, she couldn't resist. She needed to get back to the house—Tigger probably was ready for a walk—but she wanted to enjoy the scenery without worrying about wrecking Reed's luxurious little BMW. She pulled onto a paved overlook, slipped on her suede jacket and climbed out of the car.

Amazingly, she had the overlook all to herself. Just below her, Firefly Glen lay peacefully in the open palm of the mountains. For a moment the glen seemed like a living thing, as cherished and protected and safe as the kitten she had earlier held in her own hand.

Safe. She breathed deeply, trying to absorb that feeling. She'd been tense a couple of times during their shopping expedition, imagining that she saw the same expensive black sedan parked near them no matter where she went. Then she'd realized that Firefly Glen's high-income crowd loved expensive black sedans. Those and pricey SUVs pretty much dominated Main Street.

Up high in the mountains, paranoid ideas seemed completely ridiculous. The air was cold and thick with the clean smell of rich earth and growing things. How could she have lived so close to this beauty all her life and never taken the time to drive up to see it?

Even in these early stages, she could tell that the approaching autumn wasn't going to be anything like the ones she'd known in the city. On the traffic-clogged street outside her apartment, one half-choked maple had always burned orange and red like a single candle.

She had loved that tree and had appreciated its valiant effort to brighten their steel-and-smog landscape. But here—here acres and acres of that spectacular fire would roll across these mountainsides.

Any day now. She could smell it in the air. She could see it in the trees—a few red spots like a flight of cardinals in the maples; a few gold specks, like a scattering of coins, in the aspen. It was like watching an orchestra tuning up for its most magnificent symphony.

And suddenly she realized that she very much wanted to be here when the colors hit their peak. As much as she wanted them to arrest Doug Lambert, as much as she prayed for that every day, she hoped she wouldn't have to leave before fall came to this beautiful little town.

She climbed back into Reed's car, feeling a little guilty about Tigger, who had been left alone for hours. She started the ignition.

If she hadn't been checking her rearview mirror, preparing to back out of the overlook, she wouldn't have seen the approaching car at all. As it was, she got only the briefest glimpse of a swerving black sedan, taking the downhill mountain curve so fast it was little more than a terrifying blur.

Suddenly it seemed to make a sharp turn to the right.

It began speeding straight at her.

Her hand froze on the key. She had time for one half-formed thought. Thank God Spencer wasn't with her.

And then, as she'd known it would, the car hit her.

She heard the awful crunch of her back bumper, the crumpling screech of metal. Her whole body was paralyzed—her heart, her mind, even her lungs ceased to function, frozen into useless blocks of pure, solid fear—as her car lurched insanely forward.

For one horrible second she could see the steep drop of the cliff beyond the guardrail. A chaos of hemlocks, jagged granite rocks, black earth—falling away, falling down, hundreds of feet into more trees, more granite, more unforgiving earth.

And then, like a miracle, her car met the guardrail, and the guardrail held. The metal blistered outward as the nose of her car smashed into it. But it didn't break, and the car didn't fall. All at once, a headlight shattered, the airbag deployed, her head snapped back and finally everything was still.

Even the sound of the sedan roaring away faded in a very few seconds.

For a moment, the silence was so complete she thought she was deaf. But slowly her blood calmed, her ears opened, and she heard herself breathing like an exhausted runner. Heavy, rapid, desperate, from the diaphragm.

And she heard herself whispering, the same thing, over and over.

He found us. Oh, dear God. He found us.

REED NEVER DELIVERED a foal so fast in his life.

From the moment Harry Dunbar's call came through to his cell phone with news of Faith's accident, Reed could barely keep his mind on the job. If Harry hadn't assured him Faith was fine—and promised to stay at Autumn House with her until Reed arrived—he might have left Mark alone to finish the foaling, which thankfully was proceeding quite normally.

But years of professionalism helped him see it through. It also helped that he needed to remain calm for Spencer's sake. He told the little boy only the bare minimum, that Faith had been in a minor accident, that the car was slightly bunged up but Faith herself was fine. He'd even managed to smile, as if to say *Wouldn't you just know it?*

Reed must have cloaked his anxiety well. Spencer

had smiled back, without even a shadow of fear in his eyes.

Finally it was over. The foal teetered up on spindly legs, the mare watching, tired but healthy, from her stall. Mark's weathered face broke out in a cheek-splitting smile, and he pumped Reed's hand so hard he nearly pulled Reed's arm from the socket.

Spencer stared at Reed with such awestruck admiration that he felt the need to issue a disclaimer.

"This lady here did all the work," he said, stroking the horse's back. "I'm really no more than an insurance policy. I'm a just-in-case kind of guy."

It wasn't easy to get Spencer to leave. He climbed on the low rung of the foaling stall and hung there, as if he'd never get enough of watching this charmingly awkward animal discover its world.

Ordinarily Reed would have let him linger. But today was different. He had to get home to Faith. He had to see for himself that she was unharmed.

The sight of the sheriff's Jeep in front of the house reminded him that his BMW had been so mangled it wasn't even driveable. Probably totaled, Harry had said darkly.

Thank goodness he'd had it towed to the station impound. Spencer didn't need to see the wrecked metal, didn't need to picture Faith in the car as it had been hit....

Besides, he was already tense. As they approached Autumn House, and he saw the police car, the little boy clutched the dashboard with skinny, white-tipped fingers and drew in a loud, rasping breath. Then he turned, his brown eyes liquid with sudden fear.

"She's fine," Reed said again. "Sheriff Dunbar promised me. She's fine."

Spencer nodded, but he held Reed's hand as they walked up to the house. At the front door, Spencer hesitated, dragging on Reed's hand as he lagged behind.

Reed could only imagine what terrible pictures, what inexpressible fears, were darkening the little boy's imagination.

There was no point in trying to reassure him with words. Spencer knew for a fact what horrors could lurk on the other side of that door. He was just a six-year-old child, and yet he had already seen things so dreadful no adult could ever forget them.

Only Faith's voice, only her strong, living arms around him, could reassure Spencer now.

"I'll go first," Reed said. Spencer just nodded.

There must have been an anxious, unconvinced part of Reed, too, because the sight of Faith sitting on the living room sofa having coffee with Harry sent a huge swell of relief through his chest.

"Faith," he said.

She jumped up. "Reed! I'm so sorry about your car—" She looked beside him, suddenly tense. "Where's Spencer?"

"He's just outside. He was hanging back. I said I'd come in first."

She paused, and then, as the significance sank in,

she hurried toward the door. "Spencer," she called, her voice deliberately cheerful. She touched Reed's arm in a silent "thank you" as she passed him. "Hey, sweetie, where's my hug?"

As soon as she was out of earshot, Reed walked over to Harry. "Who was it?" He kept his voice low. "Did anybody see the car? Could it have been Lambert?"

Harry shook his head. "No witnesses. But she sure thinks it was."

"What do you think?"

"I think it probably was just some fool who doesn't know how to drive in the mountains. You know things like this happen sometimes, especially during tourist season. But she's scared of this Lambert, damn scared. She's practically paranoid."

Reed frowned. "He did kill her sister."

"I know. I'm not criticizing her, Reed. I'm just telling you how it is. If her lunch tastes funny, she'll think he poisoned it."

For some reason, Harry was really getting on his nerves. "Maybe that's why she's still alive. Maybe a little paranoia is a good thing when somebody is trying to kill you."

Harry gave him a funny look. "Hey, man. I understand. I'm just saying all she saw was a black sedan. It could have been anybody. Kids joyriding. A tourist from Florida who never saw a hill in his life. Could have been a drunk—"

"At two in the afternoon?"

"Hell, you know drunks. Boxer Barnes is plastered by nine in the morning."

Suddenly the two men looked at each other. Harry's mouth was slightly open.

"Oh, my God," he said. "Boxer?"

THE ADVENTURES—and the emotions—of this long day had clearly worn Spencer out. Though he had stopped taking naps at least a year ago, when Faith suggested one now he didn't balk.

He climbed up onto his bed, patted the quilt to invite Tigger to join him and settled back against the pillow with a sigh.

Faith sat on the edge of the bed and held his hand tightly while she told him about the accident. Just the most general details. She didn't mention Doug at all. She merely said that someone had been driving down the mountain road too fast, lost control for a minute and bumped into Reed's car.

Somehow, deep inside, Spencer must know that "bumped" was a serious understatement. But he gave her a sleepy smile and let his grip relax a little. He obviously wanted to believe. He was tired of being afraid.

Finally he turned on his side, his arm wrapped around Tigger's fluffy coat, and fell asleep.

Faith patted them both on the crowns of their little heads, and then she quietly left the room. She didn't have a lot of time to waste. She needed to talk to Reed.

She stopped on the lower landing, aware that Reed and Harry were conferring in muted tones by the front door. Harry was holding the portable phone in one hand, his walkie-talkie in the other.

"He said he can be here in ten minutes," Harry said, clicking on the telephone and beginning to punch numbers. "I'm going to call the café. Someone might have seen Boxer today. Might know if he'd been drinking."

Reed looked up and saw her. He murmured something to Harry, and then hurried up the first few stairs to join her on the landing.

"Is Spencer okay?"

She nodded. "He's sleeping."

"Good. The sheriff's deputy is on his way right now. Harry had an idea, and we want someone to stay with you while we go check it out."

Reed was leaving? Surely not... But she felt numb all over, and her thoughts seemed to be moving in slow motion. It was a little like being drunk. Drunk on fear.

"What kind of idea?"

"There's a guy in town who drives a car like the one you described. He's had a drinking problem for years. Boxer Barnes. It's a long shot, but it's worth checking out."

She shook her head. "Don't go," she said. "It wasn't Boxer. It was Doug."

Reed hesitated, then he put his hands on her shoulders. They were warm. If he left them there, she might thaw out a little. She might be able to think.

"Faith, listen to me—"

"If he's found us, we'll have to leave. Detective Bentley said there was no need for us to change our names yet. That they weren't even sure Doug was still in the country. Or that he was guilty at all. But now—" She took a deep breath, which was harder than it should have been. Her throat felt raw. She wondered if she might have screamed as the car hit her. She didn't remember.

"I should have started packing right away, but I wanted to see you first. I wanted, at least, to tell you how sorry I am about your car."

"I don't care about the car."

He ducked his head, and he put his finger under her chin, lifting her face so that he could look straight into her eyes. "Faith, listen to me. I know you believe it was Doug, and maybe it was. But think about it. How could he have known you'd be there, on the overlook? How could anyone have known? It's possible it really was an accident."

She looked at his rugged, honorable face and felt strangely sad. She understood why he didn't want to believe it. Until you met evil face-to-face, you couldn't accept that it even existed.

But she knew it did.

"Maybe he's been watching us. He did that for weeks before he…" She shivered, remembering how, sometimes when she pulled up in front of her interior design shop, Doug's car would be parked across the street, waiting.

"He liked to watch me."

Reed's fingers tightened on her shoulders. "Don't think about it, Faith. Not until you have to. We don't know who it was yet."

Harry, still over by the open front door, put the telephone on a table and cleared his throat. "Reed. Danziger's here. I'll fill him in, and then we'd better get going."

"Okay. Right there." Reed smiled at Faith. "Danziger is Harry's deputy. He's a good man. He'll look after you and Spencer while we're gone, okay?"

Faith didn't answer. She felt, momentarily, as mute as Spencer. What could she say? She didn't have the right to ask Reed to stay. If Doug really was in Firefly Glen, anyone near Faith was potentially in danger. The deputy was okay—he had signed up for hazardous duty. Reed had only signed up to hire a housekeeper.

And if Doug came for her here, came straight to Autumn House, what could Reed do, anyhow? He wasn't a hunter. He was probably one of the few men in Firefly Glen who didn't even own a gun. He didn't kill things. He healed them.

And yet, strangely, the idea of facing the next couple of hours without his quiet strength to sustain her was almost more than she could bear.

"Faith? What is it?" He touched her cheek. "Talk to me."

She tried to smile. "I guess I just wish you didn't have to go."

"I'll be right back."

"I know."

Harry was at the door again. He had his hat on. "Reed. Customer at Theo's says he saw Boxer this morning, and he was already fairly well pickled by noon. He told Theo he wasn't driving, but somebody else saw his car on Main Street."

"God." Reed scowled. "Have you called Parker?"

"Yeah. He's going to meet us at Boxer's house, just in case. No point having Parker yell later that we talked to Boxer without his lawyer present." He jingled his keys. "Come on. We need to shake a leg."

Reed looked back at Faith. She gave him her best attempt at a smile. "It's okay," she said. "I'm okay."

But the performance that had fooled a six-year-old wasn't good enough to fool Reed. He looked at her a minute, and then he turned to Harry.

"You go ahead without me," Reed said. "I think I'll stay here."

Harry frowned. "What the hell? A minute ago wild horses couldn't have kept you out of this posse. That's half the reason I called Parker, so I'd have someone to help hold you down if it turns out Boxer really did make a mess of your car."

Reed shrugged. "I changed my mind."

"Really." Harry's eyebrows went up. "Mr. Vigilante changed his mind."

"Hell, Harry, you should be relieved. Now you won't have to worry about my temper, and you can concentrate on Boxer. Just call me the minute you see his car. I don't need a confession first, and I don't care how Parker spins it. If Boxer's right front bumper is dented, that's all the evidence I need. Call me."

Harry looked from Reed to Faith and back to Reed. "Okay," he said slowly, with a reluctant smile. "I think I get it. Although I'm not sure there's anything in the sheriff's job description that says I have to take orders from the town vet."

Reed smiled, too. "No. That's in your job description as a human being and a friend."

Harry grumbled as he left, but Faith could tell he wasn't really annoyed. Both at the scene of the accident, and in the two long hours they'd spent together waiting for Reed, she had learned what a sweet person Harry Dunbar really was under his dour exterior. He'd told her about his wife, Emma, and how they were trying to adopt a baby. He'd misted up a little when she told him about Grace and Spencer, though he'd tried to hide it by pretending to sneeze.

And, though he had nearly choked on the coffee she made him, he'd drunk the whole thing, just to keep from hurting her feelings.

She heard his Jeep start up and drive away. She looked over at Reed.

"Thank you," she said. "I'm sorry to ask you to stay. I shouldn't have, but—"

"You didn't ask me. I wanted to stay." He grinned a little. "I'm afraid of Boxer Barnes."

"I doubt that." She smiled back, appreciating his effort to lighten the tone. "I've seen your friend Boxer."

"You have? Where?"

"He was passed out in the back of a blue Cadillac, drooling on the legs of a woman named Bridget O'Malley. He wasn't particularly terrifying."

"He's scarier when he's awake." Smiling, he took her hand and pulled her down the last few stairs. "Now. How about something to eat?"

She hesitated. "I guess I could fix something, like a…" She tried to think of anything she could make that was actually edible. So far she'd boiled a lump of pasta till it looked like a ball of sticky yarn, served an omelette so undercooked you had to eat it with a spoon, blackened toast and bacon and pancakes and muffins. She'd even baked chicken breasts until they could have been used for hockey pucks.

If it hadn't been for Theo's casseroles, they all would have starved.

"No. I meant I would fix something for you," he said. "I make a mean peanut butter and jelly sandwich, and it's well known that carbs are very calming. We can take it out on the back porch and watch the leaves change, which is about all the excitement we can handle after a day like today."

"You know, I'm not sure I can eat." Suddenly exhausted, she walked over to the sofa and sat down heavily. She put her fingers up between her eyes, pinching the bridge of her nose. "And I—I don't think I want to be outdoors, where anyone could…"

He sat down beside her. He pulled her hand down and looked into her eyes. "Does your head hurt?" He had dropped his lightly teasing tone. "Harry should have made you go to the emergency room."

"No. It doesn't hurt. The airbag inflated, and—" She tried not to remember that moment, when she had thought the guardrail would give way. It made her insides feel as if they were being sucked down into a whirlpool of terror.

"My head is fine. My nerves, on the other hand, seem to be kind of a mess." She took several deep breaths, as if she could force her body to relax. "I keep thinking I should pack, I should hide, I should just take Spencer and run."

She looked at him, swamped by a sudden feeling of helplessness, a wretched feeling she despised. It was so useless, so weak. "But then I realize—I don't know where to go."

"Don't go anywhere," he said. He shifted, and then he reached out and gently guided her into a resting position, with her head against his chest. "Not yet. Just rest here, with me, until we hear from Harry. And then we can decide what you should do."

"I can't," she said, her lips against his soft flannel shirt. She ought to sit up. It was too tempting, the thought of letting someone else shoulder the fear for a while. She couldn't afford to relax her guard. "I'm not tired."

"Of course you are," he said softly. He put his hand on her head and grazed her cheek with his knuckle. "When something like that happens, adrenaline rushes through you, and then, when it's gone, there's nothing left but exhaustion."

"I'm not tired." But she was. She was. And her cheek fit so perfectly against the curve where his chest and shoulder came together. Her neck relaxed, giving up the fight.

"How could you not be tired?" His voice was soothing. She felt herself sinking into it. "I hear you up every night, checking on Spencer again and again. I hear you walking miles across the floor of your room. I see your light burning until dawn, keeping the demons away."

His stroking fingers were rhythmic and as soft as warm silk. She closed her eyes.

"I didn't know you knew." She realized she was slightly slurring her words. She was on the very edge of sleep, coaxed there by the gentle stroke of his fingers. "Do I make too much noise? Do I make it difficult for you to sleep?"

His fingers stopped their movement for a second, and then they began again.

"Yes," he said quietly, so quietly she wasn't sure she really heard it. It might have been the rustle of the dark wing of a dream, which was rapidly overtaking her. "Sometimes the very thought of you can keep me awake all night."

SHE COULDN'T HAVE SLEPT very long. When she opened her eyes, she saw that the fire hadn't burned down much. The shadows in the room were all in the same places. The light from the windows was still the wild-rose red of an early autumn sunset.

But she was stretched out on the sofa, with a knitted throw across her legs. Reed was kneeling on the floor in front of her, his fingers on her arm. The telephone was in his hands, and he was speaking her name.

"Faith," he said as her eyes fluttered shut, then fought to open again. "Faith, wake up. Harry just called."

"Harry." Awareness returned like a wash of cold water. She struggled up on one elbow. She swallowed. "Was it Doug? Does he know?"

"He knows," he said. He smiled, and the warmth of that smile could grow daffodils in December. "He's one hundred percent certain. It wasn't Doug, Faith. It was Boxer."

Her elbow gave way, and she fell back against the soft cushions.

It wasn't Doug. That meant...

She was safe.

But that wasn't the only thought that went through her mind. It was paired with another.

She could stay.

CHAPTER NINE

Doug let himself into Faith's apartment without bothering to be particularly quiet. Who was going to hear him? In the middle of the day, these bourgeois apartment buildings were as empty as tombs. All the little worker bees were slaving away at the office, and the occasional housekeeper they could afford was sitting in front of their kitchen television, watching her favorite soap opera and eating whatever junk food she thought the boss wouldn't miss.

He probably hadn't even needed this ugly white electrician's jumpsuit, or the paint cap, or the gloves. But stealing them had been fun, and he needed all the fun he could find these days. Life at the homeless mission was not exactly intellectually stimulating.

The apartment was dark, but he knew where the light switches were. The air was stale, but not unpleasant. It merely intensified the scent of Faith, which he had always liked. Smelling it now excited him. It made him feel closer to her, closer to finding her.

He had been here before, of course, though not often. A couple of times, when he was a new and lucrative client, she'd let him in and given him dreadful coffee. After that, the next time he came, she had told him that she conducted all her business at her office, and instructed him to meet her there.

She'd instructed *him*. What a joke! He should have known then that she wasn't worth it. That she was just a bitch who didn't deserve him.

But unfortunately these things weren't logical. A woman didn't set your blood on fire because she met Sensible Standard A, or possessed Suitable Quality B. It was a chemical thing, or a metaphysical thing. It went as deep as your molecular structure, as high as your soul. You couldn't use logic to create it, and you couldn't reason it away.

If you wanted to be free of it, you had to kill it.

He took his time. He liked being here. It was frilly and female, all blues and purples and cream. She had good taste, he'd give her that.

It was not as nice as his own penthouse suite, not by a long shot. But it was better than the mission. And besides, it amused him to make himself at home among her things.

When her telephone rang, he almost answered it, just for kicks. Just because he could.

But he played it safe. The answering machine picked up after only two rings, and an uneducated voice drawled, ''Ms. Constable? This is Delilah. I know you said it would be a while, but I was just checking. Call me.''

After that he didn't even want to touch the telephone. She was so cheap, so unworthy, with her low-

rent friends. More like his mother than he had wanted
to believe. Strange that, after he'd worked so hard to
leave those sleazy, stained-linoleum childhood days
behind, he'd fallen for a woman who was so much
like his mother it made him sick.

He looked through the fussy little secretary desk
first, with its orderly pigeonholes and its prissy inlaid
flowers and scrolls. She was neat and organized. God,
was she boring. She paid every bill on time, the curse
of the middle class.

That reminded him of how many creditors were
still bleeding from the bottom line thanks to him, and
that made him smile.

He had millions. Millions. Stashed safely overseas,
just waiting for him to finish this Faith Constable
business and come and get it. Suddenly impatient, he
tossed her bills into a messy heap and moved to the
personal correspondence. The clues were in the private life.

An hour later, he was more irritated than ever. Not
a single clue. His man had already checked into all
these people. He sent the tangle of letters, cards and
e-mail addresses onto the floor with one swipe. Then
he stood up and went into the kitchen for a beer.

Just inside the pass-through counter, he paused.

This was where he'd done it.

For a minute he could hear her voice again, gig-
gling into the telephone. "I love you, too, teddy
bear." It was the stupid endearment that clinched it—
the kind of thing his mother had called her boyfriends,

all of them, so he could easily imagine what kind of low-rent half-wit she was talking to. And she had preferred a cretin like that to Doug Lambert?

Thinking back now, he realized he must have gone slightly insane, just for a moment. But at the time he had felt a preternatural clarity. He'd put the roses carefully down on the countertop, walked quietly up behind her and snapped her neck with one swift crack. She hadn't felt a thing. She hadn't even had time to be afraid.

He looked at the floor, where her body had fallen, the telephone clattering to the tiles beside her. Her thick, dark hair had been like a veil across her face, and he hadn't realized then that she wasn't Faith. He hadn't realized his mistake until, when he was leaving, he saw Faith and the brat on the sidewalk.

His fury had been a physical eruption, like a volcano inside him. The bitch had made a murderer of him—and all for nothing. The comfortable Doug Lambert life he'd worked so hard to create was over, all because of her. But Faith Constable still danced along the sidewalk, holding her nephew by the hand, as if she hadn't a care in the world.

Well, he'd fix that, and soon.

And she wouldn't go like her sister, she'd know she was dying. She'd have plenty of time to be afraid. She'd be so damn scared she'd get down on her knees and beg. He felt a small swell of arousal just imagining her eyes drowning in tears.

He took the beer into her bedroom. He'd left that

room for last, and now he was glad he had. Because he suddenly realized he wasn't quite over his need to have sex with her. He would do that first, before she died, while she still thought there was hope. He'd do everything, and she'd let him. Even the things the prostitutes refused to do, no matter how much money he offered them.

But he'd need something to gag her with. And probably tie her hands. When you were in enough pain, instinct took over, and you began to fight, even if you were trying not to, even if you were trying to pretend you liked it.

He picked up a couple of pairs of panty hose, which were the perfect handcuffs. Wasn't that ironic? If women only knew. And a pair of powder blue satin bikini panties.

He stuffed them in his pockets, chuckling. It was too perfect. She'd refused to let him get even a glimpse of her sacred underwear, and now he'd take them and stuff them into her wet, weeping mouth.

The whole idea excited him so much the jumpsuit was killing him. It was much too small for a man like him.

He unzipped the suit and freed himself, sighing with relief and anticipation. He didn't have to worry about his DNA showing up in her apartment. They already knew he'd been here.

He stood over her panty drawer, over the innocent white lace and the sinful silk fantasies. And then, closing his eyes, he entered a hot, throbbing world of terrified brown eyes and the delicious, gurgling sounds of blue-satin screams.

IT RAINED Saturday night, and then it turned cold. By Sunday morning autumn had officially arrived in Firefly Glen.

Spencer must have seen it from his loft window. He woke Faith early, his face alive with excitement. He pulled at her, tugging impatiently until she sleepily grabbed her robe and let him lead her onto the second-story porch.

The minute they opened the door, a cold mask of crystal air molded itself against her face. When she stepped out, a garnet carpet of leaves crunched under her slippers.

"What is it?" She wrapped her robe tightly around her throat, took two steps, and then she froze, speechless.

Nothing she'd ever seen in a picture book had prepared her for the magnificence of this cloisonné-colored landscape.

Magic had come in the night. Every tree suddenly was dressed in a new, exotic costume. Vermilion, carnelian, russet and rose, mandarin orange, burnt sienna, saffron and strawberry. The entire forest, from ground shrub to treetop, was jeweled and decorated and painted with fire.

Spencer stood beside her in his Lassie pajamas. His hand crept up to hers.

"Oh, Spencer," she said. "It is beautiful, isn't it?"

He nodded, his teeth chattering. She looked down and saw that he hadn't even taken time to put on his slippers.

"We should get you inside," she said. "You're going to freeze."

He shook his head vehemently. She had never seen him so excited. So instead of insisting on the sensible retreat, she picked him up.

It was the first time she'd been able to do that without even a twinge of pain streaking through her arm. A tall, thin young Firefly Glen doctor had taken the stitches out the other day, wisecracking his way through the procedure, and he'd seemed thrilled with the neat job done by the emergency room physician. But today was the first day her arm had felt completely normal.

It was reassuring to realize that her body had been doing its job all along, knitting her flesh back together while she was busy, sleeping or working or playing. Maybe the psyche was equally competent. Maybe it, too, was going about the business of healing silently, one small step at a time.

She wrapped Spencer inside her robe, and together they stayed out on the porch, marveling at the colors, until their noses and ears were numb.

After about ten minutes, Reed appeared on the lawn below them, bundled up in a wool sweater, gloves and a sports cap. He smiled up at them, tossing the football in the air meaningfully.

"Kickoff time!" he called, and those, it seemed,

were the magic words. Spencer wriggled out of Faith's arms quickly and ran inside.

"Dress warmly," she cautioned, but she didn't think he'd heard her.

She got dressed, too, but she was slower, feeling the need for little niceties like a shower that Spencer sometimes ignored. By the time she met them outside, the game was already fourteen to nothing.

"He's beating the pants off me," Reed complained. "He's as slippery as an eel. I tackle him, but he just squirts free and scores."

Spencer grinned smugly. His cheeks were two red apples, and his nose had a distinctly Rudolphlike glow. It was running from the cold. His hair was matted with bits of dry leaves and grass. But he looked happy and normal, and she wouldn't have combed that hair or wiped that little nose for all the money in the world.

"You'll have to be on my team, Faith," Reed said. "Just to even things up. He's got Tigger, who tackles with his teeth."

So they played, and they played, falling into piles of huge amber leaves that had dropped from the big leaf maple, and sending the football soaring through the crystalline air.

She and Reed scored once. At that happy moment, Reed spiked the football in the end zone, which was officially the clearing between two golden elm trees, and triumphantly yelled, "Touchdown!"

Spencer laughed, but from then on, whenever he

scored, he spiked the ball, too. He'd look over at Reed, and Reed would cooperate by hollering "Touchdown!" at the top of his lungs.

She didn't know much about football, but by the time the score was forty-nine to seven, she got the idea Reed was letting Spencer win.

"We have to," he said with a grin when she pulled him aside and accused him of it. "It would destroy his developing male ego to get beaten by a girl."

"Oh, yeah?" She brushed maple leaves from her behind. "Frankly, I haven't noticed that the male ego is all that sensitive."

He pulled a mock-tragic face. "Honest, we're very fragile." Then he dove for Spencer, who came streaking by. He missed, falling into a pile of leaves, and Spencer spiked the ball again with feeling.

"An eel, I tell you," Reed said, groaning from his pyre of leaves. "Touchdown!"

Just then his beeper went off. He pulled it from his pocket, looked at it and climbed to his feet. "Whoops. Gotta go. Emergency over at Lofton's farm."

Spencer looked crestfallen. Faith believed he could have stayed out here all day.

"It shouldn't take long," Reed said. He tossed the football to Spencer. "I'll be back for lunch, I promise."

Spencer clearly wanted to be invited, but Faith understood that Reed didn't think it was a good idea. Perhaps he didn't know what he'd find at the Lofton farm. The last thing Spencer needed was to witness an animal's suffering. Or death.

"Come on, champ," she said. "We never got any breakfast this morning. Let's go roast some marshmallows by the living room fire."

Spencer looked at her, obviously surprised. She never allowed him to eat things like marshmallows for breakfast. Not even marshmallowy cereals or doughnuts or pie.

But he didn't know that something had changed inside her yesterday, when she almost went over that cliff. He didn't know that, for the first time since Grace's death, she had understood how very much she wanted to live.

Yesterday, when the guardrail had held its ground, saving her, she had been given a second chance. And she intended to make the most of it.

No more crouching in fear and paranoia. Tragedy existed, and maybe evil did, too. But so did beautiful autumn forests and football games and marshmallows.

Detective Bentley might be right. Doug Lambert might already be in South America, far more interested in saving his own skin than in damaging hers. But even if he wasn't, even if he was still in New York, still hoping to harm her, she couldn't let terror rule her every thought. It wasn't healthy.

Not for her, and certainly not for Spencer.

And so she was going to choose life. Real messy, scary, thrilling, beautiful life.

Complete with marshmallows.

IT WAS ALMOST lunchtime when she heard the car pull up. Thinking it was Reed, Faith hurried to the back door and flung it open.

But it wasn't Reed. It was a young, beautiful blonde with wild, curly hair and the prettiest smile Faith had ever seen. Another of Reed's would-be girlfriends?

"Hi," Faith said, wiping her hands on her apron. She had finally learned that she needed an apron when she tried to cook. It didn't save the food, but it at least protected her clothes. "I'm sorry, Reed's not here right now, but he—"

"Oh, we're not looking for Reed. We're looking for you!"

"For me?"

"Yes, you're Faith, aren't you? Well, I'm Natalie Quinn. Mrs. Matthew Quinn." She grinned. "Sorry. I just like to say that. I've only been married about fifteen minutes, and I can't quite believe it yet myself. I've been meaning to come by and welcome you to the Glen, but I'm practically a newlywed—you know how that is—and my house is falling apart, and it's just been crazy. Wonderful, but crazy."

Faith smiled. "That's okay," she said. "We haven't been here long. Come on in."

Natalie wrinkled her nose, hesitating. "Maybe first I'd better tell you why I'm really here, just in case you don't really want us to come in after all. You see,

I am a good friend of Boxer Barnes. He's out there in the car, I drove him here so that he could say he's sorry about yesterday. He's afraid to come in, because he's sober, and he's pretty much afraid of everything when he's sober, that's why the poor man drinks so much. But I told him I'd come first and make sure you wouldn't hit him over the head with a spatula or anything.''

She smiled again. "You won't, will you?''

Faith felt a little light-headed. Natalie Quinn had such an amazing life force that she seemed to burn up all the air in the vicinity. But how could anyone resist that smile?

"Of course not," Faith said. "I don't even know what a spatula is.''

Natalie laughed. "Yeah, Theo told me. That's okay. I'm pretty good in the kitchen, maybe I can show you some stuff.'' She took a couple of steps toward the drive and waved merrily at the man who sat in her car. "Come on, Boxer. She doesn't bite.''

Slowly the car door opened, and the old man stepped out. He wasn't quite as imposing as the other men of his generation she'd met, the robust Ward or the roguish Granville, but he was appealing in his own way, with his dapper tweed suit, his long, wavy white hair and his sad blue eyes.

He looked a bit like an elderly poet, which apparently was a deliberate effect. He walked stiffly up to the door, put his hand to his heart and cleared his throat.

"Ms. Constable, I can't begin to tell you how grieved I am that I put your life in danger," he announced. "It was wicked of me, and I will be punished for it, both by the law and by my own guilty conscience. All I ask is that someday perhaps you may find it in your heart to forgive me."

Natalie put her arm through his and chuckled. "He talks like this when he's sober. When he drinks, he's considerably less flowery." She looked inside the door. "It's kind of cold out here. May we come in?"

Faith stood back. "Of course." As she moved back into the center of the kitchen, she smelled the now-familiar stench of burning food. "Oh, heck, the hamburgers!"

Natalie raced over to the stove, slipped on a mitt and whisked the tray of grilling burgers—now grilling lumps of charcoal—out of the oven. "I'm so sorry," she said. "This is my fault. We came at a bad time. We distracted you."

Faith shook her head sadly. "No, I do this all the time. To tell you the truth, I'm hopeless. I simply can't cook."

Natalie surveyed the kitchen. She set the tray down across the sink and looked carefully at every bowl and bottle of spice Faith had used.

"Nonsense," she pronounced finally. "Cooking's easy. It's like sex, everyone can do it, you don't need to be taught. And the difference between a good cook and a lousy cook is like the difference between a good lover and a lousy lover. If it's going to turn out right, you have to give it all your attention. You can't keep letting your mind wander off to other things."

Faith stared at her, trying to decide whether she was kidding. From the table, where Boxer had sat down the minute he entered the room, the old man made an offended noise.

"Don't you start talking like that, Natalie Granville. Sex, indeed. It doesn't become you."

"Oh, Boxer. I'm not twelve anymore." She smiled at Faith. "Boxer was one of my grandfather's best friends. He hasn't accepted that I'm a grown woman yet." She held up her left hand and wiggled her ring so that it would twinkle in the light. "A grown, married woman. Isn't that lovely? You'll have to meet Matthew. He's the sexiest man in Firefly Glen, and you may have noticed that's saying quite a bit."

"Oh, the shame of it," Boxer moaned. He put his head between his hands. "What is this generation coming to? Talking of sex in the kitchen, as if it were the weather."

Reed walked into the kitchen. "Who's talking of sex in the kitchen? Oh, it's you." He reached over and gave Natalie a big, easy hug. "I should have known. You haven't talked about anything but sex since the day you met Matthew."

"Oh, the shame of it," Boxer groaned. "Saints in heaven. Sex in the kitchen."

Natalie grinned. She leaned closer to Faith and whispered. "And in the dining room, and in the pool. And even on the roof. But you have to be very, very careful on the roof." She sighed. "Oh, heavens, marriage is wonderful. I highly recommend it to the entire world."

Reed frowned at her, but it wasn't a real frown. "God, Nat," he said, "are you drunk, too?"

"She certainly is not." Boxer raised his head fiercely. "Natalie Granville is a damn fine woman, and I'll kick the ass of anyone who says otherwise."

Natalie kissed the top of Boxer's head. "Yes, I am," she said to Reed with a grin. "I'm delightfully drunk on love."

"And what exactly are you two doing in my kitchen? Besides talking about sex?" Reed perched on the edge of the table and glared at Boxer. "I don't suppose you've come to apologize for mangling the hell out of my car."

"Not your car," Boxer said in eloquent, somber tones. "A car is merely a material possession, and as such matters little in this world. I came instead to offer my humble apologies to the exquisite Ms. Constable. I told her that if she would be so generous as to forgive me—"

"I forgive you," Faith put in quickly. No telling how flowery this fellow could get, and she still had to think of something to feed Reed and Spencer for lunch.

Boxer bowed his head. "My endless gratitude is yours."

"Well, that's very nice," Reed said, "but I'm

afraid she needs something a little more concrete than gratitude.''

He held out a small black cell phone, not his own, but a new one. ''I picked this up when I was in town. I figured you should have it, in case of emergencies. That way you can always call me, no matter where I am. No matter what.''

She understood what he meant. In case Doug showed up. He wanted her to know she could always call for help. But no one else was supposed to know the true circumstances of her life, so he couldn't spell it out. Everyone else in town just thought she was the new housekeeper.

She took the telephone with a polite murmur of thanks, but she looked at him warmly, hoping he could read the real gratitude in her heart.

Spencer, who had been in the living room watching television, must have heard Reed's arrival, because suddenly he appeared in the doorway with the football in his hand. He tossed it to Reed, who caught it easily.

''Oh, no,'' Reed said, putting the ball behind his back. ''No more football until I get some lunch. A man needs sustenance before he can endure another stomping like that.''

''Umm, Reed.'' Faith sighed. ''About lunch…''

He sniffed the air. He stared at her, his face falling. ''No.''

''Yes.'' She picked up one of the scorched burgers and held it out. ''I'm sorry, but yes.''

He closed his eyes and moaned under his breath. "Must...eat..." he whispered tragically.

Spencer, who obviously could not accept that his football game had suffered a setback, scanned the room quickly, desperately searching for an answer.

Finally he found one. Pouncing, he grabbed the open bag of marshmallows and held it up with a triumphant flourish.

Reed stared at it, and then he began to laugh. He took the bag, dug out a marshmallow and popped it into his mouth.

"Clever boy," Reed said. He grinned at Spencer, and the two of them slapped palms. "Touchdown!"

CHAPTER TEN

SPENCER LATCHED ON TO the cell phone the minute he saw it. Faith didn't know whether he liked the security of it, or whether he just thought it was a cool techno-gizmo. Spencer was all male that way. He loved anything with buttons and beeps and a digital display.

His reasons didn't really matter, anyhow. It made him happy to carry the phone around in his pocket, and that was enough for Faith. Reed didn't mind, either. He said that, as long as Spencer would fork it over whenever Faith went anywhere alone, he didn't care who played with it.

That Friday afternoon, Spencer came in to the kitchen holding an empty bread bag. He'd begun to feed the ducks every day after lunch, a ritual he took very seriously. Tigger wasn't allowed to help. He'd never quite learned to keep out of the pond, so he had to stay inside, staring a hole through the kitchen door.

Today, though, Spencer seemed to be out of food. He held out the bag and shook it to emphasize how empty it was.

"Okay, sweetie," Faith said. "I'll see if we have some more."

She put down the cookbook she'd been studying, relieved to be able to stop struggling with foreign phrases like "deglaze with wine until it is reduced by half" and "let the fat reach the point of fragrance."

The darn book particularly loved the phrase "bake until tender." Well, yeah. But how long exactly *was* that?

Naturally Melissa Fairmont hadn't owned any but the most sophisticated cooking tomes. Faith needed beginner pamphlets, like "Meet Your Kitchen" and "Making Friends With Your Measuring Spoons."

"You know," she said, slipping a fork into the book for a marker, "I think Reed said you should occasionally give the ducks real feed. Did he tell you where he keeps that?"

Spencer shook his head. He was eyeing the apples in the bowl on the table. He'd just had lunch, but he was always hungry. Especially now that Faith was doing the cooking. Thank heaven for fresh fruit and vegetables.

"Tell you what. You have an apple, and I'll go ask Reed about it, okay? I think he's out back working on the stable."

Spencer nodded. He pulled up a chair, shoved her cookbook out of the way, and dragged his teeth happily through the crisp skin of the apple. The cell phone was hooked to his belt, riding on a clip Reed had given him just yesterday.

She smiled as she went outside, thinking how smart Reed was. One of these days, Spencer would not be able to resist using that beloved phone. And there was only one way to use a telephone, as Reed well knew.

You had to talk.

She made her way across the backyard, breathing in the sweet smell of someone's nearby leaf fire. The new stable was about halfway finished. Reed worked on it a little every day, before the clinic opened, or after it closed. Because the clinic closed early on Friday, she assumed he'd be out there now.

She was right. But he wasn't alone.

As she rounded the corner, she saw Justine standing with him. Gavin was sleeping on her shoulder, covered from head to toe in a blue woolen sack with a peaked hood.

And Reed, who had his wallet open, was handing Justine a rather thick stack of money. Cash money. Big bills.

Justine twitched a little when she saw Faith. She jammed the money into her shirt pocket quickly and flicked Reed an uncomfortable look.

He seemed more nonchalant. He refolded his wallet smoothly and slid it into his back pocket as he smiled a welcome to Faith.

"Hey. I hope you've come to help." He gestured toward the pile of unused boards. "I am never going to get this darn thing finished before winter at this rate."

She shook her head. "No, unfortunately, I'm working on dinner. This isn't one of Theo's nights, so I have to come up with something edible. I actually just came to ask where you keep the food for the ducks. Spencer is ready to feed them.''

''Oh, we store that in the back of the clinic,'' Justine put in, shifting Gavin to a more comfortable spot on her shoulder. ''I'm headed back that way. I'll show you.''

In the short silence that followed, she looked at Reed, apparently realizing she might have butted in. ''I mean, unless you wanted to show her, of course. I was just thinking, you know, that this way you could keep working.''

Reed laughed and picked up another long, thick board. ''No, it's fine. You show her. If I stop now, I'll never be able to force myself to do any more today.''

Faith and Justine turned away, but after they'd walked just a few feet Reed called out again. ''Hey, Faith!''

She looked back. He was awful cute, standing there in his dirty sweatshirt, with his jeans riding low on his narrow hips, hoisting a heavy board on one broad shoulder. ''Yes?''

''If things get rough in the kitchen, there's a telephone number I want you to remember. It's 555-MAMA.''

''Okay.'' She wrinkled her brows. ''And that number would be for...''

He grinned. ''Pizza.''

She scowled at him playfully, Justine laughed, and then they headed once again toward the clinic.

In a minute or so they heard the low whine of Reed's circular saw. The noise seemed to wake Gavin up. Justine patted his back and murmured something soothing—and that seemed to break the ice between them.

"You know, I'm sure glad it was you who came around that corner just now," she said, glancing at Faith with a sheepish expression. "If my mother had seen him giving me money like that, she would have thrown a fit. God only knows what she would have thought."

Faith wasn't sure how to respond. She couldn't help being curious herself. Why had Reed been shelling out large sums of cash to Justine behind the clinic?

Justine wasn't stupid. She gave Faith one considering look, and then she smiled tightly. "You're not sure what to think, either, are you?"

Faith smiled back. "No, but the difference is it's none of my business."

"It's none of my mother's business, either." Justine's mood seemed to sour abruptly. She tightened the hood around Gavin's little face with tense, jerky movements.

"I mean, why should it be? They're not supporting me and Gavin. My father won't even speak to me. I don't owe them answers. I don't owe them a damn thing."

Faith didn't say anything. Clearly a lot of volatile emotions lay just under the surface in this young woman. It was hard to be sure what might make her explode.

"Reed is nice to me. Sometimes he helps me, okay? He's the only person in this town who would give me a job. He's the only one who isn't afraid of my father. And now he's loaning me some money to get my car fixed. That's all. I don't know why anyone would read anything dirty into that."

Faith kept her tone level. "I can't imagine that anyone would."

Justine snorted. Gavin lifted his head and looked at her curiously. "You don't know my father, then. He thinks everything is dirty. Do you know he even asked me if Reed was Gavin's father?"

She looked at Faith with bloodshot eyes. "He told my mother he thinks maybe Reed got drunk one night, and was all horny because his wife was dead, and so he slept with me."

Faith took a deep breath. What a terrible man Alton Millner must be. She hoped to God he wasn't telling everyone in town this sordid fantasy of his.

"I have to agree, that sounds a bit far-fetched," Faith said cautiously.

"It's more than far-fetched. It's completely whacked. My father is disgusting. I hate him. I'll never tell him who Gavin's father is now. He doesn't deserve to know."

Faith had vowed to stay out of this. But suddenly she just couldn't stop herself. Justine was very young and very emotional. It was possible she hadn't thought this through.

"I can understand how upset you must be. But this seems a little rough on Reed, doesn't it?"

Justine sniffed loudly, ran her finger under her nose and shot Faith a frown. "Why? Reed doesn't give a flip what my father says."

"Maybe not." Faith chose her words carefully. "But other people might. What if your father tells everyone his theory? It's a shame for Reed's reputation to be ruined, don't you think?"

"No one would believe him. They know Reed's not like that. Everybody likes Reed. Nobody likes my father."

Faith shrugged. "Maybe you're right. I'm sure you understand the situation better than I do."

They walked in silence the rest of the way back to the clinic. Now and then a fat duck would waddle right up to them, clearly aware that it ought to be dinnertime. Faith apologized, holding out her empty hands and promising that Spencer would be out soon, though that didn't seem to impress any of the ducks much.

Justine stepped around them, as if they weren't there.

It was obvious that Faith's words had made Justine think. She sighed heavily a couple of times, and then she nuzzled Gavin's ear with a lost, needy gesture that was somehow extremely poignant.

While her lips were pressed against the flannel, she

made a small sound that was half frustration, half distress. Faith thought she might be crying, and she regretted having upset her. This was all so horribly unfair to Reed, though. Surely Justine would see that sooner or later.

As they reached the door, Justine finally turned to Faith. Her blue eyes were full of tears and defiance.

"You know, nobody thinks about this from my side. What if I actually have a reason for not telling people who the father is?" She took a ragged breath. "What if I'm not just being a bitch?"

Faith looked at her calmly, though her heart ached. What a horrible dilemma this was!

"What kind of reason?"

"Maybe it would ruin the father's life if the truth got out. Like, what if he's already married? Or in love with someone else? What if his family would throw a fit? Nobody ever thinks about that."

"But, Justine, I—"

"What if it would totally mess up his life to get saddled with a kid?" Tears began to fall in earnest, and her voice was choked with misery. "What if I'm actually trying to do the right thing for once in my goddamn life?"

OUT IN THE HALL the pay phone was ringing. Doug heard it in his sleep. He shifted on the lump of stained rocks they called a mattress and tried to tune it out.

Why the hell didn't somebody answer it?

But suddenly, as the rings faded into the empty

corridor, a random, half-conscious thought flashed through his mind.

The telephone. Ringing and ringing and ringing.

In his dreams he saw a glowing number, pulsing in and out, blinking blood red, winking at him, trying to tell him something important.

And not just any number. The number of trouble, the number of fear. The number of death.

The number 13.

He bolted up, suddenly wide awake, his whole body strangely cool, as if he were made of melted ice.

Good God, he was a fool. Such a stupid, stupid fool.

The telephone.

Faith's telephone. With thirteen red messages still suspended in its mechanical bowels, recorded but unheard, fertilized but unborn. Waiting for him to come back, waiting for him to push the button that would force the machine to helplessly disgorge them all.

He'd pick through every message, every word. And somewhere in them he would find the clue he needed. He was sure of it. So sure that, for the first time in two months, he thought perhaps he could really sleep.

He wouldn't go tonight, not tonight, when all the little ants would be at home in their mound. And not tomorrow, which was a weekend. The ants would be scurrying around in the elevators and the corridors, hauling bags of groceries and cans of paint and other made-up chores to make their pitiful lives seem less pointless.

It annoyed him to remember Monday was Halloween. Too busy. All those parties and trick-or-treaters. He couldn't go then, either.

But Tuesday, when they all marched in a line back to their offices, leaving the mound untended. On Tuesday, he would return to Faith's apartment.

And he would force that silent, overlooked machine to reveal to him every one of its thirteen secrets.

HALLOWEEN WAS only three days away.

After dinner Friday night, while Reed and Faith did the dishes and Spencer drew pictures at the kitchen table, Reed suggested they might want to enter the scarecrow contest.

"It's fun," he said as he dried the last of the dinner plates. "We won't win, because Suzie Strickland always wins. She's the only truly artistic person in town. But it's still fun to enter."

Spencer looked intrigued. Reed had noticed that his freckles always seemed to get darker when he was excited, and they were practically mahogany right now. Tigger, who always mirrored Spencer's mood, lifted his head from his paws and panted enthusiastically.

Faith, on the other hand, looked downright dubious. "But if we aren't going to the Halloween festival, won't that be kind of pointless?"

Reed gave her a shocked look. "Why on earth wouldn't we go to the festival?"

Spencer opened his mouth and scowled at Faith, too. He didn't actually echo Reed's words, but his expression said it all.

Her face tightened, and she swallowed hard. Suddenly Reed knew what she was thinking—he could almost see it in her eyes. The festival would be crowded and chaotic, and people would be in costumes that cloaked their true identities. She was afraid of all that chaos, all that exposure.

But, in a few dramatic seconds, he watched her overcome that fear. She looked at Spencer's eager face. She frowned. Then she took a deep breath, blinked twice and forced her lips to smile.

"I guess you're right," she said. "Of course we ought to go."

For this little boy, she could do anything. She just might be the bravest woman Reed had ever seen. He thought of the two self-indulgent years he'd wasted after Melissa's death, weeping into a bottle and wishing he were dead, and he was ashamed.

As he passed behind her to put away a bowl, he rested his hand briefly on her shoulder. "Bravo," he said softly.

She looked up. "For what?" Then she smiled. "Oh, you mean because I didn't completely ruin dinner? Just the edges this time. I actually am getting better, don't you think?"

He took the clean platter from her hands. He had

the most ridiculous urge to say, *No, how could you get better? You were damn near perfect already.*

"Yes," he said. "It was actually pretty good. Natalie must have given you some excellent cooking advice."

To his surprise, she blushed slightly. "Well," she said with a small smile. "It was certainly interesting."

She fished around in the hot water for the last of the silverware. "But tell us more about the scarecrow contest. Spencer and I are city people. We don't have any idea how you actually build a scarecrow."

Spencer put his crayons down and watched Reed intently. It was clear he didn't want to miss a word.

"It's easy," Reed said. "Mostly you just need two poles, some straw, some old clothes and something to make a head. After that, it's all up to the designer. You can get as fancy as you want."

He reached out toward Spencer. "Got an extra crayon?"

Spencer handed over his box and sketch paper willingly. Reed sat at the table and doodled out a basic scarecrow, with crazy hair, a jack-o-lantern face and a straw hat.

"For hair, you can use an old mop, or yarn, or pipe cleaners. Anything you can shred, really. The head, well, that's the fun part. You can use a basketball, or a pumpkin, an old pillowcase stuffed with straw, or even a really big squash."

He grinned at Spencer. "Of course show-offs like

Suzie Strickland make elaborate papier-mâché masks and stuff, but most of us settle for burlap sacks and a magic marker.''

Faith cast a wry glance at him over her shoulder. ''Sounds as if you've done this before.''

He smiled, remembering the terrific designs Melissa used to create. One year she'd created a scarecrow gymnast, who appeared to be in the middle of turning a cartwheel. He never had really understood how she had pulled that one off.

But he did know she'd be happy that he was planning to enter the contest again.

''I used to,'' he said. ''I haven't lately, not for a couple of years.''

Spencer grabbed one of the crayons and began to draw a scarecrow of his own. Reed sat back, delighted to see that his idea had been a success.

''We'll have to decide what ours should be. The theme this year is 'The Guardian.'''

Spencer looked up, a question in his eyes.

''Guardians are people who protect things. Scarecrows protect the crops—corn or wheat or apples or whatever—from the big birds who might come around and eat them up. That's how they got their name. They literally scare the crows away.''

Spencer laughed. He picked up the black crayon and drew a gigantic black bird flying above his scarecrow.

Faith let the water out of the sink, and, drying her

hands, she came to sit beside them. "So if the theme is guardian, what shall we make?"

Reed thought. "How about a policeman? Or maybe a fireman?"

Spencer looked up and nodded, smiling.

"I know!" Faith clapped her hands. "How about an angel? A beautiful guardian angel."

Silence. The two males frowned.

Spencer, who was young enough to bypass diplomacy, shook his head emphatically and made a gagging noise.

"Sorry," Reed explained. "Too girlie." He turned to Spencer. "How about a dragon?"

Spencer nodded and began to draw a big red dragon next to the scarecrow on the paper.

Reed kept the ideas coming. Trolls and knights and kings, doctors and astronauts and cowboys. Superheroes who looked like bats, or spiders, or muscular green giants. The suggestions got wilder and more testosterone-driven with every minute.

Faith sat there, with her chin in her hand, smiling wryly. He grinned over at her, hoping she didn't think they were carrying this male bonding thing a little too far.

She grinned back. "I still don't see what's wrong with an angel," she muttered.

When Reed ran out of ideas, Spencer picked up his crayon one more time and began to draw. He sketched a man, a man with brown hair who wore a white coat, strangely reminiscent of a lab coat. Then he drew a crude stethoscope around the man's neck. Finally he added a basket full of kittens at the man's feet.

The implication was obvious—and a little overwhelming. In Spencer's eyes, Reed himself was a guardian. Reed was a superhero.

Oh, man.

Now what should he say?

If only it were true. He would love to be able to raise his magic sword and protect these two people from everything—from Doug Lambert to Boxer Barnes, from bad dreams to bad luck, from stubbed toes to the common cold.

Well, sure. And he would love to have been able to save Melissa, too.

But some things could defeat even heroes.

And he was no hero.

Spencer was staring up at him, a glaze of admiration in his eyes, the same kind of awed adoration Reed had seen in his gaze after the delivery of the foal.

Oh, hell.

For a dozen reasons, big and small, he suddenly saw what a mistake it was to let this needy little boy count on him too much. Spencer and Faith were only here for a short while, just until it was safe for them to go home, back to their real lives. Autumn House was merely a temporary haven.

But wasn't that a concept no six-year-old child could ever fully grasp? Sometimes Reed himself forgot that this wasn't real life.

Eventually they would go home—Faith probably woke up every morning, hoping today would be the day. And what would happen then? Soon, a few weeks at most, Reed Fairmont and Firefly Glen would disappear from Spencer's life. Just as his father and mother had disappeared.

Knowing all that, was it fair of him to let Spencer get too close?

Reed glanced at Faith. She was staring at the drawing, and her expression was very strange.

What did she want him to do? Pull back—or come closer? Insist on a hurtful distance now, or allow for the possibility of heartbreak later?

Oh, yeah, he definitely wished he were a superhero.

Right now, it would be damn useful to be able to read her mind.

FAITH HAD BEEN relieved when Reed laughed off Spencer's scarecrow suggestion and carefully shepherded the ideas in another direction.

During their few weeks here, she had of course seen how much Spencer was growing to like Reed, and she had been glad. Anything that made Spencer happy seemed by definition a good thing.

But not until she saw that drawing, and the naked admiration in Spencer's eyes, had she realized the dangers, She hadn't fully understood that Spencer might think of Reed as more than a friend. She hadn't seen that he might already be thinking of him as...

As a father figure.

Thanks to Reed's subtle guidance, Spencer abandoned the idea of a scarecrow vet and ended up believing he had wanted to make a policeman all along. Spencer kept their scarecrow in his room all weekend, through every stage of its creation.

It sat on his chair, a crude, lumpy, straw-stuffed man in a blue hat that clearly symbolized safety to the little boy. Since Grace's death, Spencer had been waking up frequently, plagued by nightmares. But that weekend, with the scarecrow and the puppy for protection, Spencer had slept the whole night through.

Until Sunday night, the night before Halloween.

At midnight, Faith was alone in her room, reading a cookbook by the last of the dying firelight, when she heard Spencer's footsteps coming down from the loft. The clatter of Tigger's feet followed, as the sleepy puppy struggled to keep pace.

Faith put her book down and glanced toward the door, expecting any second to see Spencer's frightened little face. Another nightmare, poor baby. She closed her eyes, which suddenly stung. Did he dream of Grace, lying on the floor? Or Doug, hiding in the shadows? Or something shapeless and evil that he could never put a name to?

She scooted to one side of the bed and pulled the soft green spread down, making room for Spencer to climb under the covers. But several seconds ticked quietly by on the mantel clock, and Spencer didn't come.

Where had he gone? She wasn't worried, exactly,

but any variation in his routine felt a little uncomfortable. She'd better go see.

She stood, knotting the belt of her robe tightly around her waist and sliding her feet into her slippers. She went out into the hall, which was glowing with nightlights Reed had installed as soon as he realized Spencer had bad dreams.

To her surprise, Spencer stood at the open door to Reed's office, wearing only the bottoms of his Lassie pajamas. Tigger waited patiently at his side.

By the golden glow of the office desk lamp, Faith could see Reed sitting there, his back to the door, going over veterinary journals. He often did that until the very early hours of the morning.

She started to call to Spencer, warning him not to bother Reed while he was working. But something in the little boy's posture stopped her. He had his hand on the doorknob, and, though she couldn't see his face, the muscles in his skinny back looked as tightly drawn as piano wire.

And suddenly, breaking the stillness of the midnight hallway, she heard a sound she had been afraid she'd never hear again.

She heard Spencer's high, innocent voice.

"Reed?" The little boy paused. "Reed, can I come in?"

CHAPTER ELEVEN

"CAN I COME IN?"

The sound of the little boy's voice hung like a bubble in the air. Though he was utterly shocked, Reed forced himself to put his pen down slowly, aware that one wrong move and the bubble could pop.

He smiled, but the little boy didn't smile back. Spencer just stared at Reed, his brown eyes very large and intent, yet oddly unfocused.

Once, when Reed was a child, his pet collie had run away and, somewhere on the mountain roads, had been hit by a car. Though the dog's back legs no longer moved, he had used his front legs to drag himself home on his belly. Reed still remembered the dog's eyes, black with pain but tuned to an inner, inarticulate faith that somehow Reed could help.

Spencer's eyes were like that now.

"Of course you can come in," Reed said, his tone measured. He knew better than to whoop with joy that Spencer had actually spoken. He hadn't forgotten that much about being a kid. Sometimes the mere fact that grown-ups wanted you to do something was reason enough to refuse to do it.

Not that Spencer was looking particularly defiant. He just looked lost.

Reed swiveled his desk chair so that his lap was reachable, just in case Spencer wanted to climb up. He didn't hold out his arms, though—he mustn't push. He could only wait, poised to receive whatever Spencer was ready to give.

Spencer took a couple of steps into the room. Then a few more. He stopped only an arm's length away from Reed.

His small fingers toyed with the edge of the two-hundred-year-old chestnut desk. Reed noticed that Spencer's fingernails were clean, for once, and his hair was softly shining. Faith must have won the bathtub battle tonight.

"What's up, buddy? Did you have a bad dream?"

Spencer shook his head. "No. I didn't sleep yet."

"How come?"

"I don't know." Spencer was staring at his fingers while he pointlessly picked at the wood. His hands were stiff and awkward. "I couldn't."

Reed looked at the little boy's profile. His lips pressed together so tightly the edges were rimmed in white. He breathed fast and ragged, as if he were fighting tears.

Waiting silently for Spencer to continue required more self-control than almost anything Reed had ever done.

But it paid off.

"Sometimes it's hard to sleep." Spencer poked his

finger into a small scratch in the wood. "I keep thinking about Mommy."

"Yeah." Reed concentrated on keeping his body relaxed. No signals of stress, no alarming overreactions. "I bet you miss her a lot."

Spencer nodded, staring at the desk as if his job was to memorize every whorl. He took a breath, but the breath broke, and he just nodded again.

No, no, no. Reed wanted to say. *Don't go back to that. Keep talking to me, buddy.*

But somehow he made himself keep waiting.

Finally, after seconds so long they seemed to be made of hours, Spencer looked up. His brown eyes shone, glassy and helpless.

"It's my fault, you know," he whispered through those stiff white lips. He made a choking sound. "It's my fault my mom died."

Reed felt his own eyes burn. It was impossible to look on such naked grief and not feel your own heart crack a little. But he refused to let the burn become anything as self-indulgent as a tear. This pain belonged to Spencer. And he'd been carrying it around for far, far, too long.

"Your fault?" Reed said calmly—surprising himself with his own control. "That's kind of hard for me to believe."

The little boy lifted his chin. He was fighting like a man to keep his own tears from falling. Reed wanted to take him into his arms and tell him it was all right. When you were six, and your mother had been murdered, it was impossible not to cry.

But the kid had courage. He had self-reliance. He'd been using it like a shield for almost two months now. Reed wouldn't rip that away from him before he was ready.

He wouldn't automatically dismiss his guilt, either. Whether it seemed rational to Reed or not, the guilt was Spencer's reality. And, like any genuine emotion, it had profound power. It deserved respect.

"Tell me why you think so," Reed said. "Tell me why you think it was your fault."

"I—" Spencer knitted his brows together hard, digging deep lines in that young, unmarked brow. "I was supposed to take care of my mom. Everybody said so. After Daddy died. Everybody said I was the man of the house now. They said I was supposed to take care of Mommy."

He looked at Reed. And finally the tears, which had been massing like an army behind his eyes, won the war. They poured down his cheeks in shining white lines, and his chest began to heave.

"But I didn't," he said, his voice high as he tried to push it through a throat narrowed with pain. "I didn't take care of her. I wasn't even there."

To hell with "handling" the situation cautiously. With a low sound, Reed reached out and picked up the sobbing little boy. He held him close. The kid didn't have on his pajama shirt—probably the heater had been set too high. But on his bare, wiry back,

Reed could feel the bones of his shoulder blades, and the knobby vertebrae of his spine. It was strangely poignant. It was as if Reed suddenly realized that this rough-and-tumble child was actually made of very fragile, mortal building blocks.

As, in the end, all human beings were.

Spencer didn't resist him, not even for an instant. He curled up in Reed's lap, grabbing his shirt, and tucked his head against Reed's shoulder, the way a bird might duck its head under a sheltering wing. And he wept without any more holding back.

Over the little boy's racked body, Reed suddenly saw Faith, standing in the hallway, staring into the room. She squeezed her hands against her chest, as if she needed to apply pressure to her heart to keep it from bleeding. She wasn't crying. She seemed to be beyond tears.

He met her gaze across the dimly lit spaces. He nodded his head, just a little, just enough for her to see. *It's all right,* he said with his eyes. *Let him cry.*

It probably went against every nurturing instinct she possessed, to let her nephew weep and weep, and keep weeping, to the point of exhaustion, and not try to stop it. But Reed knew these tears had been inside too long. They'd poison Spencer permanently if he didn't let them out.

And thank goodness Faith seemed to understand— or if not to understand, at least to trust Reed's instincts. She didn't move a muscle.

Gradually the sobbing grew quieter, and Reed thought

Spencer might just fall asleep, which would be okay, really. He'd come so far tonight. They could make the rest of this journey later, when he had more energy.

But soon, tired and strangely flat, his little voice spoke again.

"I'm right, though, huh? It was my fault, wasn't it?"

Reed took a minute, as if he were weighing the question seriously. He could sense that Spencer was hoping against hope that Reed could persuade him it wasn't true.

Reed met Faith's eyes again. She almost appeared to be praying, but her eyes were locked on him, and for a moment he knew real fear. What if he screwed this up? If psychiatrists and their dozens of years studying "maladaptive stress reactions" hadn't been able to help, what made him think he could?

But he didn't have a choice. He had to try. He sent Faith a look that promised only that. He would try.

He took a deep breath.

"No," he said finally. "I actually don't think it was your fault, Spence. You see, I know that wasn't what everybody meant when they said you should take care of your mom."

Spencer sniffed dubiously. "It wasn't?"

"No, it wasn't. Little boys aren't supposed to take care of their mothers in that way, in a practical, physical way. They aren't supposed to earn money, or fix dinner, or get the car repaired, or even watch out for bad guys. They can't. They're too young. They're still learning how to do all those things.''

Spencer lifted his head. His eyes were bleary, but focused. ''Then what are they supposed to do? How are they supposed to take care of their moms?''

''They're supposed to make them happy.''

Spencer frowned and sniffed again. He rubbed the back of his hand across his eyes. ''That's it?''

''That's a lot. Some little boys don't make their families happy at all.'' He gave Spencer a serious look. ''But what about you? Do you think you made your mom happy? Did you ever let her play games or draw pictures with you?''

Spencer nodded. ''Yeah. We played 'I Spy,' and we tickled a lot. And we colored together every night before bed. I drew dogs, she drew cats. We'd pretend to make them fight.''

''Good.'' Reed remained somber. ''And did you ever make her laugh? Did you give her lots of hugs and kisses?''

''All the time.'' Spencer almost smiled. ''She was like Aunt Faith, she wanted millions of hugs and kisses.''

Reed gave him a guy-to-guy nod of understanding. ''Girls are like that. But mostly we don't really mind, do we?''

Spencer wrinkled his nose. ''Mostly we don't,'' he said. ''Unless Chad Mixler is looking. But Mom knew about Chad Mixler, so she didn't kiss me much at school.''

With a sudden sigh, he let his head drop back onto Reed's shoulder. He sat there quietly for a while, sniffing now and then but mostly just thinking. Faith was still watching, still frozen in place—but tears were falling now, winding crazy crystal paths down her cheeks. Those beautiful tears of joy.

"I'm pretty sure I made her happy," Spencer said after a while. "She called me her sunshine. But not in front of Chad Mixler."

"Well, of course not. Your mom wasn't dumb."

"No, she wasn't." Spencer tilted a look up. "That's what sunshine means, isn't it? When you call somebody sunshine, it means they make you happy."

Reed had to take an extra breath himself before he could answer.

"It sure does, buddy," he said. His gaze locked with Faith's. "It means you make them happier than anything else in the world."

AFTER THEY PUT HIM TO BED, Faith sat with Spencer for almost an hour.

They talked about little things, easy things, like Tigger and the Halloween festival, and the color of the autumn leaves. They didn't talk about Grace, or Doug Lambert, or when they were going home.

Those subjects were for later, when they were both stronger. Tonight, it was enough to share the simplest of words and thoughts and hugs and smiles.

When, at nearly two in the morning, it began to rain, he seemed finally to realize how tired he was.

Even the elation of being able to talk freely had worn off. Spencer's eyes drifted three-quarters closed, and his chattering slowed to a murmur.

Faith watched him, her heart full of inexpressible things. He looked so young. So peaceful, now that some of the guilt had been lifted. They had a long way to go yet. But the journey toward recovery had begun.

Finally she pulled up the covers and kissed him softly, swallowing back the lump in her throat.

"Go to sleep, pumpkin. Tomorrow's a busy day, you know."

Spencer smiled sleepily. "Yes," he said. "It's Halloween. Say good night to Tigger."

"Good night, Tigger."

"And to Sergeant Braveheart."

She looked over at the scarecrow, who flopped against Spencer's armchair, his button eyes shiny brown over his Magic Marker smile. Spencer had adamantly insisted on brown buttons instead of the black Faith had first offered. More shades of Reed, she'd thought. Reed's brown eyes were very special. So full of kindness and understanding.

"Good night, Sergeant Braveheart," she said, smiling as she straightened his straw body a little. He smiled back at her, unblinking. "I didn't even know you had a name."

Spencer chuckled and yawned at the same time. He checked under his pillow, where he always kept

Faith's new cell phone. "Of course he has a name. Good night, Sergeant."

Faith was all the way to the door, ready to dim the light, when Spencer spoke again.

"Aunt Faith," he said softly. He paused. "I'm sorry I stopped talking to everybody."

She slid the switch down slowly, deepening the shadows until the room was soft and gray with rainy moonlight.

"That's okay, sweetheart," she said, resisting the urge to sweep back into the room and clutch him one more time. "I knew you would talk when you were ready."

Right after that she went looking for Reed. After the four of them—Reed, Faith, Spencer and Tigger—had walked together up to the third-floor loft, which was Spencer's special sanctum, Reed had thoughtfully left them alone.

But he wasn't in his office, or in his bedroom, or anywhere on the second floor. Faith hesitated, wondering if he might have gone out to the clinic, when she heard the low throb of soft music coming up through the stairwell.

He must be down in the great room. She'd seen him there on other nights, very late, staring at a dying fire and listening to jazz on a stereo turned down so low she wondered how he could enjoy it.

She walked down the twisting wooden staircase now, and, by the time she reached the second landing, she could see him. He sat on one side of the large, soft green sofa, so utterly still she couldn't tell whether he was awake or sleeping.

She tiptoed down the last few stairs just in case. But he heard her. He turned his head as she approached. The amber firelight played across one cheek. The other was dark, reflecting the midnight rain from the picture window behind him.

"Is Spencer sleeping?"

She nodded. She went over and sat beside him on the sofa. She kicked off her slippers and hugged her knees to her chest. She was so excited, so flush with relief, that she didn't know if she'd ever sleep again.

"I don't know how to thank you," she said. "I— There aren't even words for how happy I am. It's a miracle."

He shook his head. "It was just the right time. He was ready, and I was there, that's all."

"Please don't minimize what you did. It was wonderful." She wished so much that he would accept her gratitude. It was like a river swelling inside her, and she needed to let it flow naturally to its destination—this extraordinary man who had changed Spencer's life forever, and by extension, hers.

"I don't know how you knew what he needed. But everything you said was so wise. So perfect."

He smiled and shrugged lightly. "I'm glad it worked," he said. "And I'm glad you don't mind that he spoke to me first. I know you've been a little concerned that he might be getting too attached."

She flushed, and was relieved that the darkness

probably kept it from showing. "It's not that, exactly, it's just that—"

"It's okay. I understand. I'm concerned about it myself. But I think tonight was different. He just needed someone objective to talk to. He knew you'd say he wasn't responsible, but he'd always think you said it out of blind love. I think it was easier to open up to someone on the outside."

"I don't care who he talked to first. I'm just ecstatic that he was able to talk at all."

He smiled, then. A real smile. "Me, too," he said.

"And I'm so grateful you were willing to listen. But how did you know what to say? How did you know what he needed to hear?"

"I didn't." He turned briefly to look at the fire. The saxophone was dwindling off now, like the echo of someone crying. Outside, a rumble of thunder spilled across the cloudy night. "I guessed, that's all. I thought maybe it would be the same for him as it was for me."

She wished the light were better. Fading firelight was tricky. It suggested movement where there was none. She touched his arm, which was stretched out along the back of the sofa.

"You mean when your wife died."

"Yes." Even if she hadn't felt the muscles tighten under her hand, she would have recognized the tension in his voice. "When Melissa died, I was sick with guilt. Sicker, really, than Spencer has been, because I didn't have his courage. I felt that I'd failed her. I thought I should've been able to save her."

"But she died of cancer, didn't she? No one can really—"

"I know. But I loved her. I thought I should have been able to do something. Bring in a new doctor, unearth a cure, coax a true miracle out of God himself. She'd been gone for nearly two years before I accepted the truth."

"And what is that?"

He shrugged. "That life simply doesn't come with guarantees. We have no idea what's around the corner for any of us. All we can do is try to make each other happy for whatever time we're given."

"And did you?" She had heard no weakness in his voice, no threat of tears, but suddenly she heard those things in her own. She took a breath and tried to sound stronger.

"Did I what?" His looked at her, his eyes sparkling in the fluid light from the rain-spangled window.

"Did you play games with her and make her laugh? Did you give her lots of hugs and kisses? Did you make your Melissa happy?"

He didn't answer for a moment, and she wondered if she'd trespassed. Perhaps she should not have spoken Melissa's name. But she felt so close to him right now, like people who had been through a war together. She felt as if she could say anything to him.

"Yes," he said. He smiled, and she knew it was all right. "Yes, I honestly think I did."

She squeezed his arm, and then they sat together without speaking for a little while, watching the fire burn down. The tongues of flame grew smaller and finally disappeared, leaving behind just a painted orange glow in the wide stone hearth.

The CD changed with a tiny click, a subtle whirr. Another jazz disc began, but this one was less mournful, more romantic, with an unapologetic, sweeping duet from saxophone and violin.

Reed held out his hand suddenly.

"Let's celebrate," he said. "Dance with me."

She wasn't much of a dancer, but she couldn't have said no, not tonight. He turned up the volume a little, just enough to fill the room with soft notes and slow drums. He stood, and then, tugging on her hand, he pulled her up and into his arms.

He was so tall. Barefoot, she barely reached above his shoulder. But their bodies fit well in spite of that, and the music wrapped itself around them like a soft blue ribbon of sound. The Navajo carpet under their feet was soft and warm.

They moved easily together, small movements that were almost dancing but not quite, their bodies doing only what the music said they must and no more.

The rest was just touching. Just being close and being safe. No longer being afraid. And no longer being alone.

She shut her eyes, absorbing the moment through

her fingers against his chest, through her hips where his fingers rested lightly on her. Through her nose, where the cedar and pine scent of the room mingled with the clean, intoxicating man-smell of him.

It was bliss. Outside, the sky flashed with lightning and the wind tore at the tired red leaves, but in here everything was still and sweet. Spencer slept quietly above them, high in his sheltered loft, and all was right with her world.

Somewhere, though, in the middle of the song, when she was too relaxed to see it coming, too drugged to mount a defense, the peace and pleasure spiked into something sharper, something with teeth and fire.

His breath changed, and so did hers. Their bodies grew restless and, without conscious thought, they found themselves pressing a little harder, shifting with small fevered nuances, seeking the perfect connection.

They danced less, searched more. Reed's hands tightened on her hips, pressing, and her hands fisted into his shirt, pulling. He lowered his head, and his mouth touched her ear. His breath sizzled down her neck, down her spine, like an invisible fall of air that spilled into a pool of bubbling awareness hidden deep in the center of her body.

She turned her face toward his, murmuring wordlessly. She found his neck, where a swollen pulse beat slowly, and then his jaw, which was hard, jutting satin and so sweet she found herself tasting it, running wet lips along its angled planes, up to his ear. She kissed his ear, taking the small, tight lobe between her teeth.

He groaned, the sky flashed and suddenly he was kissing her. It wasn't a gentle sugar-apple kiss, not like the first time. This time it was hungry and wild, hot with lightning and wet with rain. It was deep and rough and so miraculously alive she felt alive, too. Alive, and gloriously immortal.

She couldn't get enough. She opened her mouth. She put her hands behind his head and drew him closer, deeper. She stood on tiptoe and begged for more with every outstretched inch of her body.

But suddenly, without warning, he lifted his head and pulled away. Just an inch—but the inch that mattered, the inch that meant the kiss was over. He shook his head, such a tiny motion that she thought—wanted to think—she had imagined it.

But she hadn't. Slowly, so slowly, he peeled her arms from around his neck. Holding her hands at her sides, he carefully disengaged, gazing down at her the entire time with a painful tenderness.

Her whole body protested the loss of him. When she said his name, her voice was taut with thwarted need. Little pinpricks of disappointment flashed where once she had felt him against her.

Gradually, though, the flashing died down, just as the fire had slowly disappeared in the hearth. No fire could last forever, not without fuel, not without anything to burn.

And though he looked the same as ever, an invisible shield seemed somehow to have risen up around him, deflecting her desperation, rejecting her emotions. They bounced back to her as surely as the sounds of his CD, that sad saxophone and that low, lonely violin, bounced off the pine walls of this big, beautiful room.

He wasn't unkind. He was merely unreachable.

Finally, when he must have seen that she could breathe again, he spoke.

"This isn't a good idea," he said.

She looked at him, feeling the lovely sexual heat dying away.

"You know it isn't," he said. "Don't you, Faith?"

She made herself think more clearly. Made herself think of something other than that primitive drive toward life and sex and the momentary oblivion she could have found in his arms.

She made herself think about Spencer, and Doug and Grace, and Melissa and New York City, and her career and Firefly Glen. And death. And all the things she simply didn't know about tomorrow.

"No," she said softly. "It isn't a good idea."

He reached over and clicked off the CD player. The room fell suddenly silent. The only sound was the beating of the rain against the windows. It would be very, very cold tomorrow.

"We should get some sleep," he said. "It's late."

"Yes," she said numbly. What else could she say? "I suppose we should."

"Tomorrow is a big day. Today, really. It's Halloween already, isn't it?"

She had gathered her senses enough to notice that he was now treating her very much as she treated Spencer. Like a child, someone to be protected. As if he knew she would, if left unguided, do dangerous and foolish things.

And she would have. Oh, yes, she would have.

Ironic, really, that all this time she'd been worrying about Spencer—Spencer misunderstanding their status here, Spencer growing too attached. Spencer wanting more from Reed than he had any right to ask, more than Reed was interested in giving.

Ironic that not once, in all these weeks, had she seen where the biggest danger really lay.

Right here.

In her own body.

Right here in her own heart.

CHAPTER TWELVE

AFTER SUCH AN EMOTIONAL night, Faith was afraid she'd never fall asleep, but when she finally did, she slept well, and she slept hard. When she woke up, the cloudless, ice-blue Halloween morning was almost over. The clock by her bed said eleven-forty.

Oh, dear. She hadn't slept this late since she was Spencer's age. She jumped up with a groan.

And came face-to-face with a smiling brown-eyed man.

A man who was, thank goodness, made of straw.

Sometime during the morning, Spencer had brought Sergeant Braveheart in and arranged him on her chair. He had a plate of pumpkin muffins balanced on his lumpy lap.

Around his neck hung a sign hand-lettered with wobbly orange and black crayons. Happy Halloween, it read. And then, down in the corner, a bold adult hand had dashed in a postscript. ''Carving jack-o'-lanterns in the clinic. Come play.''

Suddenly as excited as a child, Faith showered quickly, threw on her most comfortable jeans, fur-lined boots and a thick gold turtleneck sweater, wolfed down a pumpkin muffin and hurried downstairs.

It was hard not to dawdle just a little, once she got outside and saw how spectacular the day was. A million leaves had fallen in the night, turning the ground into a brilliant red, green and brown oriental carpet. The air was cold and raw and made her shiver in a delicious, magically alive sort of way.

She laughed out loud, startling the ducks, who were hunkered down in the grass irritably, obviously not half as enchanted with the weather as she was. Their pond was as glassy as silver ice.

"Sorry, guys," she said. "But I love it." She spun in a circle, just once, for no reason at all, and then continued on toward the clinic.

Reed had planned to close at noon for the holiday, and only one car was left in the parking area. When Faith opened the clinic door, she was surprised to see that the entire lobby area was covered with newspapers, and at least six grinning, scowling, winking, fully carved jack-o'-lanterns already sat on the waiting-room chairs.

Spencer and Tigger squatted on the floor, scooping out yet another bright round pumpkin. They both looked up as the clinic door chimed out her arrival.

"Aunt Faith! We thought you'd never wake up! We've only got three left." Spencer pointed excitedly at the jack-o'-lanterns. Tigger walked over and sniffed one, just to show her where to look. "See how many we've already done?"

Justine was at the receptionist's desk, but she, too, was working on a pumpkin. "Yeah, Faith," she drawled lazily with a teasing smile. She pointed her tiny, serrated knife reproachfully. "How come you're such a lazy-bones today? The rest of us have been carving our little hearts out for hours."

"Sorry," Faith said, bending down to give Spencer a kiss. He was sticky all over. Fat beige seeds and strands of orange pulp stuck to his cheeks and hands. "I didn't know we had a pumpkin party planned."

Spencer gave her a long-suffering look. "It's Halloween," he explained patiently. He had a pumpkin seed in his hair, and he wriggled impatiently as she tried to pluck it out.

She had to laugh. "Oh, yeah? I don't remember you feeling the need to carve a hundred pumpkins last year."

He shook his head. "We're in Firefly Glen this year," he said, as if that explained everything. "Glenners are a little bit obsessive about their holidays."

That must have come straight from Reed. She'd never heard Spencer use the word "obsessive" in his life. And the way he said "Glenners." It was one-hundred percent possessive. He might just as well have said "We Glenners."

But she couldn't bring herself to worry about all that today. Today was for celebrating. She smiled over at Justine. "Where's Reed?"

Justine rolled her eyes. "With a patient. Suzie Strickland. Only person in Firefly Glen self-centered enough to make poor Reed work on Halloween. As if her dogs couldn't get their shots any old day. But they're almost done, thank goodness. After that, I'm sliding that sign to Closed, and we're out of here!''

Suzie Strickland. Faith had a sudden image of a gamine, dark-haired beauty, furiously stalking away, leaving Mike Frome helplessly ensnared in Justine's net. Suzie Strickland, who was one jagged corner of the painful teenage love triangle Faith had glimpsed in front of the pet store that day.

Uh-oh. Maybe she should take Spencer outside to feed the stoic, frozen ducks. It might be better to miss the tense encounter when Suzie came out to pay her bill.

But she had no time to put her thought into action. At that instant the door to the patient's room opened, and Suzie came out, with two large, gorgeous golden retrievers straining at their leashes, eager to meet Tigger.

Tigger, who had no idea he was just a half-pint puppy, went trotting up to introduce himself. Spencer tried unsuccessfully to hold him, but luckily Suzie's dogs were friendly. They did a lot of embarrassingly intimate sniffing and finally decided the new guy was okay.

Justine made a face. ''Yuck,'' she said. ''Dogs are so gross.''

That, of course, was the wrong thing for any employee of a veterinary clinic to say to anyone. But it was particularly insensitive to say to Suzie Strickland, who obviously adored her two dogs. They were glossy and healthy and well behaved. They had clearly been given a ton of intelligent love.

"Not as gross," Suzie said, scowling, "as some people I know."

Justine smiled. She might be thoughtless, but she wasn't stupid, and she'd seen that response coming a mile off. "Yeah, well, you always did hang out with some pretty skanky people."

That did it. Faith guessed that, even at the best of times, Suzie Strickland didn't have a tenth of Justine Millner's dexterity with the conversational rapier. A politician's daughter, Justine had been bred to the quick, smiling thrust. Suzie was a street fighter, and she bled messily when she'd been hit. But she hit back.

She stared at Justine now, breathing heavily. Justine kept smoothly writing out the bill for the dogs' shots, munching placidly on her gum.

"You know what, Justine?" Suzie said between clenched teeth. "You are a trashy bitch. I can't even tell you what a mean, trashy tramp I think you are."

Justine tore off the bill at the perforation and handed it to Suzie. "You said trashy twice," she observed. "Vocabulary meltdown?"

"No, there just aren't enough words to describe how awful you are." Suzie had her gloves off now, and Faith could see this was going to end ugly.

Spencer was watching curiously, though he didn't come over to hide behind Faith, which was a good sign. All three dogs began to pace nervously, smelling distress in the air, perhaps, and going on the alert.

"And as long as I'm being honest here." Suzie kept her voice low in spite of her obvious fury. She probably didn't want to bring Reed out to see what was wrong. "Let me tell you something else. You need to stop playing games with people's lives. You need to stop trying to use your own child to keep Mike Frome from slipping away. He hates you, but he can't get free because he thinks your awful kid might be his."

Justine's face tightened. "You don't know what you're talking about, Suzie-freaka. Mike Frome is a free agent. If he doesn't want to be with you, maybe you should look in the mirror for a reason. Don't blame it on me."

"I do blame it on you. Because you know darn well he's breaking his heart wondering if he's Gavin's father, and you won't have the decency to let him know he isn't."

"And are you so sure he isn't?"

"You bet I am. I don't know if it's that redheaded ski instructor you were hanging all over last winter, or the high school janitor or every disgusting no-neck monster on the football team. I do know it isn't Mike Frome."

Suzie's anger, which had at first been just a hot eruption of emotion, had finally begun to go cold and focused. And dangerous. She straightened her spine and narrowed her eyes at Justine.

"You're so low you don't even care what this is doing to your little boy. He's become the town joke. Did you know people are making bets down at the Duckpuddle Diner on what color Gavin's hair is going to be when it comes in?"

Justine didn't answer. She opened her mouth, but nothing came out.

"And poor Dr. Fairmont, who has always been so nice to you. Your dad's spreading it around that maybe he's the father."

She flipped a twenty-dollar bill on the counter and hitched her purse over her arm tightly. "You're a horrible person, Justine. You're poison for any man who gets near you. Up to and including your own son."

She gathered the leashes and began to walk her dogs toward the door, carefully avoiding the newspapers full of pumpkin guts.

Justine stared for a long moment. Faith, who was facing her, saw that her lovely blue eyes were slowly filling with tears.

"So what was the point of all this, Suzie?" Justine blinked hard. "Did you just come here to hurt me, or what?"

Suzie turned around. Faith could sense that, in spite of her inexpensive clothes and her awkward manner, Suzie Strickland had real steel in her spine, far more than poor, pampered Justine Millner had ever dreamed of. Faith suddenly felt very, very sorry for both of them.

"I don't give a damn about you," Suzie said. "I just want you to stop playing games about who Gavin's father is. Whatever the truth is, just say it. Just be an adult for once in your life and say it."

Justine lifted her chin. "No matter what the truth turns out to be?"

"Of course."

"What if you don't like it?"

Suzie shrugged. "It's called reality. I don't like a lot of it, but I deal with it anyhow."

"Okay," Justine said thickly. She took a deep breath, then bent down, reached into the baby carrier and picked up her son. She put him over her shoulder and patted his sleeping back with shaking fingers.

"Then here's a nice big dose of reality for you to choke down, Suzie. Reed Fairmont isn't Gavin's father, and neither is the red-haired ski instructor, or the janitor or anybody on the Firefly High football team."

She took another breath. "Mike Frome is."

REED NOTICED that Faith was a little subdued when they first left the clinic for the festival. He didn't know if she was just skittish about going out for such a public occasion, or if she might still be uncomfortable about what had happened between them last night.

But, whatever was bothering her, he set out to make it go away.

He had plenty of help. Halloween was one of the most exciting days of the year in Firefly Glen. Because the turning foliage attracted thousands of tourists, the carnival was a major event, a real moneymaker for the city, complete with midway and small rides, two haunted houses and the best food in three states.

The city went all out. The town square was strung from treetop to streetlight with garlands made of autumn leaves and twinkling gold, orange and red lights. Hundreds of jack-o'-lanterns and scarecrows and stalks of corn lined rows of booths selling arts and crafts. Bands played, one after the other, from the band shell, and the air smelled wickedly of fried dough and sauerkraut, onion rings and corn dogs and cotton candy.

And of course, Reed's secret weapon in the assault on Faith's mood was Spencer. As long as Spencer was happy, Faith was happy. And the kid was having a ball. He laughed and chattered and demanded to play every game, ride every ride, eat every piece of junk he could see.

His enthusiasm was irresistible. Within half an hour Faith had shaken off whatever was bugging her. And then the real fun began.

Reed hadn't been to the carnival in about three years, not since Melissa got too sick to come. He had forgotten how fantastic it was.

Spencer stopped dead in his tracks at the cotton candy booth. "Can I have some of that? The pink kind."

"Not this early, sweetheart." Faith eyed the big

puffy sticks of sugar with a frown. "You'll get it all over you, and then you'll stick to everything you touch for the rest of the day."

"Please. I'll be careful, I promise."

Naturally, the kid won, even though Reed knew Faith was right. Reed would probably have to buy a paper cup of water and haul Spencer over to the side of the road for a mini-bath.

But nobody really cared about any of that. Not today. Today there were no rules. Just foolish fun and mindless pleasure.

As the little boy walked away with his treasure, Reed surreptitiously pinched off a piece of the cotton candy cloud. He held it behind his back, and then shoved it into Faith's mouth when she opened it to admire a grapevine wreath.

Her eyes widened, and then, in mock anger, she clamped down on his finger with her teeth and refused to let him go.

"Ouch," he said dramatically. He appealed to Spencer for help. "Hey, your aunt's going to bite off my finger."

Spencer's eyes sparkled with unholy delight. "Do it, Aunt Faith! Bite his finger off!"

Reed scowled down at him. "I think I liked you better when you weren't talking."

Spencer just laughed. Reed looked at Faith. "I'm warning you. Just eat the cotton candy nicely now, and let that finger go."

Spencer was watching, so she really didn't have

any choice. She closed her lips and sucked gently. She was going for minimum sensuality, he could tell. Her tongue massaged his finger hesitantly, removing the candy with as little contact as possible. Still, he felt every soft tug, and the tip of his finger began to throb.

Other stuff began to throb, too.

Brilliant. Now what? About a thousand people milled around, and he was having trouble standing up straight. This definitely, definitely hadn't been his best idea.

He'd meant it as a joke.

Or had he? Last night, when they were dancing— another one of his bad ideas—he'd come face-to-face with the truth. He wanted Faith Constable. He wanted to make love to her until neither of them could speak or move or even breathe.

Yeah, he wanted her so bad he couldn't think straight. But he wasn't going to have her. He wasn't going to let himself even try. Abstinence. Self-control. Common sense. Courage. Those were the words to live by, at least until she went home again.

Then, the very next day, he suddenly decided it would be fun to put his finger in her mouth and let her suck on it? Who was he kidding? He was just trying to get around the whole self-control thing. He'd just wanted her to touch him. He wanted to feel the velvet warmth of her tongue against his skin.

So, frankly, he deserved whatever discomfort he got.

And he got plenty. Even when things stopped throbbing, he stayed on edge, as if the slightest thing could set him off again. Who would have thought a Halloween carnival would be such a merciless pit of sexual temptation?

If she paused suddenly to look at something, and he collided with her, front to back, he was in serious trouble.

If the wind blew her hair across her lips, he was sunk.

If centrifugal force pressed her shoulder against his in the Scrambler, he was dead.

And if she smiled at him, her eyes sparkling like cinnamon fairy dust in the fall sunlight, he was an absolute, helpless goner.

He did his best. He kept Spencer between them while they walked. He suggested they alternate accompanying him on the rides. Reed had all the adrenaline he could handle. He didn't need the Tilt-a-Whirl to turn him inside out. Faith did it every time she spoke a word or moved a muscle.

Finally, when Spencer had ridden everything twice, he decided he wanted to play some midway games. Good, Reed thought. They definitely wanted to avoid the Haunted House, which might be too scary. Besides, maybe throwing darts at balloons, or pennies at saucers might work off some of this tension.

Yeah, right. He could throw that gigantic Ferris wheel clean off this goddamn mountain, and he'd still be a wreck, still humming with awareness and aching with frustration.

But at least he'd be making Spencer happy. That mattered. It mattered even more than his own pathetic sex life—or lack thereof. The kid was something special. He was gutsy. He was going to get over this tough break, and he was going to be fine.

The first booth they hit had a squirt gun aimed at a grinning clown. If you could shoot straight enough to make the clown rise to the top of his ladder faster than everyone else, you won. Spencer and Reed each grabbed a gun. Faith hung back, watching.

Reed won six times in a row, each time trading one stupid stuffed toy in for a bigger stupid stuffed toy, until finally they got to the Super-Duper level. A hideous purple hippo.

Spencer hugged the gigantic toy as if he'd wanted it all his life. Then he turned to Reed. "I thought you couldn't shoot anything. I heard you tell Aunt Faith you couldn't."

Reed slipped the gun back in the plastic bracket and moved aside to let the next sucker try his luck at winning a lovely hippo.

"I said I didn't own a gun. Not that I don't know how to use one." He wondered if that had frightened the little boy, thinking he was being protected by a loser. "I don't hunt. I don't think it's fun to shoot things. But I can bring down a purple hippo with my trusty tranquilizer gun if I have to."

Spencer's eyes lit up. "Yeah? Can I see it? Where do you keep it?"

"Where little boys can't find it," Reed said, reaching out and ruffling his head. "Now where to?"

Next on Spencer's list was the balloon-dart thing. Three darts, three balloons. If you popped them all, you began the climb toward some disgusting toy all over again. This time, Reed let Spencer play alone.

He was pretty good. He hit two of the three balloons the first time. Then, with just the slightest adjustment in his release, he got them all.

"Touchdown!" Spencer cried as bits of balloon fluttered to the shelf.

"Touchdown," Reed agreed. They gave each other a high five.

The midway huckster took down a horrible hairless pink mouse. "Here you go, kid. And just so you know. When it's darts, you call it a bull's-eye."

Reed and Spencer exchanged grins, pitying the uninitiated. Even Faith was smiling.

Reed handed over another dollar for three more darts.

"Keep your mouse, mister," he said loftily. "Where we come from, everything is a touchdown."

BY NINE O'CLOCK that night, as they pulled Reed's truck out of the crowded parking lot, the starry night was as cold as black ice, the Halloween party was in full swing, and Spencer was absolutely exhausted.

On the way here, the little boy had ridden in the

flat bed with Sergeant Braveheart and the many jack-o'-lanterns, which had been donated to the Haunted House. But it was too cold to ride outside now, so the three of them crowded into the front seat, Spencer in the middle, half-asleep.

Reed stretched his arm out across the back of the seat. Faith leaned her head against it and shut her eyes, smiling.

"Thanks," she said softly. "I had a wonderful time."

He touched the side of her face lightly, brushing her hair and tucking it behind her ear. "Me, too," he said.

It was true. In spite of the shaky beginning, watching Justine and Suzie argue over poor Mike Frome, the day had been nearly perfect. She couldn't remember a lovelier afternoon, not ever in her life.

They hadn't won the scarecrow contest. As Reed had predicted, Suzie Strickland won, which pleased Faith, who knew better than anyone that Suzie's mood could probably use a boost right now.

It pleased her even more to see that Suzie's entry was a papier-mâché guardian angel. The angel had huge feathery wings made of pieces of petticoat netting glued to wire frames and sprinkled with glitter. She had a halo of silver and white pipe cleaners. She was incredibly beautiful, attached high on a black stake so that she seemed to be flying, her arms outstretched, as if showering blessings on everyone in Firefly Glen.

"I told you we should have made an angel," Faith had said, pretending to pout, enjoying the moment tremendously.

Spencer had made a rude sound. "Yeah, like ours would have looked like that anyway."

But nobody minded that they didn't win. It had been enough just to be a part of the whole wonderful fantasy of it all. Faith realized she'd almost let herself forget how nice it was to be part of real, bustling life.

Suddenly Spencer wriggled in his seat. "Aunt Faith? I have to go to the bathroom."

She looked over his head at Reed. "We'll be home soon," she said. "Can you wait?"

"I don't think so. I think I had too many corn dogs."

Reed chuckled. "I won't say I told you so," he said. "No. Wait. I think I will. I told you so, sport. Any way you look at it, four corn dogs is too many corn dogs."

"Well, I still have to go to the bathroom. Now."

Reed didn't seem annoyed. They hadn't left Main Street yet, so he stopped the truck in front of Theo's Candlelight Café.

"I don't think I can find a parking space within two miles of here," he said. "Are you comfortable taking him in by yourself? Theo won't mind."

"No, I'm fine." She didn't feel a bit of fear— amazingly, she hadn't felt afraid all day, though she had moved constantly among mummies and witches and monsters. Besides, she loved Theo's café, with its elegant silverware and candles on every table. And she loved Theo, too.

She nudged Spencer. "Come on, porky. Let's see if Miss Theo will let you use the rest room at her place."

The café was packed, and right away Faith saw several people she knew. Natalie Quinn was in the corner, whispering and stealing hungry little kisses with a hunky guy who undoubtedly was the legendary Matthew Quinn. Faith looked at him carefully. Even on the roof, huh? Wow.

Ward Winters waved at her from the back, where he was sharing a hot chocolate with Madeline Alexander, who obviously had aced the audition for a spot in the Cadillac. Madeline smiled, gesturing that they had an empty spot, but Faith waved back, shaking her head. She pointed toward the rest rooms, and then to Spencer. Madeline nodded, sympathetic.

It was nice, Faith thought, to see so many friendly faces—to sense that, even in some small way, she had begun to fit in here. She felt as if she'd been gone from her own life, her own home and her own friends, for a very long time.

She wondered, suddenly, why she didn't miss it all more.

While she kept guard outside the bathroom hall, she found herself standing next to the pay phone. Had any of the people in her old life missed her, she wondered? Had they been calling, maybe even worrying? She had had time to notify only a few special friends before she left, and she'd been very vague even with them.

It hadn't seemed to matter much. With Grace gone, she had no family left. No one who would really worry. No one who really had to be told the truth.

She dug in her pocket and pulled out a few quarters. And then she dialed her home number. When the machine picked up, she entered her code.

Yes, there were messages. Fourteen of them. The dry cleaner, the housekeeper, her exercise instructor, the woman who would have taught her belly dancing. A couple of clients, a fabric supplier. A couple of friends, a couple of men she occasionally dated. Nice men. But she could hardly remember their faces now.

She erased all the messages with a strangely hollow feeling. Was that it? She had lived in New York City since she was born. How was it possible that not one of these people, not one of these messages, had seemed to be worth saving?

That had been her life. How weird that she didn't really miss it.

Spencer finally came out. "I'm better now," he said, rubbing his eyes and yawning. "Let's go home."

She took his hand. They walked through the café, talking to some people, waving at others. And when she opened the door and looked out onto the bustling, twinkling town square, when she saw Reed's clean white truck waiting patiently by the curb, she realized something shocking.

Something that made her hold her breath, overcome by a new and terrifying kind of vulnerability.

Of course that apartment didn't feel like home to her anymore.

Autumn House did.

CHAPTER THIRTEEN

DOUG LIKED TO THINK of himself as a patient man, but this time he couldn't force himself to wait. He needed to listen to Faith Constable's messages. Halloween or no Halloween, he'd have to risk it.

Not that it was such a big risk. He washed his hair, put in his dentures. He wore a pair of khakis and a polo shirt with an expensive logo, to look like the dream daddy. He added a Casper the Friendly Ghost mask—Dream Daddy in touch with his inner child. He carried a huge bag of candy—Dream Daddy overindulges the neighbor kids.

Most people were dumb as rocks anyhow. They might notice that Dream Daddy had no kid, but they wouldn't really think about it. They'd make some easy assumptions—kid was at a party, kid was down the hall, kid was inside apartment with Dream Mommy. And then they'd go on with their own lives, which were all they really cared about anyhow.

As it turned out, he rode the elevator alone. This apartment house was the "in" spot for young, trendy singles. Halloween apparently wasn't that big a deal around here. He chucked the Casper mask before the third floor.

The minute he opened Faith's apartment door, he could smell the difference in the air. It wasn't just Faith's scent in here anymore. His was here, too. He liked that. He thought he might just spend the night and work on it some more. Before he was finished, his scent would be dominant. As it should be.

Besides, he was sick of the homeless shelter. The kick of fooling the cops had long since worn off. He was tired of vermin, whether six-legged or two-legged. He was tired of bad food and mildewed mattresses. He was tired of no privacy, no comforts, no women.

Frankly, the longer he had to live there, the worse Faith Constable was going to suffer. So if she knew what was good for her, she'd better have left some decent clues on that damn recorder.

He went into the bedroom, kicking aside the underclothes he'd tossed around the last time. He looked down at a bra he'd torn in half and tentatively stroked the front of his pants. Nothing. Stupid bitch didn't even get him hard anymore. He was so ready for her to be dead.

But when he looked down at the machine, he thought for a moment he must be losing his mind. The red light was steady, unblinking. The number it showed him was zero.

Zero. A big fat goose egg.

He knew he had seen messages there before.

What the hell was going on here?

Had someone beaten him to it? Impossible. He

knocked the telephone off the table. Then he sat on the edge of the bed and tried to think.

Who could possibly have come in here and retrieved those messages?

The answer, when it finally came, was as simple as it was beautiful. No one could have come in. If anyone had been in here, if they had seen the empty beer cans and the wrecked bedroom, they would have called the cops. And a guy with a badge would have been watching that door tonight.

So if no one had come in, what happened to the messages? Obviously, Faith herself must have called in, from wherever she was, and played them. And then she had erased them.

He picked up the receiver from the floor, made sure there was a dial tone, and then he punched in three lovely buttons. Star. Six. Nine.

A mellow female voice spoke to him. She had no choice, she was programmed to give the information he wanted. "The last number to call your line," she said gently, "was..."

He didn't need to write it down. He had a wonderful memory. He got another dial tone, and then he punched in a new set of numbers. Long distance, but not all that far. Somewhere in upstate New York, judging from the area code. A few hours drive at most. He'd have to steal a car, but that was no big deal. And now that he knew where she was, he could take his time.

It rang only twice. And then, amid a lot of clanking

and talking and laughing, he heard an older woman's voice.

"Candlelight Café, the finest food in beautiful downtown Firefly Glen," she said with a cheerful flourish. "Theodosia Burke here, answering the pay phone when she ought to be taking care of her customers!"

He hung the phone up quietly. And when he lay back on the bed, among the torn silk and ravaged satin, he laughed to himself.

What a good girl Faith was. She had made it so easy for him.

Maybe it had been deliberate, he thought, and felt his first stirring of the evening.

Maybe she really wanted him to find her.

FAITH TRIED NOT to go downstairs. But she couldn't help herself. She was so restless, so unsettled and edgy, that she knew she'd never sleep without help. A warm glass of milk might do it. Or maybe just an aspirin.

When she found the kitchen empty, with just the range hood light glowing, she felt a keen disappointment. She realized how much she'd been hoping Reed would be down here, too. Hoping that they could talk. She'd like to tell him what she'd discovered tonight.

She thought she might tell him that she'd probably never go back to New York City again. Not even if they caught Doug Lambert. Not even if it was one hundred percent safe.

No, what was she thinking? She couldn't tell him that. It might sound too much as if she were asking for…what? An invitation to stay? To make Autumn House her home instead?

She wasn't angling for any such thing, of course. That would be ridiculous. She'd only known him a month—even though it had been an amazing month.

She knew he liked her. They both had acknowledged there was a sexual spark between them that could easily be fanned into a fire.

But friendship and a little electricity didn't add up to anything permanent. And, now that she was Spencer's surrogate mother, she wasn't able to consider anything temporary. So, however sweet, in this case friendship and electricity added up to nothing.

Nothing but an edgy, sleepless night with no end in sight.

She opened the refrigerator and took out the milk, then poured some into a pan and lit the front burner. She got out the aspirin, too, for good measure. And maybe she should put a little brandy in the milk.

She saw his gray sweatshirt tossed over the table, the one he often wore when he was constructing the shelter out back. She picked it up and smelled it, then put it down quickly, feeling like a fool.

A *lot* of brandy might be even better.

He opened the back door then and came into the kitchen. A gust of cold air blew in with him.

She saw him before he saw her. He had his shirt off and was wiping his face with it, which gave her a few seconds to take in the beautiful, naked chest, the broad shoulders and narrow hips.

It was freezing out there, and yet he was sweating. She wondered what he had been doing. Surely it was too late to be working on the shelter?

"Hi," she said softly. "I see you can't sleep either."

He looked up. His hair was tousled from his vigorous rubbing. Brown waves fell onto his forehead and tickled his eyebrows. A dusting of the same soft brown hair made a narrow vee on his chest.

There was something so completely male about his body that she felt herself answer it by softening inside, growing strangely, painfully more female.

She tried to cover the odd sensation by tightening the belt of her robe. She moved briskly toward the stove, talking cheerfully.

"I couldn't quite sleep," she said. "So I thought I'd have some warm milk. You must be freezing. Would you like some, too?"

"No, thanks," he said. He put down the shirt. "I think I'll just have a glass of water."

"Let me get one for you," she said.

But they reached the cabinet at the same instant. Their hands both grabbed for the small ceramic knob, and his fingers closed hard over hers. He pulled them back sharply.

"Sorry," he said. "Really. Don't stop what you're doing. I can get it."

It was a large kitchen, but from that moment on it

seemed much too small. They couldn't seem to avoid each other. When he crossed the room, she found herself in his path and couldn't choose the right way to shift to avoid him. When she moved to the sink, he was on his way to the refrigerator, and they collided.

It was as if, on some subconscious level, their bodies were magnet and metal, and invisible polar forces were drawing them together.

When she clumsily dropped the kitchen towel, for a moment neither of them dared to pick it up, sure that their hands would meet, or that their eyes and lips would come too close, and the magnetic field would take over.

"I'll get it," she said finally, and added a small, disappointingly artificial, laugh. He nodded, backing up against the cabinet to give her extra space.

The light from the range hood spilled like buttermilk across his rippling chest. She remembered putting her head against that chest as they danced. She remembered how strong it was. How his heart beat just there....

Her fingers closed hard around the towel.

"Got it," she said, holding it up stupidly, as if there had been any doubt. He must think she was an idiot. He couldn't know that, for a moment, as she looked at him, she'd felt so weak she wasn't sure she could make a fist.

He stopped moving around the kitchen altogether, as if he knew that no square inch was truly safe. He held his position by the cabinet, next to the light. He bent his golden-muscled arms back, propping the heels of his hands on the countertop. His grip on the granite was so tight his knuckles had gone white.

When her milk was ready, she took it to the sink and poured it carefully into a mug. She was proud that she didn't spill a drop. She could feel him watching her, and the touch of his gaze made her blood pulse in her veins so violently her fingers trembled.

"Well, that's ready. I guess I'll just go, go back to bed. Upstairs," she said, giving him another strained smile. "Try to, you know, get some sleep."

He nodded. "Good night, Faith," he said.

She hesitated, wishing she could tell him at least one of the million things she had wanted to say. She'd like to thank him again for the oasis of today. She'd like to thank him for the gift of Spencer's voice. She'd like to say she was sorry she'd invaded his home, made him uncomfortable in his own kitchen.

But none of those simple things belonged in this thick, heavy moment. The only language in this room right now was passion. And that was the one tongue they weren't allowed to speak.

"Well," she said. "Good night." Her voice sounded flat and toneless. She smiled to try to soften it.

He didn't smile back.

"Faith," he said suddenly. "Before you go, tell me you know I want you. Tell me you understand how desperately I want to make love to you right now."

She caught her breath against a stab of heat in her belly. "I think I do," she said.

"I'm on fire with it," he said. He glanced down at his hand. "If I touched you right now, my fingers would burn your skin."

"I know," she said. She let her eyes drift shut, imagining it. Ripples of cold fire raced across her arms and legs, and she shivered.

She opened her eyes and looked at him. "Why don't you do it, then? Why won't you come over here and touch me?"

The muscles in his shoulders flexed as he tightened his grip on the counter. "Because my job is to protect you."

"No."

"Yes." He smiled with a ragged tenderness. "You're so beautiful, Faith. Every man who sees you is going to want you. Doug Lambert wanted you. I have to be different. I have to show you that a man can want without taking."

Dear God, was that the only thing holding him back?

She put the milk down on the countertop. She began walking toward him. He was shaking his head, a hundred muscles tightening, preparing to reject her. But she didn't stop until she was so close her robe drifted softly between his legs and her hands could easily find their resting place on his chest.

She covered the wild knocking of his heart with her palm.

"I already know you're different," she said. "I've seen your restraint, and it's true, in the beginning I needed to see it. It comforted me. It helped me to remember that sexual attraction isn't always dangerous, it isn't always about power and terror and control."

His heart kicked. "God, Faith! If I could kill him, I—"

She laid a finger across his lips. "But I don't need your restraint now. Not anymore."

He looked at her, his eyes dark. "What do you need? Whatever it is, I'll give it to you if I can."

"I need your lips," she whispered, looking at them. "Your arms." She ran her hands down their clenched length. "Your whole body."

He was strong, but he was a man, and she knew, as if she could read the Morse code of his racing heart, that he was on the edge of surrender.

She stepped in closer and felt where the heat was gathering, where his need was strong and straining. "I need you and me together, Reed. Just for tonight, I need there to be an *us*."

"Faith, I—"

But there were no words, and he knew it. He groaned, releasing the countertop roughly. He let his arms find their way around her, let his lips claim hers, let their aching bodies come together with such perfect force that she cried out her relief.

She'd been so afraid he'd say no.

He kissed her until the room spun and her lips were

swollen. He untied with dexterous fingers the knot of her robe and dragged it down over her shoulders, past her trembling arms, beyond her shaking fingers, and let it fall.

He bent his head to her breast, his mouth so hot the cotton of her gown was no real barrier.

She stopped him with uncertain fingers.

"Here?" she whispered helplessly. If he said yes, here, she couldn't stop him. But somewhere in the back of her mind she remembered caution, remembered Spencer, although she was forgetting fast.

He smiled.

"Here first," he said.

And then he bent his head again, bringing the cold darkness and the white, pointed stars inside the room. She clung to his shoulders, shivering, and filling with stars.

When she could hold no more, he reached softly between her legs. She gasped, melting. His fingers seemed to be tipped in light. He drew quick circles for a few delirious minutes, or perhaps only seconds.

It was impossible to slow her body's reactions, though she tried. A slight change of pressure, a gentle shift, and everything spiraled out of control. She broke around him so easily, like a fragile silver firecracker. She doubled over, clutched at his arm and throbbed with fiery light.

As it slowly ebbed away, he murmured her name and pulled her gently against his naked chest. Stroking her back, he let her gather strength there for a long, blissful minute.

It wasn't enough, she thought hazily, listening to his heart, smelling the sweet cedar he'd been working with, and feeling her body tightening all over again. It was heaven, but it wasn't enough.

And then she remembered.

First, he'd said. *Here first.*

And then…oh, yes. And then more.

"Reed?"

He twisted from the torso, still holding her with one strong hand, and fumbled with the other in the drawer behind him. The first-aid drawer, where the aspirin she had come down here for was stored.

"Reed?" But she didn't finish the question. She was really too weak to wonder, too drugged with passion to do anything but trust. When he held up the condoms with a smile, she could only nod. *Yes.*

When she could walk again, he took her hand and led her quietly across the living room, through the darkness to an interior, windowless room that was tucked away in the nook formed by the twisting stairs.

He moved a switch, and a small bedside lamp glowed like candlelight.

It was a simple guest room. Reed had shown it to her when she first arrived, explaining that it was something of an architectural mistake, left over from poorly planned expansions decades ago

It hadn't needed even her meager cleaning efforts. It was never used. It was very plain—just a charming

Victorian bed, an empty hope chest at its foot, a sloping, pine-beamed ceiling and four bare pine walls.

"This has always been called the safe room," he said softly. "Tonight, if this is what you want, it will be our room."

She nodded.

"I want you to be sure." He paused. "You may not want to go any further. Maybe what happened just now was all you needed. Maybe it was just enough relief to help you sleep."

She tried to turn and look at him. "Reed, you—"

"Faith, listen to me. There will be an 'us' here tonight, either way." He held out the condoms. "We don't have to use these. They are not a condition of the 'us.'"

He was standing behind her, with his hands on her shoulders, giving her the choice. But there was no choice. Did he really believe she could be satisfied with that one, tantalizing glimpse of heaven?

She could feel the swollen heat of him, the promise of his power, just inches behind her. She felt a little dizzy, knowing what was to come. Inside her, things were already coiling back into position, desperation and need building to a higher pitch than before.

She reached back and let her fingertips graze him, thrilling at the harsh gasp that told her how completely his need matched her own.

"Come with me," she said softly. She let go and walked into the room. She sat on the high Victorian bed and began to unbutton her gown.

"You don't have to do this," he said tightly from the doorway. "I hope you believe me, there are no strings. Take only what you need, and no more."

She smiled as she peeled off her gown and laid it on the creamy bedspread. He watched, pale and tense, every muscle clenched, as if he couldn't breathe.

Oh, it was going to be so sweet and fierce and wonderful.

"Then you'd better hurry, Reed," she said. "Because the night is short, and I'm going to need it all."

WHEN IT WAS OVER, when they had wrung every last drop of passion from the long, shadowy night, he held her drenched body up against his to rest. Their hearts were pounding, and, for him, the sound was strangely comforting. It was the sound of being alive. Alive in every way.

He hadn't made love to anyone since Melissa's death. He had sometimes wondered how it would feel. He had imagined he might hold back, saving something of the perfect joy he'd known with his wife. He thought he'd feel the need to protect something for her memory—to prove that he was not letting another woman take her place.

The reality had been so different.

With Faith, he hadn't dreamed of holding back, and he wouldn't have been able to, anyway. His body gave its all, and his heart, too. He could offer nothing less to this rare and beautiful woman, this magical creature who had arrived at his clinic broken, vulnerable, hunted—and turned to him for healing.

And, miraculously, when he touched her soft, trembling body, he suddenly realized that caring for Faith was no threat to Melissa after all. Melissa's place was permanent and untouchable—because her place was in the past.

Faith was very much in the present. They made love over and over, sometimes hungry and hard, sometimes sweet and slow. In this hidden, windowless room the light never changed, no clocks ticked their time away. He had no idea how long they explored each other. Every time he entered her, it was like starting life all over again.

But finally, exhaustion claimed them. And then, as they lay there, sated, he realized her shoulders had begun to shake. And the moisture where her cheek met his arm was not the sweat of tangled bodies. It was tears.

He tucked her in tighter. It saddened him to know she was crying, but it didn't surprise him. This kind of lovemaking, so raw and real and revealing, tore down all a person's defenses. She had nowhere to hide anymore, from her grief or her fear—or, like Spencer, from her guilt.

"Talk to me," he said into the nape of her neck. "Tell me what you're feeling."

He felt her hold her breath briefly, then swallow hard.

"I was thinking about Grace," she said. "I was

thinking that she'll never have this. She'll never lie in any man's arms again.''

He didn't respond. It was true, and it was tragic. It would be wrong to deny the enormity of even that one small fact among so many bigger facts. But he also sensed that she hadn't yet voiced the real pain, the one that now brought the tears.

He waited. It would come.

''It's my fault,'' she said after a few minutes of silence. Her chest was moving again, roughly. ''I brought Doug into her life. If it weren't for me, she would still be alive.''

Over the past few weeks, he had sometimes wondered how long it would take her to face this dreadful thing. This crushing burden of guilt, so like the one her little nephew had been carrying. She was so brave—she had faced everything but this.

Maybe this was the real reason she had needed an ''us'' tonight. Perhaps it took an ''us'' to conquer something this desperate.

He let her keep talking, keep crying, without interruption, just as he had allowed Spencer to do the same. He let her spill the misery onto his arm, onto the pillow, into the soft pine-scented air of the safe room. Like Spencer's guilt, hers was real to her, and he would not deny her the right to it.

But he also knew something she did not yet know. He knew that, once it had been spoken, once it had been brought out into the light, it would lose much of its potency.

Because it simply wasn't true. Doug Lambert was an evil man. He was to blame for Grace's death, no one else.

Someday Faith would see that. But not tonight.

Tonight she just needed to cry, and then to sleep. And to know that someone was watching over her. Someone else was standing guard.

When she had exhausted her tears, her body began to go limp. As she drifted into sleep she twitched once, her muscles reacting to some lingering phantom.

He tightened his arms and kissed the skin at the edge of her shoulder, where the scar from her wound was still dark pink and tender.

"I'm here," he said.

She murmured and settled herself closer against him.

"Yes," she said, the sound slurred and dreamy. "This is the safe room."

CHAPTER FOURTEEN

"AUNT FAITH? Aunt Faith, where are you?"

Reed came to consciousness slowly. He wasn't sure at first whether the muffled voice was real or part of a dream.

But then he heard the light bumping overhead. Someone was coming down the stairs. Someone small and light-footed, moving slowly, as if he were a little nervous.

Spencer.

Spencer was awake.

Reed rubbed his eyes, trying to think clearly in spite of a thick head that felt like a hangover. He had slept very little, probably less than an hour, all told.

But falling asleep at all had been a mistake.

The last thing he wanted was for that poor little kid to open this door and see Faith and Reed lying here, their clothes on the floor and their naked arms and legs tangled beneath rumpled sheets.

If they were going to tell Spencer they were more than friends, they'd want to do it slowly and diplomatically, couched in generalities that left out any unsettling adult details. And they would probably wait a while, looking for the perfect moment, when Spencer was most receptive. Faith would of course want Spencer to view it as a happy thing—not another confusing curve ball thrown by a fate that didn't ever consult him first.

Though she'd begun her sleep in a curled-up, near-fetal position, sometime during the night Faith had rolled onto her back. She'd thrown one graceful arm over her head. The sheets covered one breast, but the other was exposed, its curving swell as creamy white as the sheet, its pink tip as lush as a rose petal.

Such an open, unguarded position was touching. He wished they had another night, another hour, even another minute, so that he could wake her by taking that sexy breast into his mouth and...

But they didn't have another night. And right now every minute counted. This room was hard to find, but not impossible.

He touched Faith's cheek, rubbing his knuckle softly against its peachy blush. "Faith," he said. "Wake up, sweetheart."

She stirred then, and stretched like a kitten, pulling the sheet even farther down, exposing her other breast. She opened her eyes halfway and smiled. "Hi," she said thickly.

He leaned over and kissed her lips, which were warm and full. Sleepy lips.

"We'd better get up," he said. "Spencer is awake."

She made a drowsy, uncomprehending murmur,

and twisted toward him, as if she weren't quite ready to absorb words yet. "Hmmm?"

"Aunt Faith?" The little boy's voice was shockingly close. He must be just above them on the stairs. He was close enough for them to hear clearly the anxiety in his tone. Tigger's tags were clinking as he followed the little boy down the stairs. "Aunt Faith, where *are* you?"

Reed could never in a million years have imagined her reaction.

· She pulled back sharply, as if she'd been slapped. Her eyes were wide open, though still slightly unfocused. And then, in a sudden flash, he saw comprehension strike her like an electric current.

Her panic was painful to watch.

She stood, holding the sheet to her nakedness as if it were something wretched and shameful. She scoured the tousled bed with frantic hands, searching for her nightgown.

And all the while she murmured frantically under her breath, the words expelled on a rush of unadulterated fear.

"Oh, no," she said. "Oh, no, no."

Reed found her gown—his hands were surer, less numbed by overwrought nerves. She whispered a thank-you, and began to fumble with it, searching for the neck. She finally found the opening, and, checking to be sure it wasn't inside out, she slipped the gown over her head.

She looked around the room, buttoning as fast as her fingers would fly.

"Your robe is in the kitchen," he said quietly.

She grimaced. "Oh, God, that's right."

"Aunt Faith? Reed?"

Running her fingers through her tangled hair, she turned to Reed, who sat on the bed, watching her, his shoulders against the carved Victorian headboard, the sheet carefully up around his waist.

"He mustn't see us," she whispered. "I'll take him into the kitchen. You can come later, is that all right?"

He nodded. What else could he do?

"Of course," he said.

And then she was gone. She shut the door very softly. He heard her voice in the hall.

"Spencer," she said with a certain forced gaiety. "Hi, sweetie! Hi, Tigger! Are you guys hungry? I was just thinking about some breakfast."

Their footsteps faded away toward the kitchen, but Reed stayed where he was for several long minutes.

Don't overreact, he told himself. What else could she have done? She felt guilty, having slept through Spencer's waking. She was embarrassed, confused...afraid that the slightest thing might cause a setback in Spencer's recovery.

It didn't necessarily mean that she wouldn't ever want Spencer to know that she and Reed were...

Were what?

They had been lovers last night. But today?

Today they would go back to being friends. Had she ever implied anything more than that?

He remembered the horror she'd shown the night when they'd been making apple pies, when she thought Spencer might witness an innocent kiss. He'd registered the sting of it even then, her automatic assumption that there could never be anything serious between them, and therefore it was wrong to let Spencer get "ideas."

This was much more dramatic, of course. Now she had nakedness and passion to hide. But, at the core, wasn't it essentially the same thing?

She still didn't want Spencer to get his hopes up. She didn't want him to start thinking Reed might become a permanent part of the family. A friend, yes. A "father figure," absolutely not.

Which seemed to give him the answer to the question he'd never dared to ask. Yes, she was still planning to leave here as soon as she possibly could. She had no intention of starting anything serious. Anything permanent.

And why should she? Was he really so egotistical that he thought one night of animal loving with Reed Fairmont, and a woman would be ready to kiss her city, her home, her friends, her very life, goodbye? It had been spectacular sex, at least for him. But it was still just sex. It could hardly stop a woman's world in its orbit.

Hell, he couldn't even say she'd misled him. She

had asked for one night. He remembered her words distinctly. "Just for tonight, I need there to be an *us.*"

Just for tonight. She wasn't asking for a real love affair, with implications for the future. She asked for one night, a passionate, no-holds-barred coupling that would give her momentary physical relief. A temporary refuge from a loneliness that had become unbearable.

That his disappointment was unreasonable didn't make it any less sharp. He'd had no real evidence, except the feelings that had been building inside him. Still, he had believed that what was happening between them was something extraordinary. He had even believed it might be the beginnings of...

He stood up and began pulling on his jeans.

He remembered his own words from last night, too. Yeah, he'd been pretty smooth, promising her whatever she wanted.

There are no strings. Take only what you need, and no more.

It *had* been a promise. A vow that he wouldn't make her life any more difficult than it already was. If she needed a friend, he'd be a friend. Arms to hold her chastely through the night? He had 'em.

If she needed the temporary anesthetic of lovemaking, he could provide that, too. And would exact no payment in the morning.

He took a deep breath, fingered his hair into submission, and opened the safe room door.

Vows like that could not be broken.

So it was back to being friends.

But damn it.

He wasn't ready for this.

TWO DAYS LATER, Detective Bentley called Faith again, as he had done twice a week for the past month. Again he had the same story. No real news.

As usual, Doug Lambert had surfaced everywhere and nowhere. Six tourists in an Atlanta bar swore they'd bought him a pint. Three drunks insisted they'd seen him in a toy store in Manhattan, buying a Casper the Friendly Ghost mask. A hippie in downtown Seattle had called collect to tell them he'd seen Doug's ghost at the bus station, standing on the bare backs of a pair of galloping greyhounds.

Green galloping greyhounds, in fact. Whatever that one'd been drinking had left him prone to alliterative hallucinations.

It went on and on. Liquor, unfortunately, seemed to be the only common denominator.

"You might want to start thinking," Detective Bentley said after a pause, "what you'll do if he's already left the country. If he simply doesn't turn up."

Faith was momentarily speechless. He couldn't be serious. She tried to look into that future, a future of never-ending fear, of seeing Doug's face in every crowd, of hearing his step in every creak, his whisper in every gust of wind.

A future without love, because what kind of

woman would ask a man to marry himself to danger and doubt?

A future of never knowing for certain that Spencer was safe.

She tried to look at it, but she couldn't. It was like looking into the blinding black center of Hell.

"You have to find him," she said, holding the telephone so hard the joints of her fingers burned. "Please, Detective, find him now. Give me back my life."

When she returned the telephone to the cradle, she realized that Reed was standing in the hallway, close enough to have heard every word.

"Bad news?"

She tried to compose her face. "No worse than usual. They just can't find him, that's all."

He looked very sympathetic, but he didn't enter her room. She didn't expect him to. In the two days since they had made love, he'd been as distant as a stranger.

A delightful, friendly stranger. Unfailingly thoughtful, amusing and kind. In every way his gentle, normal self.

But it was that very sameness that told her how wrong things really were. They had been lovers. They had shared the kind of night few people ever know.

Things should not ever have been the same between them again.

And it wasn't just a facade to protect Spencer, though that was what she'd told herself at first. Reed was cool, distant, polite and kind in front of Spencer, yes. But whenever he found himself alone with Faith, he was doubly so. He was suddenly as unreachable as Sergeant Braveheart with his unreadable brown eyes and his painted-on smile.

Foolishly, she had resisted understanding his message for a long time, a whole anxious, nerve-racking day. She'd waited for a sign, searched his words for clues and his eyes for a spark. Humiliatingly, she'd even tiptoed down to the safe room at midnight, just in case he was waiting for her there.

The bed was empty. Only when she saw that raw, naked mattress, stripped of its sheets and left exposed to the night, had she understood what he was trying to show her.

One night, that was all she'd asked for—and that was all he'd promised. Well, she'd had her night. It was over now, and there would be no more to come.

So she made her peace with it. She didn't allow her disappointment to turn to bitterness. He was still Reed. He was still the guardian who had sheltered her and made her laugh and, when she desperately needed to, allowed her to cry. He was the miracle worker who had brought Spencer back to her.

She would always be grateful for those things. Grateful that Reed Fairmont had come into her life.

The rest of it wasn't his fault. He hadn't asked her to seduce him.

And he definitely hadn't asked her to fall in love with him.

"I know the wait must be frustrating," he said

gently now. He leaned against the doorjamb, his hands in the pockets of his blue jeans, and his gaze soft on her face.

"I heard what you said about getting your life back. It must seem as if you've been exiled for so long, cut off from your home, your city and all your friends."

She looked at him, wondering what she should say. If she had a home like Autumn House, a city like Firefly Glen...then that would be true. But the vague thought she'd first had on Halloween night had become a certainty. She knew for a fact that she and Spencer would never return to New York City. There was nothing waiting for them there.

But apparently there was nothing for them here, either. Nothing permanent.

"It's strange," she said. She refused to lie to him outright, and yet of course the truth was unspeakable, too. "You start to be confused about where home really is. You start to feel as if you don't have one at all."

He got that shuttered look again, the expression she'd started, in her private thoughts, to call his Sergeant Braveheart look.

"Yes, I can imagine how difficult it must be," he said politely. "I'm very sorry."

A sudden, hideous thought occurred to her. Was it possible he found Detective Bentley's lack of progress disturbing for more personal reasons? Had she and

Spencer outstayed their welcome? Was he tired of having outsiders in his house?

She hadn't thought so. In fact, she had been pretty sure he had begun to enjoy their companionship a great deal.

Until two nights ago. Until Halloween.

Oh, how stupid she'd been to give into her mindless desires that night. It was quite possible that, by doing so, she'd loused things up forever. It was possible that she'd tipped the delicate balance that allowed them to enjoy one another, and that her presence now had become uncomfortable. A burden.

"You know, you don't have to worry that we'll just camp on your doorstep forever," she said. "Detective Bentley was saying that, if he doesn't find Doug pretty soon, we'll have to make other plans."

She looked at Reed and tried to smile. "So really, please. Don't worry about being stuck with us indefinitely."

He smiled back, as mechanically polite as ever.

"I haven't ever for a minute considered myself stuck with you, Faith," he said. "Please, stay as long as you need to."

REED WAS HAVING one of the worst days of his life. Justine had mixed up all the appointments, and everyone was pissed. Spike was boarding again, left with strict instructions to be checked regularly for signs of depression, and right off the bat the damn lizard had tried to take a chunk out of Reed's left thumb. He'd been sorely tempted to give the spoiled reptile something to be depressed about.

And then, for the past hour, Gavin had been squalling. Every animal who came in was edgy and uncooperative, unsettled by the noise. Reed himself was getting a killer headache. It was taking all the emotional equilibrium he had to muddle through this thing with Faith. He just wasn't in the mood for any more stress right now.

When he finally got a break in the action, he went out to Justine's desk, ready to raise some hell.

But what he saw stopped him in his tracks.

Justine was bent over her blotter, crying her eyes out. And Mike Frome was standing in the waiting room, as stiff as if he were facing a firing squad. He held Gavin awkwardly in his arms, and the baby was throwing a fit, screaming and stretching his whole body back toward his mommy.

"Justine." Reed put his hand gently on her shoulder, but his tone was no-nonsense. "What's going on out here? Go get your son. He's upset."

Justine looked up, her eyes bloodshot, her pale skin blotchy, streaked with watery brown lines of mascara. Reed was shocked. Justine had been a beauty queen so long she knew how to cry quite prettily. He'd never seen her like this.

And that's when he knew the rumors must be true. Mike Frome must really be Gavin's father. No wonder the boy looked so damn poleaxed.

Oh, man, what a mess.

"Justine," he said again, his voice extremely firm. "Gavin."

"Mike's got him." She dragged in a wet breath. "He's so sure he wants to be a daddy. Let him see what it's really like."

"This is not what it's really like," Reed said. "Gavin doesn't know Mike, that's why he's crying."

He strode over and plucked the wailing baby from the poor kid's arms. Mike still didn't move. He even kept his hands up, though now they were empty. He looked as if he'd been turned to stone.

Gavin calmed down a little almost instantly, now that he recognized the hands that held him. He still cried, but the terror and fury abated. Reed patted him a minute, then brought him back to Justine.

"Teach Mike a lesson some other time," he said. "When it's not at Gavin's expense."

To her credit, she looked ashamed. She folded her baby into her arms, bent her head over him, and cooed soothingly.

With her makeup all cried off, she looked much too young to be anyone's mother. Reed looked into Gavin's big watery blue eyes and felt a little sick. The poor infant had no idea he'd just become the rope in a heartbreaking tug-of-war between these two teenagers.

Two frightened kids, who were too damn young to know how to fight fair.

And he wondered, for the first time, whether Alton Millner's desire to see this baby put up for adoption might not have been as selfish as he once thought. Maybe, just maybe, Alton had believed it would ensure a smoother life for Gavin.

But, in spite of the fact that there might be some rocky times ahead, Alton was wrong. Justine loved this child. Reed had seen it every day. She didn't know much about parenting, but that skill could be learned. The capacity for love was either in a person, or it wasn't. In spite of her wretched home life—or maybe because of it—that capacity was definitely in Justine.

Motherhood just might, in fact, be the making of her.

"Look," he said. "You two clearly need to talk. Take the rest of the afternoon off. I can handle things here."

She shook her head stubbornly. "He just wants to badger me. But he might as well forget it. I'm not going to marry somebody who doesn't love me."

Mike looked furious. "Damn it, Justine. Who says I don't love you?"

"I say." She nuzzled Gavin. "I've learned a few things about love in the past year, Mike. Things you've never dreamed of."

"And whose fault is that? I haven't had a chance to learn anything about being a father, because you wouldn't let me. You still don't want to let me."

"Damn right, I don't." Her eyes teared up all over again. "You think I want to marry a guy who's got the hots for somebody else? No way, Mike. I grew up with people like that, and take my word for it. It's a rotten way for any kid to live.''

''Got the hots for—'' Mike flushed. ''What— You're talking about Suzie?''

Justine didn't even answer. She was probably crying too hard to get any more words out anyhow.

''I—'' To Reed's surprise, instead of getting hopelessly defensive and flustered, Mike seemed to stand a little taller. ''I like Suzie, I'm not saying I don't. I like her a lot. I was even starting to think we might—''

He broke off. ''But that was before I knew about the baby. Now the baby comes first, before anything. Suzie will understand that.''

He looked uncomfortably toward Reed, then turned back to the weeping young woman.

''Look, Justine, we need to do what Dr. Fairmont said. We need to go somewhere and talk. Maybe you're right, we shouldn't get married. But we have to do something. Gavin is my son, and I'm going to be a part of his life one way or another.''

Reed gave the kid an admiring look. *All right, Mike,* he thought. *All right.* When something was this important, you just had to find a way.

Even Justine seemed to recognize the sudden determination in his voice. She dried her eyes on a tissue, sniffed hard and turned to Reed.

''Do you want me to go get Faith?'' She gestured to the pile of scattered telephone message notes and chaotic appointment cards. "She probably wouldn't mind helping you out in here."

"No, that's okay," he said. Watching Mike just now, watching the kid take his first step toward becoming a man, Reed had remembered something important. He had remembered that, though life was rough as hell, sometimes giving up just wasn't an option. "I can manage."

When the subdued teenagers finally left, with Gavin bouncing on Justine's shoulder, oblivious to the tension around him, Reed sat down at Justine's desk and picked up the telephone.

He called the sheriff's department, which was one of the preprogrammed numbers. He got lucky. Harry answered right away.

"I need the name of the best private detective you know," Reed said without preamble. "The police can't seem to catch this Lambert guy. I don't care if he's living in an igloo at the top of the North Pole, I want him found. He's not getting away with this."

"Damn, Reed. Are you sure? It could cost a fortune. The police will have worked all the obvious angles." Harry hesitated. "It may not be realistic to think there are any more unturned stones."

Reed looked out the clinic window. Faith and Spencer were playing tag with Tigger by the pond. The ducks were ignoring them, paddling placidly through a floating sea of red and gold leaves.

Faith was smiling—she always smiled at Spencer. She had tied her hair back with a bright green ribbon.

But her eyes had dark shadows under them, and her face was very pale. He remembered the desperate tone in which she had begged Detective Bentley to give her back her life.

If he'd had any doubts about where her heart lay, about whether she could ever come to think of Firefly Glen as "home," that tone had eliminated them. There was no question that Faith was suffering. And that was something he simply couldn't bear.

Harry spoke carefully. "This is just how it goes sometimes, you know. Sometimes the bad guy doesn't ever get caught."

"This one's going to. Faith wants to go home, Harry. And, one way or another, I'm going to see to it that she can."

CHAPTER FIFTEEN

DOUG HATED KITSCHY little eateries like this. Mediocre food at best, but pretensions up the wazoo. Candlelight Café, his ass. Cloth napkins and candles and fresh flowers and a bossy old lady in an apron didn't change the fact that this was essentially just a tacky tourist-trap mountain dive.

However, he wasn't here for the food. He was here because this was where Faith Constable had made her amazingly naive call home to check her messages. He was here because this was where the trail began, and he needed to catch the scent.

So he ordered Theo Burke's coffee, which surprised him by being tolerable, and took his time drinking it.

He kept his ears pricked. Within an hour, he knew he'd hit the mother lode. Believe it or not, this little dump was the heart of Firefly Glen social life, the place where all the really good rumormongers congregated to smack and drool over the freshest, juiciest gossip.

And what a little soap opera it was! Some socialite had married her handyman, the sterile sheriff and his wife were trying to adopt a baby, the widower vet had finally fallen in love again, the mayor's daughter had been knocked up by somebody, there seemed to be some debate over exactly who.

And on and on and on. These yahoos would blather on about anything to anybody. The concept of discretion apparently hadn't made it this far north.

But nobody mentioned Faith Constable. And after a couple of hours Theo Burke was beginning to look at him sharply. He had to order dinner just to buy some more time.

She poured him fresh coffee. "So. You here for the leaves?"

He looked up at her with a charming expression. He didn't mind if she noticed him particularly. It wouldn't help anybody to hear her describe the nice redheaded backpacker who had come in the other day. No one would hear that and think *Doug Lambert*.

"Yes, ma'am," he said with a smile that showed off the brilliance of his white teeth. "I've been hearing for years that Firefly Glen had the best foliage in the northeast. This is my first chance to take a look for myself."

She nodded, apparently satisfied, and moved on to the next customer. But Doug was not satisfied, not at all. He had suddenly realized the disturbing implications of what he'd said.

People did come up here as tourists. Lots of them. Even now, the overly precious downtown streets of Firefly Glen were clogged with several thousand simpletons who apparently thought a few red maple trees constituted the eighth wonder of the world.

What if Faith had been one of them? If she'd been here just to gawk at nature, if she'd just stopped by once to use the phone, no telling where she might have escaped to by now.

It had been stupid not to think of that. And Doug was rarely stupid. This whole Faith thing was getting to him. He needed to settle it, and soon.

But he wasn't quite ready to give up on Firefly Glen just yet. Just a few minutes ago, Theo had been chatting to a pretty little brunette with a baby in her arms. And Theo had said something—he couldn't quite hear what—about someone named Spencer.

Now there were plenty of Spencers in the world, he knew that. It wasn't much to go on. But it was enough to make him stay another hour or so, choking down Theo's horror du jour, chickenshit stew, and listening.

Finally—before he had to order dessert, thank God—his patience paid off.

A sexy blond number came in and sat down next to an uppity black-haired teenage girl Doug had noticed before and discounted. Even if Faith was in Firefly Glen, she wouldn't bother with ghastly little geeks like that.

And at first the conversation sounded pretty damn dull. If Doug hadn't found the blonde easy on the eyes, he might have ignored it altogether.

"I'm telling you," the blonde said. "Reed Fairmont is absolutely positively one hundred percent in love."

The teenager scowled. "Natalie, get a grip. You think everybody's in love just because you are. Last month you wanted to fix him up with Pauline. Face it. Reed's still in love with his wife. He's never going to get over that."

Shit. Were they back to the cow doctor's pathetic love life? Doug had already heard all this. Frankly, he didn't care if the widower vet got it off with his new housekeeper, or with one hand on himself and the other on his dead wife's memory.

All Doug cared about was finding Faith. And if something didn't turn up soon, he was going to tear this podunk town apart.

"Besides," Suzie went on. "I was just there the other day. Vincent and Claude needed their shots. I didn't see any signs of a romance. You're dreaming."

"I am not. I saw them at the festival, and I promise you. Reed Fairmont is flat-out in love with Faith Constable.'"

Doug dropped his spoon.

Suzie, the geeky teenager, turned to eye him, still scowling. He gave her his winning smile, but it felt funny. He felt funny. She turned away without returning the smile. *Little bitch.*

"Yeah, well, even if you're right, so what?" She rolled her eyes at Natalie. "Love sucks."

"It has its harrowing moments," Natalie agreed,

grinning. "But it's worth it in the end, I promise you. When you finally get it right, it's—"

Suddenly her cell phone rang. She dug in her purse for it with comic excitement.

"It's Matthew," she said, looking at the digital ID. Her tone implied the name was synonymous with God.

She cooed into the phone for a second, and then she stood up. "Gotta run. Love calls. Apparently there's something called a pneumatic drill, and it's very exciting."

Suzie rolled her eyes. "Gross." Then she stood up, too, her bill in hand. "Anyway, if he can get his mind off drilling things for even a second, tell him I said hi."

Natalie hugged Suzie quickly, chuckling, and hustled out of the café. Doug was annoyed. He'd planned to follow her. He needed more information. He needed, among other things, the vet's address.

But he had a bill to pay, too, and obviously the stunning Natalie would be flying down the street on wings of love to where her husband waited with his big new drill.

So he had to settle for the skinny, homely Suzie. He stood behind her at the cash register and tried to make engaging small talk.

"The food here's pretty good, isn't it?"

Maybe the stress really was affecting him more than he realized. Two months ago, if he'd smiled at a boring bag of bones like this one, she'd pretty much puddle at his feet. But Suzie just gave him a cold eye and said, "Yes."

He tried again out on the sidewalk, where he found her wrestling with two large golden retrievers. The recently vaccinated Vincent and Claude, no doubt. They were nice-looking animals, and she was talking to them as if they were her children.

"Handsome fellows," he said. Unfortunately, for some damn reason, his upper plate wasn't holding tight. Maybe that fool dentist had been right—maybe he should have gotten implants after all. His dentures started to separate in his mouth, and he had to force the plate back into place with his thumb.

Suzie looked at him as if he were some kind of pervert.

"Yeah. Thanks."

Her tone infuriated him. Now he knew he was starting to lose it. What difference did it make what this twit thought of him? She had no sex appeal, no brains, no breasts, no nothing. If he were feeling normal, he'd just laugh her off.

But he wasn't feeling normal. He was feeling damn strange, and for some reason her attitude violently insulted him.

He had a sudden vision of hurting her, and he had to physically stop himself from acting on it. Wild thoughts like that worried him. They weren't Doug Lambert. Doug Lambert was focused and disciplined and always worked from a plan. That was why he always succeeded.

Patience. Brains. Self-control. That's what Doug Lambert was all about.

So he followed Suzie and her dogs for a block or so, until they stopped to sniff a scarecrow in front of the bookstore. She saw him, then, and gave him a dirty look.

"Look, mister—"

But he ignored her this time. Because he'd had an idea. An idea worthy of Doug Lambert.

Pretending he hadn't noticed her *back-off* tone, he reached over to pet the dogs, fussing over them, making an elaborate show of admiring their personalized tags. Suzie whipped the animals away within five seconds, but five seconds had been enough.

"Weirdo." She walked briskly into the crowd, looking back every few feet, clearly afraid of him. But that didn't matter.

Because now he knew where the dogs lived.

He felt himself relax. His blood pressure normalized. He thumbed his dentures, making sure they were tightly affixed. Then he put his hand in his pocket, appreciating the solid feel of the knife.

Yes, he felt much better now. It was always better to have a plan.

And, as usual, it was going to be almost too easy. Poor, stupid Faith. She should never have gotten herself mixed up with a veterinarian, of all people.

Because, see, that was the thing about vets. They were apt to get called out at all hours of the night.

IT WAS ALMOST MIDNIGHT. Reed wasn't sleeping. Faith wasn't sleeping, either, he knew. He'd heard her go downstairs half an hour ago to get a drink. He'd wanted to follow her down so bad he had seriously considered tying himself to the desk with his computer cord.

But he didn't. He stayed where he was, adding up numbers and entering them into the spreadsheet. It was mind-numbingly dull. Trying to keep his thoughts off Faith with something like this was as useless as trying to stop a river with a rope.

If it hadn't been so cold, he would have gone out to work on the shelter, which was almost finished. All those extra hours lately—staying out of the house, working off frustration—had definitely sped things up.

But he'd probably freeze some body parts off if he went out there tonight. Last time he'd checked, the thermometer had read about eighteen degrees and the stars had looked like icicles in the sky. And while he would like a few of his body parts to go into a temporary coma, if possible, he wasn't quite ready to relinquish them altogether.

All of which explained why he was almost relieved when the telephone rang. He didn't want any animals to be in trouble, but at least it was something to do.

Suzie Strickland, sounding absolutely terrified, was on the other end. ''Dr. Fairmont, something's wrong with Vincent. Can you come look at him, please? I'm really worried about him. He threw up, and now he's just lying there, and he doesn't respond to me."

Reed began closing the file on the computer, saving the information he'd just typed in. "Is he breathing?"

"Yes, but it sounds funny. Please, Dr. Fairmont. I know it's late, but—"

"I was awake. Can you bring him to the clinic?"

She began to cry softly. "I tried already. But my parents are out of town in their car, and my car won't start. I would have called Mike, and asked him to bring me over, but he—we—"

"That's okay," Reed said. He knew all about what was happening between Mike and Suzie. Poor kid, all alone there and scared to death. "I'll be there in a few minutes. Stay with him. Keep a phone with you."

"Okay," she said. Her voice trembled. "Okay. I'll wait. Thank you, Dr. Fairmont. Thank you."

Reed pulled on his jacket as he walked down the hall to Faith's room. She was sitting up in bed, reading a book. She was wearing a different nightgown. This one was yellow, and he suddenly realized that her brown hair had a lot of gold highlights.

Her face was strained. Probably the sound of the telephone ringing had alarmed her. She was so vulnerable—she never knew what kind of news might be coming.

His heart tightened. He wished there were some way he could take the fear from her. But he couldn't. He couldn't do a damn thing, not unless she asked him to.

And she wasn't asking.

"I need to go out for a few minutes," he said from the doorway.

She folded her book, marking the place with her index finger, and looked over at him. "Is everything okay?"

"I hope so. Suzie Strickland is worried about one of her dogs. She can't get here, so I need to run over and check it out."

She nodded. This hadn't happened often, but it had happened a couple of times since she'd been here. He usually wasn't gone long, and she had always seemed quite comfortable with the idea.

"Yes, of course. Don't worry. We'll be fine."

"I won't be long." He paused. "You've got the cell phone, right?"

She smiled. "Well, at the moment it's under Spencer's pillow, but it's all charged up and working. Besides, I've got this one—" she gestured toward the bedside phone "—if I need it. But please don't worry, Reed. I'm fine."

"Okay." But then he remembered about the Petermans. "Oh, hell," he said. "The Petermans might be coming home tonight, and if they do, they'll want to pick up Spike. He's in his terrarium, out in the utility room. They'll call first and—" He stopped. "No, forget it. I don't want you opening the door to anybody while I'm gone. You don't even know the Petermans when you see them."

She smiled. "No, but I do know Doug Lambert when I see him."

"No, forget it. If they call, just tell them I had an emergency, and they'll have to get Spike in the morning. It won't kill Jeanne Peterman to spend one more night without her lizard."

Faith smiled again. "Okay, whatever you think is best."

"Okay, then. Good. I'll lock up and set the alarm."

God, they were so polite. How could anything so civilized be so painful?

He wasn't sure he could stand this much longer. Maybe tomorrow, if they got a minute alone, he would try to talk to her. No pressure, just an honest discussion of how he really felt.

Or maybe not. Maybe he'd just get in touch with that private detective. Maybe he'd just find the courage to stick to his decision and leave the poor woman alone.

But that decision was for tomorrow. Right now he had a frightened girl and a sick dog to think about.

"Good," he said again, trying not to look at the way Faith's breasts curved under the lace of the nightgown, trying not to see the soft, dark circles that lay just below her tired eyes. "I guess I'll see you in the morning, then."

IT WAS FOOD POISONING, he would bet on it. Reed did what he had to do, and he did it quickly. In a very few minutes, once the dog's stomach was empty and he'd begun the temporary IV drip, Reed began to see some changes.

Vincent's gaze cleared a little, and he tried to raise his head from the pillow Suzie had placed under it.

"Not yet, buddy," Reed said softly. He stroked the dog's glossy coat. "You just rest."

Suzie, who had been sent out of the room on a contrived errand, stuck her head back in the door. She blanched at the sight of the IV. "Is he going to be okay?"

"I think so." Reed stood to stretch his legs for a minute. "I think he may have gotten into some bad food. Has he been in the garbage?"

She shook her head. "No." She sat on the floor next to her dog and laid her hand on his back. "They both spend a lot of time out back. They love the cold weather. But there's no garbage out there."

Reed didn't like the sound of that. It was always disturbing when the culprit couldn't be easily identified. There was always the chance of bad canned food, which might hurt other dogs, as well. Or half a dozen other troubling scenarios. But when he got Vincent back to the clinic, he could make a better diagnosis.

"He's going to pull through fine." He smiled at Suzie. "So, otherwise, are you doing okay?"

She nodded. "If Vincent's okay, I'm okay."

"I meant about Mike. I know there's a lot going on right now, and it must be pretty rough on you. You guys were getting pretty serious, weren't you?"

She sighed and rolled her eyes. "I'm not gonna saddle him with another kid, if that's what you mean. I'm not sleeping with him. I'm not that dumb."

He laughed. "The thought never crossed my mind."

"It didn't? Hmmm… That might be a little more than I can swear to," she said, chuckling.

At least she still had a sense of humor about it, Reed thought. It couldn't really have destroyed her if she could still laugh about it.

Okay, now back to business. He took a breath, scanning Suzie's neat kitchen, where she had made a temporary bed for Vincent. Claude was locked in the utility room, but they could hear him pacing and whining softly, wondering why he couldn't come out and play. Reed didn't like the idea of Suzie alone here all night, but maybe Claude could be both watchdog and companion enough.

"I need to take Vincent back to the clinic. I believe he's going to be fine, but it might be a good idea to watch him."

She looked stricken at the thought. "I need to be with him," she said thinly. "I'll go crazy if he's there, and I'm here. It's almost three in the morning anyhow. There's not that much night left. I'll sit up with him, and then, in the morning when I get my car fixed—it's probably just a battery—I'll bring him over for you to double-check."

It was a rushed collection of logical arguments. She looked so tragic, sitting there with her black leggings and black turtleneck sweater, her face pale and devoid of makeup.

"Okay?" She turned big, dark, pleading eyes his way. "Okay, Dr. Fairmont? He can just stay here with me, right?"

He didn't see how he was going to have the heart to say no. But he needed to keep Vincent where he could deal with any unexpected developments. He was within an inch of inviting Suzie to come camp out in the clinic next to her dog.

Luckily, at that moment, he saw Mike Frome's bright red Jeep pull up in Suzie's back driveway. Suzie saw it, too. She went even whiter, and though she set her jaw tightly, her eyes began to shine.

Reed knew the visit was problematic, in a lot of ways, but he didn't care about that right now. It was time for Mike Frome to step up to the plate again and be a man. He owed this girl an apology, and maybe he owed her some company, too, some companionship to get her through a tough night.

He opened the door. "Mike. I'm glad you're here, buddy. Vincent is sick. He's going to be fine, but I've got to take him back to the clinic. I'm not crazy about leaving Suzie alone here. Can you stay for a little while?"

Mike, who obviously had already seen Reed's truck in the driveway, didn't look shocked. He just looked serious, and very subdued.

"I'd be glad to, Dr. Fairmont." He flicked a glance

at Suzie. "If Suzie will let me. I needed to talk to her anyhow."

Suzie's face was still pale, still tense. "I'm not sure this is a good idea," she said.

Mike came over and looked her straight in the eye. "Listen," he said. "I'm not here for anything funny. I'm here because I've got a lot of things I need to talk to you about. I'd like your advice."

He exhaled, and the sound was very tired and strangely adult. "Suzie, please. You're the most levelheaded person I know. I need someone I can trust."

She wrinkled her nose. "Um, in case you hadn't noticed, I'm not all that levelheaded where you're concerned."

"Yes, you are," he said, smiling. "You've always seen right through me."

"Hey, I could use some help here," Reed said. They were just making noises now—it was clear they'd reached an agreement.

"Mike, can you take some blankets and make a comfortable spot for Vincent on the front seat of my truck? I'm going to be carrying him out in a minute."

Mike snapped to attention. "Of course," he said.

"Good. He's going to need—"

He stopped. The cell phone in his pocket was ringing. He held back a sigh. Another emergency? He was tired. He wanted to go home. He wanted to be sure Faith was all right.

But he didn't have that luxury. If someone needed

him, he would have to respond. He pulled out the cell phone and looked with resignation at the caller ID.

For a moment he didn't recognize it. It wasn't a number he had ever called....

His heart began to beat heavily against the wall of his chest. It was the number to the cell phone he'd given to Faith. The cell phone that always lay beneath Spencer's pillow as he slept.

"Hello?" But there was only dead air, and something that might have been breathing. *"Hello?"*

A small sound, perhaps a sob.

His heart stopped. It just plain stopped.

But his mind didn't. He grabbed his bag and his jacket.

"Moving Vincent is going to have to wait," he said. "Take care of Suzie, Mike. I'll call you as soon as I can."

Mike and Suzie looked bewildered, but he didn't have time to explain.

"Hello?" he said again. He was already running toward his truck, driven by mindless instinct and adrenaline. And a terrible, terrible fear.

He shoved his key into the door lock. "Spencer? Is that you?"

A thin, frightened sound trembled over the airwaves. "Yes."

"Spencer, are you okay?" He had the ignition going. "Spencer, is anything wrong?"

"Please come home."

The little boy's whisper was pure terror. Fingernails of dread clawed their way down Reed's spine.

"Please," Spencer said again. "Come home. There's somebody in the house."

CHAPTER SIXTEEN

THE FIRST TIME she heard the noise, Faith didn't pay very much attention.

In the weeks she'd lived at Autumn House, she'd learned that, like most old houses, it made a lot of settling, creaking noises during the night. Especially windy nights like this.

Even the second time she heard it, she wasn't particularly alarmed. She thought perhaps Jeanne Peterman had forgotten something. The woman had shown up at Autumn House not long after Reed left, apologetic but determined to get her cherished lizard safely home.

Faith had let her in without any anxiety. Mrs. Peterman had come to the back door, as all Reed's patients knew to do. And she was obviously Spike's owner. Spike, who was in the utility room, began trying to scramble up the glass walls of his terrarium in his excitement. Faith had laughed a little. Apparently lizards did have readable facial expressions. This was one happy lizard.

After that, even though Reed had told her not to let anyone in, how could she resist? Faith herself might not be crazy about lizards, but this woman clearly was. Keeping her from Spike tonight would be as cruel as telling Spencer that Tigger couldn't sleep in his bed.

The woman had chattered, thanking Faith over and over, and making an amazing fuss over the lizard. She had to check and double-check his bag. Did he have his drops, his treats, his favorite jungle-sounds cassette tape? The whole rather surreal transaction had taken at least half an hour.

So when, a few minutes after she returned to her bed and her book, Faith heard the odd noise from the back door, Faith immediately thought of Mrs. Peterman.

She put her book down with a sigh. What now? Had Spike left his teddy bear behind?

But then she heard the noise a third time. And suddenly every nerve end began silently to scream. It wasn't Mrs. Peterman. It was the sound of breaking glass.

It was, quite clearly, the sound of danger.

Though her instinct was to fly from the bed, to fly straight up to the loft, up to Spencer, she forced herself to think clearly. The few seconds it took to dial 911 were, the literature always said, frequently the difference between life and death.

And so, breathing slowly to try to clear her mind, she picked up the bedside phone and put her index finger squarely over the nine so that she couldn't tremble and miss her mark.

But there was no point in dialing anything. For one

horrible second Faith stared at the phone, disbelieving. No wonder Mrs. Peterman hadn't called first, as
she'd promised to do. No wonder Reed hadn't phoned
to check on her, though he'd been gone more than an
hour now.

The line was dead.

Even then she tried to force herself to think. Spencer had the cell phone. If only she had time to race
up to the loft, to grab the phone without making
enough noise to wake Spencer, who might call out
and alert the intruder, without waking Tigger, who
would begin whining and shuffling, excited to see
her....

Maybe, somehow, she could even get them all to
the safe room. Doug wouldn't even know the room
existed. He'd never find them there.

But what if she didn't have time? What if, by going
upstairs, she led Doug Lambert straight up to the loft,
where there was no way out except back down the
stairs? What could she do to help Spencer, then, in
that tiny little room, where Doug would have all three
of them trapped with absolutely nowhere to hide?

No, she must not go upstairs, no matter what happened. Instead, she needed to make enough noise to
wake Spencer, so that he'd know there was danger in
the house.

And then she could only hope that he wouldn't
come out. She had to pray that, at six years old, he'd
have the presence of mind to call Reed, or 911, and

to do it quietly enough that Doug Lambert would never suspect anyone else was in the house.

And finally, most importantly, she had to pray that the police, or Reed, could make it here in time. In time for Spencer, at least.

The logic seemed a slow, excruciating process in the weird, melting time of fear. In reality she'd made her decision in less than a second. She was already hurrying down the hall, scanning it as she went for anything that could be used as a weapon.

She didn't bother with the most desperate prayer of all—that it had been the wind, or a falling tree branch, or a raccoon. That it hadn't, after all, been Doug who broke the kitchen window.

Why wish for that? In her soul, she knew it was Doug. She knew it by the way her flesh had turned to shivering waves of raw fear. She knew it by the way her body temperature dropped to a cold, lost winter, and her heart froze like a ball of ice.

Of course it was Doug. She knew it even before she saw him on the stairs. She knew it even though his hair had been dyed a ridiculous strawberry-red. She knew it even though she'd never before seen him in ratty jeans and sweatshirt, certainly never seen his face looking so caved in and unfocused, like a street person, like an insane person.

Like a murderer.

He was already halfway up the stairs, though he wasn't coming very fast, as if he knew he had all the time he needed. He was looking at her without blinking, his eyes catching the gleam from one of the dozens of little nightlights Reed had put here to guide Spencer's way in the dark.

Crazy, she thought on a wave of nausea. This man was completely crazy.

She'd known that, of course. But the last time she'd seen him, he had been hiding it so well. He had looked normal. He had always sounded normal, persuasive, even occasionally charming. It had just been his compulsive attentions—and a slight creeping of her flesh whenever he came too close—that had given him away.

But now his strangeness was written all over him. His quality of being completely *other*. And somehow that was even more terrifying. It might have been possible, just barely possible, to reach the old Doug Lambert with logic, a bribe, a treat. This new, wild-eyed man was no longer on her planet. If she spoke, she wasn't even sure he'd hear her.

But she had to try.

She planted herself at the head of the stairs. He had one more landing to clear before he was on the second floor. He would not get farther than that, she vowed to herself. He would never make it to the top floor. Not as long as she was alive.

Her knees seemed unreliable. She held on to the balustrade and tried to look calm.

"Get out of here, Doug," she said. "I've already called the police."

He had slowed down even more the minute he saw

her. His eyes were narrowed and glinting. He was working his mouth strangely. But he didn't answer her.

His hand twitched, and suddenly Faith saw the knife flash in the moonlight. She felt momentarily dizzy. Who made knives like that—so long and so cruel? That knife was made for killing things. And for enjoying it.

"Get out," she said again. "The police are coming."

But if he had cut the lines, he'd know the phone wasn't working.

"I have a cell phone," she said. Maybe Spencer would hear her say that. Maybe he would understand what she was trying to tell him.

"I have a cell phone, Doug. I've called the police. They're on their way."

He seemed to smile at that, but his mouth was so new and so wrong, she couldn't be sure. His open mouth was just a black hole, instead of those charming white teeth. The teeth must have been false, she thought. Like his charm, like his protestations of love. Like his sanity.

A door somewhere above her opened. She heard the sound of clumsy feet coming down the stairs. *No, Spencer,* she wanted to scream. But there still was hope. Hope that Spencer would turn around before Doug could see him...

"Reed?"

Spencer's voice was trembling, but hopeful. He peeked his head around the corner of the staircase. And he froze. His eyes were suddenly as empty and blank as a doll's.

"Spencer, sweetheart." Faith didn't look at him for long. She wanted to keep her gaze on Doug, who was still hesitating on the last landing, as if he wanted to prolong the moment, as if a slow anticipation was part of the plan. "I want you to go back into your room right now. I want you to lock the door."

Doug smiled at that, a real smile, as if the idea struck him as very amusing. But, thank God, Spencer didn't argue. He just obeyed. He made one strangled sound, and then he ran up the stairs with pounding feet. He slammed the door to the loft, twisting the lock so hard it thundered in the silence.

Then Doug began to move.

He made a deliberate, arrogant ascent to the second floor. Faith still didn't take her eyes off him, but she began to back up, inch by inch, maintaining the distance between them desperately, although she knew that eventually she'd run out of room.

In her mind's eye she scanned every item in the hallway. She needed something heavy. Or sharp. Or both.

Before she could decide, there was noise and movement, a whirl of confusion. And suddenly Tigger, who for once had not followed Spencer everywhere he went, was between them. The puppy crouched, snarling at Doug, baring his little teeth like the loyal guard dog he would some day grow up to be.

But not yet. Not tonight. Tonight his yapping ferocity was just a joke.

Still smiling, Doug reached down, as if to pet him. The knife flashed again. Tigger let out a brief yelp of pain, then sank to the ground.

Oh, God…

Behind her back, Faith's hands closed over a heavy pewter sculpture of a rearing horse. And then, in a startling burst of motion, she hurtled toward Doug, who had just reached the top step.

She swung the sculpture high and hard, aiming for his head.

But he was so tall. And she wasn't quite tall enough.

She connected with his shoulder instead. Something cracked, but it wasn't his skull. He roared with pain, he staggered back. But he didn't fall.

Spencer, she thought, her thoughts confused as the world turned red with fear. She swung out again, reaching high but knowing it would not be high enough.

Oh, Spencer, sweetheart. I'm so sorry.

Something else cracked—was it Doug's cheek? He put his hand to his face and cursed, and then, with a sudden vicious determination, he swung, too.

His hand with the knife came toward her. She moved away just in time, but like a motorized dervish it came back again. And again. Even as she ducked and twisted, she knew that, eventually, in all this frenzied fury, the knife would find her.

He jammed it into the wall, and he had to stop to rock it out. In that vulnerable second, she hit him again, and blood poured into his face. But he was so strong, insanity made him oblivious to pain, to fear, to anything but his need to drive his knife through her body.

And he would, of course. She had nowhere to go. He blocked the stairs to the first floor, and she refused to back up any farther than the entry to the loft staircase. As long as she lived, she would stay between him and Spencer's door.

Besides, she wasn't really fighting for survival anymore. Now she was just fighting for time.

Time for Spencer to use that phone. Time for someone, anyone, please, God, to come and save him.

But time, like an overturned hourglass, had run out. Doug had her against the wall, his arm across her throat. His breath smelled horrible. It smelled like madness and death.

Oh, Grace, she thought with an immense sorrow as she instinctively shut her eyes against what was to come. *Spencer.*

And then…*Reed.*

Suddenly, the force of Doug's arm slackened strangely, and, though it shouldn't have, the miracle of air rushed back in. She opened her eyes. Doug was staring at her, but he wasn't a man anymore. He was a statue, a frozen, wide-eyed, terrible statue. His face was smoothing out weirdly, melting into a hideous, slack-jawed caricature of shock.

He turned his head slowly, looking behind him with a wide-eyed disbelief. His mouth moved, as if he wanted to speak but couldn't.

He dropped the knife. It clattered to the floor noisily. He shook his head, frowning, looking down at his open hand as if it confused him.

And then, as if he had abruptly fallen asleep, his eyes dropped shut. His legs crumpled under him, and, without even trying to save himself, he tumbled like a rag doll down the stairs.

Bewildered, but shaking so hard she, too, could hardly stand, Faith dropped the sculpture and grabbed for the banister, hoping it would hold her up. Her legs no longer could be trusted.

She looked over the banister, blinking, trying to clear her vision, and the last thing she saw before the world disappeared was Reed.

She smiled, half-aware that she was about to pass out.

Oh, Reed.

He was so beautiful. He might look fierce, grim and determined. He might even be holding a large, strange-looking gun.

But she knew he was really an angel.

Her sweet, sexy, superhero guardian angel.

CHAPTER SEVENTEEN

WHEN SHE WOKE UP, she was lying on the couch in the great room. The whole house seemed to be full of people.

But the angel was gone.

She felt strangely unfocused, as if she weren't quite awake or quite asleep. Not quite alive, and yet certainly, thanks to the angel, not dead.

A crowd of men stood over by the fireplace, conferring in very quiet tones.

Sheriff Harry Dunbar was there. And his deputy, too. And Parker Tremaine, who had brought her to Firefly Glen, it seemed like so long ago. Others, too—she couldn't quite make them out. Ward Winters and Granville Frome, in their full, robust white-haired power, were standing by the door, guarding it.

She decided dreamily that the collection of brave men looked a little bit like a posse.

Not that she'd ever seen a posse.

Suddenly she heard Spencer's voice. She turned her head curiously, studied the men a little more closely, and finally found him. He was standing in the middle of the fireplace crowd, still in his Spider-Man pajamas. His hair stood practically in spikes, and the fire shadows danced over his freckles, making them seem to wriggle as he talked and grinned. Every inch of him was so beautifully, blessedly alive.

He was holding his cell phone like a trophy.

"And then I heard noises and stuff outside, so I called Reed. On my cell phone. I just called him right up, I wasn't even scared or anything."

She smiled and shut her eyes. What a beautiful sound a little boy's voice could be.

But where was Reed? And Tigger? A darkness moved through her. Did Spencer know about Tigger?

And where...where was Doug Lambert?

She must have slept a long time. Absolutely everything had changed. The grim, frightening night shadows were gone, and so was the hum of fear in the air. The house blazed with lights, and the mood was cheerful, like a party, though everyone talked softly, as if they didn't want to wake her.

A handsome blond man, one of the fireplace group, was laughing. She heard someone call him Griffin.

"I'm telling you, you should have seen Reed," Griffin said. "It's the state police, right, and the guy says he needs to take Faith's statement immediately. So Reed, who has this Rambo look on his face, he comes up to the cop. He's still got the tranquilizer gun in his hand, and he tells the guy Faith's resting, the statement is going to have to wait. And the guy, who mind you has a *real* gun, takes one look at that face and says, sure, no problem, pal, tomorrow is fine.''

Everyone laughed, including Spencer.

''Where is Reed?'' Faith said.

Half a dozen male faces turned toward her with expressions of varying degrees of surprise and gentle concern. They clearly had thought she was still asleep.

''Where is he?'' she said again. She was so strangely tired, and out of this whole jumbled mess, that seemed to be the only question important enough to bother asking.

''Aunt Faith! I thought you'd never wake up!''

Spencer came bounding over.

''Reed shot him with a tranquilizer gun, just like he was a bear. The police took him away, and I saw it. He was out cold, but they put handcuffs on him anyhow.''

Faith smiled. ''Hi, sweetie.'' She held out her arms, holding back the relieved tears that the sight of Spencer seemed to summon.

The little boy rolled his eyes, but he sat down beside her and rested his head against her breast.

''I love you,'' she said. She held him and let the warmth of him sink into her like rain into dry earth.

''I love you, too,'' he said with a suspicious quaver in his voice.

''I think you were so brave, and so smart to know you should call Reed.''

He nuzzled more tightly against her. Then he lifted his face and whispered. "I was scared," he said. "That was really him, wasn't it?"

Faith nodded. She knew what he meant.

"Yes," she said. "That was him."

He sighed, as if he were only now beginning to process some of the real implications of this night. Then he glanced over at the posse. "Don't tell them I was scared, okay?"

She lifted her hand and made an *X* on her chest. "Cross my heart," she said.

The others had been watching and now, as if he knew Spencer was ready to share her, Harry peeled away from the group and came over. He sat on a chair someone had pulled up to the couch.

She smiled. She liked Harry. He was so somber, and so kind.

"Reed's in the clinic," he said softly. "He's working on your Sheltie." He seemed to notice her expression, because he reached out and patted her hand. "He'll pull through. Reed is a miracle worker. Besides, though it looked pretty bad, Reed said no vital organs were hit. The little fellow will have a lot of stitches, but he'll be fine in the end."

Faith let her head fall back against the couch, relieved. Reed was a miracle worker, everyone obviously knew that. And Tigger was a fighter. It would be okay.

"That's right," Spencer said. "Reed promised.

Tigger will have a lot of stitches, and I'll have to take good care of him. But Reed promised he'll be okay.''

She smiled, and murmured a soft, relieved sound. Now that she was sure, she might go back to sleep. Though she couldn't quite remember exactly what had happened, everything seemed to be under control. And she was so tired....

Suddenly an auburn-haired young woman came over. She sat on the edge of the sofa and looked into Faith's pupils with a small light. She worked around Spencer's little body easily. She was the calmest person Faith had ever seen.

"I'm Heather Cahill," the woman said with a very sweet, very soothing smile. "Dr. Cahill. I gave you something for the pain. Reed insisted. Apparently you fainted right there at the end. I guess you tumbled down quite a few stairs before Reed could catch you.''

Faith nodded. She didn't remember falling, but she did remember the feel of Reed's arms around her. She would always remember the exquisite relief of being able to relinquish all fear, all pain, even all consciousness, into his strong, waiting arms.

And then, in spite of how much she wanted to stay and find out more, her eyes drifted shut, and, with the warm, soft feeling of Spencer up against her, she felt herself slipping away again.

IT SEEMED only the blink of an eye later, but it must have been a long time, because when she woke again a dawn as gold as an autumn elm was shining through the windows.

And Reed was there.

Reed, beautiful, magical Reed, was bending over her, stroking her hair back from her cheek, which she suddenly realized was extremely raw and tender. She must have bumped it very hard.

But Reed would make it better. Reed made everything better.

The posse was still hanging around, a visible, human symbol of this little town of Firefly Glen's complete and limitless support.

Funny, she thought, that even though many of them still believed her to be just the housekeeper, they rallied around her. She couldn't have felt more important if she'd been one of them for years. She couldn't have felt more valuable if she'd been one of their millionaire elite. Ward and Granville watched that door like twin pillars of the queen's guard.

A queen.

She had felt like a queen once. In Reed's arms. The night Reed had made love to her. That wonderful, healing night…

When she shut her eyes, she could smell Theo's cooking wafting out from the kitchen. She could hear the gentle ripples of conversation, the warm waves of soft laughter. As if they sensed Spencer's need to turn this nightmare into a happy dream, the people here were still making an admiring fuss over him.

When she'd drifted off to sleep, he must have wandered back to them. Obviously he'd merrily returned to bragging.

The sound of his voice was like music.

But, though the solidarity of these kind people meant a lot, ultimately, for Faith, Reed was the only man in the room.

She opened her eyes and looked at him. His face, his rugged, handsome face, was so dear to her, it almost made her want to cry. Which was silly, because she was so amazingly happy.

"Hi," she said.

"Hi, yourself," he said thickly. He bent over her, as if he wanted to cover her with his body, with his protection, with his strength.

She smiled up at him. His hair was shining in the dawn light. He still looked like an angel.

"Thank you so much for coming back," she said. "He was… It was…" She gave up and simply smiled again. "You saved my life."

He continued stroking her hair. His hands were slow and rhythmic.

"Thank Spencer," he said. "If he hadn't used that phone…"

He closed his eyes and shook his head slightly. "I don't like to think about how close it was. I almost lost you."

Yes, they had almost lost each other. She looked at him, remembering how his name had been the last word that blazed through her mind. For that one second, the sorrow at knowing she'd never see him again had been even stronger than her fear.

She put her hand on his arm, absorbing the strong, warm feel of it, the concrete proof that they were both very much alive. And together. That was all that mattered. They were together. Suddenly the entire crazy world was really as simple as that.

"I love you," she said contentedly.

His hand stilled on her hair. In fact, for a moment it seemed as if the whole room had gone quiet, as if everyone had heard her.

He looked down at her, and his face was strained. For a moment, she was confused, unnerved by a new, completely different, flicker of fear. Maybe she shouldn't have said that. It must be the drugs Dr. Cahill had given her. She suddenly remembered she had vowed not to say that.

But that misguided vow had been made before Doug Lambert came. Before she looked at death and realized how miraculous life really is. Before she saw that love is life, and should never be denied.

So she said it again, more clearly. "I love you, Reed Fairmont."

The room held its breath.

Finally, with a long, rough sigh that held a thousand words, he smiled. It was a smile of such warmth and promise that it brought foolish tears to her eyes.

He took her hand into his. "I love you, too, Faith Constable," he whispered. With a deep, hungry grace, he bent his head and kissed her fingers. "I love you, I love you, I love you."

And from the center of the shamelessly eavesdropping posse, a little boy's voice suddenly rang out, crowing with laughter.

"I knew it!" Spencer stomped triumphantly and raised his arms in the eternal male symbol of victory.

"Touchdown!"

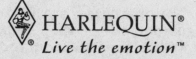

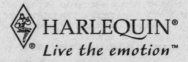

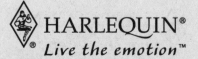

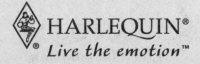